THE
STREET

THE
STREET

SUSI HOLLIDAY

Text copyright © 2023 by Susi Holliday
All rights reserved.

Published by Thomas & Mercer, Seattle

www.apub.com

Amazon, the Amazon logo, and Thomas & Mercer are trademarks of Amazon.com, Inc., or its affiliates.

ISBN-13: 9781542037532
eISBN: 9781542037549

Cover design by The Brewster Project
Cover image: ©Valentina Razumova / Shutterstock;
©Varavin88 / Shutterstock; ©JamesBrey / Getty Images

Printed in the United States of America

To Luca & Cally.
Challenge accepted.

I am not at all the sort of person you and
I took me for.

—*Jane Welsh Carlyle*

One

She stood on the back doorstep sipping coffee, gazing across the Firth of Forth towards the coastal towns on the other side. Sunlight glistened on the waves, and the colourful sails of the windsurfers in the bay made the view reminiscent of a painting that you might buy on a day trip to the seaside. The setting was glorious, and she knew she should be grateful to be here.

Not that she had any choice.

After everything that happened, the brief stint in horrible temporary accommodation had been a huge eye-opener and she was glad to be away from it. She hoped that a sense of normality would return soon. Swapping London for a small, sleepy town on the east coast of Scotland wasn't what she'd hoped for. But she was just going to have to adapt.

The Street wasn't even *in* the small town. It was on the site of an old power station that had been demolished several years ago – a conveyor belt of possible developments mooted and discarded until finally the council had agreed to let it be turned into housing. Luxury housing. An exclusive gated community with a private beach, boasting views of Arthur's Seat – that volcanic lump in the middle of Edinburgh – and the iconic Forth bridges. How had they ended up in a place like this? Their London life had been comfortable, sure, but this was another level. Or so it seemed so far.

They were both fortunate to have portable jobs, so they wouldn't have to start again from scratch. Her husband would probably have welcomed something new – he was already having to adapt more than she was. His work needed specific space and equipment that might not slot so easily into this fancy new home; she had a feeling that he was no longer happy with his choice of career, sensing his restlessness even before they'd started to prepare for this move.

But she'd only ever been a writer and she wasn't sure she was mentally equipped to do anything else.

A life like this was actually perfect, given that she literally made things up for a living. She'd written thrillers and romance novels under various pseudonyms, and she knew she could turn her hand to newspaper articles, maybe a bit of ghost-writing. She could reinvent herself over and over again, and she could transform herself from city girl to country girl, couldn't she? She had already started to edge away from the busy social life that she'd tried to cultivate during her career. The endless networking had become tiring after a while. But she was still sad to leave some people behind. People who had been important to her. To both of them.

Once upon a time.

But she was curious and open-minded about this new chapter, and more than happy to make new friends, although she wasn't sure how close she'd be allowed to get to anyone in this place. Her husband seemed a little less enthusiastic, but he would be busy soon enough, learning how to adapt his own work. Switching from cabinet-making to crafting wooden toys was not his preferred option, but there was no space in the new property for a big workshop, so he would just have to deal with it. They would both just have to deal with it. Because this was their new life and the old one was gone. She hoped it might cheer him up a bit too. He'd been on edge for months, snapping more than usual. Not like himself at all.

Thump.

She turned to find yet another box on the kitchen floor, and her husband, red-faced and slightly out of breath. 'Jeez, *Anna*. Are you actually planning to do anything, or am I "the staff" now in this new life of ours?'

She flinched at his emphasis on her new name, but it was just something else she would have to get used to. Any new pseudonyms she planned to write under would need to link to this name too. Something for her future agent to deal with, assuming she was able to find one to take her on. She hadn't been allowed to keep her old agent, and still felt awful about lying to him about giving up writing. Her royalties would sit in her old business account until she found a way to get them transferred to her new one without leaving a trail.

She stepped back inside and put her empty mug down on the counter next to his full one. An oily scum floated on the top. 'Your coffee will be cold, *Peter*.'

'*Patrick*,' he muttered under his breath. 'My mother would be turning in her grave at this awful replacement.' He puffed out a sigh. 'If you'd just help with the last few boxes, we can ditch the coffee and crack open the wine. I sure as hell need a glass, even if you don't.'

'Sir, yes, sir!' She gave him a little salute, trying to lighten the mood. She didn't much like him snapping at her, but it was definitely becoming a *thing*. She needed to make a big effort here to get them back on track. The new names might even help. New names, new couple. They could rinse away all the stress and strain in that sparkling blue sea. Besides, she wasn't being lazy. She'd hoped that with them not actually bringing much from their old life it would

3

mean there wouldn't be much unpacking to do. Glancing around the room at the stacks of boxes, she realised that she may have underestimated the effort involved. Moving house was moving house, no matter the scale. She was pleased they hadn't had to bring any of the furniture. Everything they had before looked perfect in a Victorian terrace, but none of it would fit in this shiny, white new-build.

'I saw someone across the road having a good gawp,' Peter said, as she followed him outside. They had a new car too, of course. The windscreen was peppered with the tiny corpses of hundreds of black flies – casualties from the four-hundred-mile trip up the A1. Her beloved racing-green vintage MG had been replaced with a silver Renault Grand Scenic. More 'beachy', apparently. But there was the practical aspect that all the seats folded flat for transporting the numerous boxes and suitcases they had filled with inappropriate clothing. She would have to go shopping for jeans and sweaters and multiple pairs of trainers, but there were some of her favourite 'going out' things that she couldn't bear to part with, even if it was unlikely that she'd ever wear them again.

'I hope we get to meet the new neighbours soon,' she said, knowing it wasn't a good idea to be overly sociable. *Keep to yourselves*, the little voice in her head whispered, and a wave of sadness slowly washed over her before retreating rapidly away.

Peter didn't hear, or else he chose to ignore her. Another thing he'd started lately. He dragged a bag out of the back of the car. 'I think it was a kid. A teenage girl.' He nodded towards the house opposite. 'She was just standing there at the upstairs window.'

'Bored, probably. I can't imagine growing up in a place as quiet as this.' She really couldn't imagine it. She'd spent her whole life in different parts of London, amongst the traffic and the sirens and the endless thrum of *people*.

Peter shoved a small box towards her. 'I expect so. Although I grew up in a small town and it didn't do me any harm.' He slammed the boot shut. 'Let's get inside.' He pressed the key fob and the car locked and beeped. 'Tonight, *darling*, we are ordering a takeaway and we are starting on that case of wine you insisted on bringing – for which I am now eternally grateful – and then we are going to bed, and I intend to sleep for twenty-four hours straight.'

The *darling* had sounded forced. He was not one for affectionate pet names. But she liked the sound of this plan. It had been a long day, and the last few weeks – *months* – had seemed infinite.

They returned inside, and as she was closing the door she felt a tingle creep across the back of her neck. She took a final glance at the house across the street, in time to see a light flick off in one of the upstairs windows, leaving the silhouette of a figure standing there. Watching. She shut the door firmly and double-locked it.

'Stop it, *Anna*,' she chided herself quietly.

You are safe here.

Two

StreetChat WhatsApp Group

~Lorraine #7
Well, well – they're here! Fancy car, looks brand new.

~Brooklin #2
What is it? I can't see from here and it might look a bit suss if I go out on the front grass just for a look.

~Lorraine #7
Renault Scenic, Kev says. 25 grands' worth. Nice for some.

~Mary #3
Some people have good jobs, Lorraine. What are you supposed to do with your money if not spend it?

~Brooklin #2
Damn right, Mary, hen. If I had that kind of cash I'd have a fancy car too. I still cannae believe I'm living in this posh hoose, to be honest.

~Asya #2
Shut it, you. Are you coming up to watch that film with me in bed?

~Lindsay #8
OMG you saddos need to get a life! Messaging each other on here from different rooms – LOL! Anyway, we'll go and check out the new folk, eh? I'll tell them to stay away from you bunch of judgey gossips 😜

~Lorraine #7
You are LITERALLY the nosiest person on this street, Linz.

~Lindsay #8
Nah that's @~John #4 – he just pretends he's no' interested.

~Beth #5
Maybe you should let them settle in a bit first, Lindsay?

~Lindsay #8
Actually, I meant to tell you all about a weird thing that happened yesterday . . .

~Lorraine #7
Beth's right. Remember what happened last
time.

~Brooklin #2
What happened yesterday, Linz? Ye cannae
keep us in suspenders . . .

~Asya #2
OH MY GOD would you get off your phone
and come upstairs??!!

~Lorraine #7
Linz?? You still there?

~Bradley #1 is typing . . .

~Beth #5
Lindsay?

~Bradley #1 is typing . . .

Three

ANNA: FRIDAY

Anna found wine glasses in one of the kitchen cupboards. A set of six had been provided along with high-ball tumblers, mugs, dinner plates, side plates and two types of bowls. The crockery was basic but good quality, speckled white with a grey trim. A cursory check of the deep drawer under the spotlessly clean oven revealed a set of brand-new pots and pans. Peter pulled open the drawer under the sink to find cutlery, utensils and, most importantly, a corkscrew.

'Wow,' he said, uncorking the wine. 'They weren't exaggerating when they said everything would be provided.'

Anna held out the glasses. 'It still feels a bit surreal.'

'It'll feel like that for a while.' He poured the wine into the glasses then took his from her still-outstretched hand. 'Maybe always.'

The tingle from earlier crept down her spine. Everything had changed now. But that didn't have to be a bad thing. Thoughts of what had gone before swirled around in her head and she tried to make them go away. It was her fault that they were here. She just hoped that Peter could pull some positives from it, just as she was trying her hardest to do.

'Well, maybe it'll turn out to be the best thing that ever happened to us.' She took a small sip of the wine. It was a soft, blackberry-ish red. The case of six was a gift from her agent last Christmas. The last gift she'd ever have from him, as it turned out. 'Let's go outside. It's still warm.'

Peter had already disappeared out of the back door before she'd finished talking. She stopped for a moment, turning to take in her surroundings. So much to get used to in this new house. Something caught her eye on the living-room unit, just as her phone beeped from her pocket. She wasn't sure who could be calling or messaging her. It was a brand-new phone with a brand-new number, and she had barely looked at it since she got it. Having it in her pocket was purely habit.

She pulled it out and checked the notification screen. A new Wi-Fi network had been detected and she'd been automatically connected. She clicked through to the home screen just as an app finished downloading. A blue square with just an 'S' in the centre. She frowned, walking slowly into the living room as she peered at the screen. She didn't remember clicking on any new apps.

Peter's voice was impatient. 'Are you coming out or what?'

She lifted her head again. 'One sec.' The white envelope was in front of her now, lying on the wall unit. It was addressed to Anna and Peter Clarke. She wondered if Peter minded having to change his name. It was less of a big deal for her; she'd changed her surname once already, when they'd got married. But Peter had been forced to change his birth surname. He hadn't said so, but she had a feeling he was annoyed about it. Another reason for him to be grouchy.

She opened the envelope and pulled out the single folded sheet of paper.

Dear Anna & Peter,
I'll catch up with you both very soon, but I just wanted to welcome you to your new home. You'll probably have noticed by now that the Wi-Fi connects automatically. You don't need a password,

but don't worry – it's secure. It will only operate within the boundaries of your own home – don't ask me how that works, I'm not that technical! There's the app too – StreetMate – it will automatically download on to your phones – it's connected to the Wi-Fi, I think. Again, don't ask me! But if you do want to know the details, I can find out for you, if you're interested.

The house is safe and secure, as is the street. You'll see the gates at either end of the beach. Get yourself out there exploring – the fresh air will do you good after all that London smog you're used to breathing!

I'll recap more when I see you, but I know you'll remember all the things that we discussed. You can go about your business as usual, but just remember why you're here . . . Be careful and stay alert! Anything seems odd, contact me straight away. Leave me a message and I'll get back to you – any time, day or night, OK?

I've made sure there are basic provisions in for you, but you'll probably want to get some shopping in soon. There's a Lidl just along the road in Prestonpans – I've never been in it but apparently it's good!

Hope your journey up was OK. I'd have heard by now if there were any issues . . .

All the best,

Jasper

Anna slid the letter back into the envelope. Of course he would have heard. They had a tracker in their car, and she knew that one of Jasper's colleagues was following them too. Not that she'd spotted them, but he'd explained it all when they'd last met. It was that or be driven, and she knew this situation was weird enough for Peter without that.

She put the letter back on the unit and laid her phone on top, then she headed out to the garden to join her husband. It was after eight o'clock but the sun was still bright, just the hint of a pink aura, the beginning of the sunset to come. The garden was a neat square, a patch of lawn framed by colourful borders, a small, tastefully painted shed at the bottom that would serve as Peter's new workshop. But the icing on the cake was the view. The back fence was not a fence, it was some sort of Perspex wall, completely transparent from the inside but from the outside – she had gone out to look at it earlier – it was shiny and black so that no one could see in. Not even if they were standing on the private stretch of beach that bordered the back gardens of the row of houses. Four houses had this direct beach access, the four houses behind them – or in front of them, depending on the way you looked at it – had raised balconies so that they didn't miss out, and they had beach access via a footpath at either end of the block.

'We need some garden furniture,' Peter said, sitting down on the doorstep. 'I reckon we'll be spending a lot of time out here. I will, anyway. I suppose you'll be glued to your laptop, as usual?'

'There might be some in the shed,' Anna suggested, sitting beside him and ignoring his tone. 'They did say everything we needed would be here.' She hadn't really explored upstairs yet, but she was hoping that bedding and towels were provided as part of *everything*. Shower gel would be nice. Toothpaste too. She wasn't feeling particularly fresh after the eight-hour drive and the service-station snacks.

Peter stood up, just as a pair of voices drifted over the fence from the house on the left. Male and female. Laughter. The dividing fences were wooden, not Perspex. Privacy between the gardens was as you'd expect it to be. He sat back down again and they gave one another a secret look – a moment of what things had been like before, when they were happy and in tune with one another. They were both thinking the same thing. *I hope the neighbours aren't awful.* They had been so lucky in their old place. Enough privacy to keep themselves to themselves when they wanted to, but on both sides they'd had the kind of neighbours that they liked to spend time with. She would miss them. They both would. But they might get lucky again. The Street was a high-end development and would presumably attract a certain type of person. The chances of them having things in common was high.

They stayed quiet and sipped their wine, trying not to catch one another's eye in case either of them laughed. They'd been together long enough that they could communicate easily without words: neither of them wanted company right now. Anna was enjoying the closeness of the moment, after so much tension before. At times like this she was able to convince herself that they hadn't been struggling back in London – even *before* things had gone really, really bad.

The voices next door turned to whispers, followed by another burst of laughter. Footsteps. Then someone was knocking on the gate at the bottom of their garden. The gate was next to the shed, and it was not transparent like the rest of the fence.

Peter looked at her, widening his eyes. She bit her lip, thinking. It might be nice to have some company. Have a laugh. Take their minds off things. The knocking came again. Anna shrugged and stood up, and Peter tried to grab her wrist, but she shook him off. *What's the worst that could happen?*

A lot, actually.

She dislodged the thought from her head, and handed him her glass before heading off down the path.

'Anna . . .' He said it under his breath, but she didn't reply because she'd decided she actually *did* want to meet these people. The whispers and giggles from their back garden suggested that these neighbours might be just like them. *But what if they aren't the same people we just heard in the garden?* She pushed away this thought, just like the earlier one. She refused to succumb to paranoia on top of everything else.

'Anna!' He'd stood up. She continued to ignore him. *Yes, yes, Peter. I know we're supposed to be careful.*

She unlocked the gate and pulled it open.

The giggling stopped, and a surprised-looking young couple stood in front of her, brandishing a bottle of wine and two glasses. By the look of them, they'd had a few already.

It's Friday night. This is exactly what we need.

'Hi, I'm Anna,' she said, smiling. 'I'm guessing you're from next door?'

The woman stepped forward, the man holding back, looking a little sheepish. Maybe they hadn't expected her to open the gate at all. Well, maybe Anna wasn't going to do what people expected of her any more. New house, new life, new Anna. It started now.

'Oh, hiya!' The woman beamed. 'I'm Lindsay and this arsehole is Ritchie. We've been so excited about you arriving! I hope you don't mind us just turning up like this? Your house has been empty since we moved in.'

Anna wondered how they knew they were coming. But given that someone must have been inside recently, setting things up for them, it probably wasn't much of a stretch to assume that people were moving in. 'Do you want to come in?'

'Does a dolphin piss in the sea?' Ritchie laughed at his own joke and Lindsay rolled her eyes, and then the two of them stepped into the garden and Anna closed and locked the gate behind them.

Peter had pasted on a smile. He was good at wearing his game face when required.

'Just arrived, eh?' Ritchie said. His accent was thicker than Lindsay's and Anna found herself instantly drawn to it. She had always liked a Scottish accent, although she had no idea if this was local or if they were from somewhere further afield. The *management* – she couldn't really believe they insisted on being called that – hadn't really said much about the others who'd moved into the development before them. All they knew was that they were lucky to get the place, as the previous couple had to pull out. It wasn't everyone who wanted this sort of set-up.

'Yes, we came up from London,' Peter replied. 'I think we were lucky with the traffic.'

'Oh, aye? Where in London?'

Anna flashed Peter a look. *Now it's you who needs to be careful.* He blinked, resetting himself. 'Oh, just one of those suburban places. More Surrey than London, really. You probably don't know it.'

Good. This is good.

'Right, aye. I don't actually know anywhere down south, to be honest. We're both from Dundee.'

'Is that far north?' She had a vague idea where it was but wasn't sure she could place it on a map.

Lindsay waved an arm towards the beach. 'Over there and round the corner.' She laughed. 'You cannae really see it for the Paps.'

'The Paps . . . ?'

'The Lomond Hills,' she said. 'Locally known as "The Paps of Fife" because, well . . .'

She let her sentence trail off. Ritchie ran his hands over his chest, cupping them over invisible breasts and almost spilling his wine down his t-shirt.

'Oh . . .' Peter grinned. 'Nice mounds.' Ritchie sniggered and the two of them chinked their glasses together, then Peter handed Anna's back to her and the four of them did a round of 'Cheers'.

'Welcome to The Street,' Ritchie said. 'Everybody needs good neighbours.' He half-sang the last part, the theme tune to the long-running soap. Then laughed again at his own hilarity.

'Top-up?' Lindsay offered the wine bottle she was still clutching, and Anna held out her glass. She wouldn't normally mix two wines, but it didn't really matter right now. They weren't on a wine-tasting course. Although they might need to order some food soon, because the glass she'd had seemed to have gone straight to her head.

'So, how long have you lived here?' Anna asked, taking a sip. 'And more importantly, have you got the number of a good Indian takeaway? I. Am. *Starving*.'

'Now we're talkin'!' Ritchie pulled his phone out of his pocket. 'Best Indian in Scotland, this one. They'll do us a mini party banquet with beers. Fancy that?'

Anna grinned. She was so glad she'd invited them in. She took a step closer to Peter, took his hand and squeezed it tight. 'Yes, please,' she said. 'That sounds perfect.' After a long moment, he squeezed back.

Four

ANNA: FRIDAY

If Anna had been concerned about making new friends, the doubts were washed away as soon as the food and beers arrived. The four of them attacked it like they'd never seen food before. Ritchie had called it a mini party banquet, but there was nothing mini about it: samosas and bhajis, chicken madras, prawn bhuna, skewers of paneer tikka, aloo gobi, several different rices and naan breads, a stack of poppadoms . . . plus four big bottles of Cobra – each. There was no squabbling, no complaining, just four people enjoying good food, drinks and having fun. If love at first sight was a thing that could be applied to platonic relationships, then they were all smitten.

The chat came easily. When anything arose that Anna and Peter weren't comfortable with, they managed to effortlessly steer things in other directions, avoiding the awkwardness that often slides in when people are just getting to know one another.

They started off in the kitchen, the men leaning against the worktops, drinking beer from the bottles, Anna and Lindsay sitting at the kitchen table with theirs poured into glasses. Lindsay told them that she and Ritchie had moved from Dundee when they'd heard about the development of the old power station. Ritchie's business was portable too – he was a window cleaner who also did lawn maintenance and external house cleaning. Very lucrative, apparently. And Lindsay's job selling Avon products was just a bit of fun. She had some savings too, she'd said. Anna had been a little surprised at their jobs, wondering how they afforded this kind of house – but such things were none of her business, and the last thing she wanted to do was pry – because it was the last thing she wanted anyone else to do to her.

Peter told the couple about the wooden toys business that he was just starting, and they were impressed when Anna told them she was a novelist.

'That's so exciting,' Lindsay said. 'I've never met a real writer before. Do you get to go to fancy launches with champagne? Is it amazing seeing your name on the bookshelves?'

Anna took a breath and smiled. 'Well, I mostly write under a pseudonym. I've got a few, actually—'

'What, like a made-up name?' Ritchie said, after a mouthful of beer. 'Why would you do that?'

Anna clutched her hands together under the table, squeezing tightly. 'It's quite normal for writers to do this. I write different kinds of things so it's mainly to stop the readers getting confused.'

'Oh, like J. K. Rowling and that Galbraith one she uses now,' Lindsay said, nodding. 'I get it. Ignore Ritchie. He's never read a book in his life.' She grinned. 'So, tell me your pseudonyms – I'll go and find your books in Waterstones at The Fort.'

There was a brief awkward moment when Anna said nothing. She gripped her hands together tighter, feeling her nails cutting into her skin. Why had she mentioned writing novels? If she'd simply stuck to the story that she was a freelance copywriter, the conversation would have blown out in a moment. But it was hard to just erase the novelist side of herself like that.

She was about to blurt out more, try to dial it back somehow, when Ritchie, seemingly oblivious to the tension, saved the day. 'Didn't Rowling write that series with the mad police chick who cut all her hair off into a sink then went undercover homeless? Jeez, that was ridiculous . . .'

Lindsay laughed. 'No! That was *Marcella*, and you know I loved it. Rowling-slash-Galbraith wrote that other one about the cute private eye with the false leg.'

Ritchie turned to Peter and shrugged. 'I cannae keep up.'

Anna let out a sigh of silent relief, and the moment passed.

It turned out that everyone in The Street had moved in around the same time, about six months before, and as the drinks flowed, Ritchie and Lindsay started to open up about the other residents. They'd eaten at the table, but they were back in the garden now with the rest of the beer and wine. The sun had set, and both Anna and Peter had been suitably awed by the myriad hues as it dipped down over the hills.

Ritchie had helped Peter to get the garden chairs out of the shed, and now the four of them were sitting in a circle on the lawn.

'Right then,' Lindsay started. 'Let's go through the street of freaks.'

Anna groaned. 'I hope you're joking . . .'

Ritchie laughed and popped the lid off another bottle of beer. 'Only partly.' He paused, turning to his wife. 'Although . . . it's maybe not fair to spill too many beans, eh, Linz? I'm sure Peter and Anna will be getting to know all the others soon enough.'

'Oh, don't be such a spoilsport, Rich.' Lindsay was talking more slowly than before, trying not to slur her words. Like all of them, she'd had a fair amount of alcohol.

Anna's head was spinning a little, and she was aware too of what she was saying now. Trying not to say things she hadn't intended. They were in the danger zone with the amount of alcohol they'd consumed. She knew she needed a break, should drink some water, but she didn't want to ruin the fun.

Lindsay waved a hand towards Ritchie, as if swatting a mosquito. 'OK, "freaks" was maybe a bit strong. But, right . . .' She stopped talking, her face screwed up in confusion. 'What was I saying?'

Anna realised that Lindsay was even more drunk than she appeared.

'Linz . . .' Ritchie leaned over to put a hand on her knee, but overstretched and tipped the chair, face-planting himself into the grass.

Lindsay burst out laughing, while Ritchie scrabbled around on all fours, trying to get back on to his feet. Peter held out a hand to help, but he was shaking with laughter. Anna took it all in, and then she started laughing too and couldn't stop.

It took a while for them to calm down again.

'Jeeeez, Rich.' Lindsay was wiping tears from her cheeks. 'Well, that sobered me up.' She sat up straight on her chair. 'Where were we?'

'How about there?' Peter, still trying to catch his breath, pointed to the fence on the right.

'Ah, yes.' Lindsay put on a BBC newsreader voice. 'To our right, we have Number Four, The Street. The wholly good and righteous Mr John Alfred. Thirty-something, single. Works for a charity in town. Either closeted, a virgin or both – we can't decide—'

'Lindsay!'

'What? Are these not the facts, Rich?'

Ritchie flattened his mouth into a line and rolled his eyes to the sky. 'I think we'd better take you home.'

'Take yourself home. I'm just getting started.'

'Linz . . .'

There was a warning tone to his voice, but Lindsay waved a hand, dismissing him. Anna was intrigued. She and Peter had plenty of reason to be cagey about things, but what was Lindsay and Ritchie's story? It was only a bit of fun, wasn't it? Anna was sure she'd get to know the neighbours for herself soon enough. It wouldn't be long before her false backstory started to sound real, even to herself. They'd already passed the test with Lindsay and Ritchie, hadn't they? Even the awkward pseudonym chat had slipped away quite easily.

Lindsay popped the cap off another beer and flicked it across the grass. She poured a bit into her glass and took a swig of the massive frothy head. 'Next to John you've got Brooklin and Asya Knight.' She spelled out both of the first names. 'You can probably tell a lot about them by the ridiculous names and how they've spelled them . . .'

Anna was about to say something about not being able to choose your own first name, then stopped herself. She knew from personal experience that was very much untrue.

'He reckons he's some sort of app designer, and she's an animal influencer.'

Peter laughed. 'How does she influence animals? Do they even have social media?'

Lindsay vanished off into hysterics again, leading them all to follow suit. Even Ritchie seemed to have forgotten his earlier concerns about his wife's lack of discretion. 'She takes pictures of her dog! Some stupid wee fluffy thing. Apparently she gets sent loads of dog accessories to promote—'

'And a lifetime supply of Pedigree Chum. Although I reckon Brooklin tucks into a bit of that.'

Lindsay roared with laughter, then held her fingers up to her lips, her face becoming serious. She made a small gesture with her head, towards the camera that was fixed in the corner above the back door. 'The hills have eyes,' she said.

Ritchie snorted, shaking his head. 'The walls have ears, you mean . . .'

'Aye, whatever.'

Peter shifted in his seat and Anna felt a chill in the air that she hadn't noticed earlier. She shivered, rubbing her bare arms. 'Maybe we should go inside?' She picked up her empty glass and a couple of the beer bottles, and headed for the back door.

'We should be getting home,' Ritchie said. 'It's late.'

'Maybe a coffee first? I'm OK now, honestly, Rich.'

Lindsay sounded a lot more sober than she had earlier, and Anna wondered again what was going on with the secrecy and now the change in atmosphere. Why was Ritchie so bothered by her joking about the other neighbours? What did he mean about the walls having ears? There were security cameras on the houses, of course there were, but they were visual only, right? No audio. And even if they were, so what? They were in their own back garden. Lindsay hadn't said anything too outrageous. They were just having a laugh, weren't they?

Anna stole a glance at Peter to see if he'd picked up on the change, but he wouldn't catch her eye. That momentary closeness she'd felt with him earlier had slipped away again, and she felt uneasy now. Had she said something wrong? Did Lindsay and Ritchie suspect that she was lying about things?

Stop it, Anna. She hated this creeping paranoia that was seeping into her bones. No one knew anything. Ritchie just didn't like his wife being indiscreet after a few drinks. That was all it was, wasn't it?

Maybe Lindsay had a moment of clarity and had stopped herself before it all went too far. But Anna was still intrigued about the other residents of The Street. She'd thought that was the most unimaginative name for a new development she'd ever heard, and yet when she'd arrived, it had somehow just seemed to fit. Despite the luxury, it was bland. Anonymous. It could be anywhere, and yet it stood out, somehow – this gated development wedged in between a couple of nondescript little towns.

The Street. Something about it made her shudder.

The others were all sitting in the living room when she brought through the coffees. The earlier tension had disappeared again, and they were laughing about something that Peter had said. Anna laid the tray of hot drinks on the table and told them to help themselves to milk and sugar.

'So,' she said, after taking a sip of her own coffee, relieved that the evening was back on track. Her head was spinning a bit from the alcohol, and she knew she needed a pint of water, two paracetamol and a good night's sleep – but first, she wanted to know about the neighbours. Their names, at least. 'Give us a quick rundown of the others then, Lindsay? Please? It'll make it easier when I go round and introduce myself.' *I will have to do that at some point,* she thought. *It will just look strange if I don't.*

Lindsay smiled. 'I bet you twenty quid you'll get your first visitor tomorrow. The Street is meant to be a classy, discreet development where no one bothers anyone uninvited, but she won't be able to help herself. Mark my words, Mad Mary from Number Three will be round with an inedible fruitcake and a whole list of moans about the village shops—'

'Oh . . . well, that will be nice. I think.' Anna could think of nothing worse. She needed more time to sort things out, unpack. Get settled. Make sure that she and Peter were on an even keel, with their stories straight.

Lindsay waved a hand, dismissing her. 'Don't worry about it. Just don't answer the door. That's what I'd do. It's bad enough in that WhatsApp group—'

'Right, you . . . we're off.' Ritchie stood and took Lindsay's hand, pulling her from the couch and cutting her off mid-flow.

'Great to meet you both,' he said. 'I reckon this one needs a good night's sleep.'

Lindsay shrugged him off. 'I told you I got woken up last night by some racket out on the beach.'

'Aye, whatever . . .' He dragged Lindsay across the room and out the back door, mouthing a 'sorry' as he went.

Anna followed them down the path, closing and locking the gate behind them. Wasn't the beach private? Why would anyone be out there making noise in the night?

A shiver ran over her all of a sudden and she rubbed her arms against the chill. She thought again about the figure across the street, watching, and about Mary, desperate to come round. And what was so special about this WhatsApp group? Why had Ritchie stopped Lindsay from saying more about it?

Anna wasn't quite sure she was prepared for this. She could really do without local busybodies wanting to know her business, or even talking about her on some private local gossip group. For their safety as much as hers.

Five

ANNA: SATURDAY

Anna woke to an incessant ringing sound that might've been her phone, except she hardly ever had the ringer volume up and she never kept it in the bedroom anyway. Or it might've been the front doorbell, but it wasn't a familiar sound. Theirs played the theme tune to *Happy Days* and it always made her want to do a little dance when the postman pressed it, but it did her head in after the third delivery man of the day had jammed a finger on it for longer than strictly necessary. And why was it so bloody dark? Anna had always hated sleeping in a dark room. It freaked her out when she couldn't even see her own hand in front of her face. She sat up and the room spun.

She poked at the figure lying beside her. 'Are you awake?'

No response.

Anna sunk back into the pillows. Soft, feathery like giant squishy marshmallows. Not her pillows. Not her room.

'Are we in a hotel?'

Bits and pieces of the night started to form in her tangled mind. She took a deep breath and tried to keep calm.

'Peter!' She remembered who she was with, at least.

'Christ, keep it down a bit, will you?' He rolled away from her and pulled the duvet over his head.

The unfamiliar ringing had stopped, but it started again now and she felt like the sound was penetrating her skull, making it vibrate. She had a vague recollection of taking a sleeping pill, which, on top of all the alcohol, had been a really, really stupid plan.

She felt woozy as she climbed out of bed, feeling the soft, thick carpet beneath her bare feet. Her house had stripped wooden floors in every room. The occasional rug, but nothing like this. A sliver of light shone to the right of her, like someone had pulled a strip light off the ceiling and propped it against a wall. It took her a moment to realise it was a gap at the side of a heavy blackout blind. She hated blackout blinds. Preferred to wake up with the sun, no matter the season. Too early in summer, too late in winter. It made no difference – she worked her writing schedule around it and she always felt better for keeping her biorhythms in order. Her body clock was definitely not in sync right now.

She yanked up the blind, squeezing her eyes shut against the bright light, then opening them slowly and ignoring Peter's protestations from the bed.

She squinted out at the sun bouncing off the sea. *What the . . . ?* And then she remembered. A cascade of disjointed memories tumbled around inside her head.

You're not in Kansas now, Dorothy.

If she had ruby slippers she would give the heels a click, but she knew there was no point.

There's no place like home . . . and this is yours, for now.

The day and night before continued to slot into place. The drive, the unpacking, the wine, the neighbours. Food. Too much drink. The pill. She was pissed off about the pill. No more of that shit, she had vowed. She should have flushed them away. Fresh start, fresh head.

Stupid. Stupid. Stupid.

Hell of a view, though.

She picked up yesterday's clothes from where they'd been left in a ball on the floor, and pulled them on.

'I'm going to make some coffee. Might drink the entire contents of the water tank too. Want anything?'

Peter grunted from beneath the duvet that was still over his head. She would bring him something to drink. Maybe some food too. She felt ropey as hell, but she'd dealt with worse. Much worse. What was a few too many drinks and one stupid little pill between friends?

Lindsay and . . . Roger? No. Ritchie. Lindsay and Ritchie Walker. The neighbours couldn't have given them a better welcome, although Anna couldn't remember much of the detail of what they'd talked about all night. She hoped she hadn't said anything inappropriate, but then again, chances were the other couple wouldn't remember either. She was pretty sure she hadn't, but she vaguely remembered Lindsay being hushed up by Ritchie. Had *she* said something out of turn? But that made no sense. It was her and Peter who had the skeletons in their closet.

They were the ones in witness protection, after all.

Maybe she'd take them round a bacon sandwich. They might appreciate it. Or was that too pushy? She didn't even know if she had any bacon. Or bread. She'd have to venture out and find the nearest shop as soon as possible. Lidl. Was that what it said on Jasper's letter?

She would need to re-read it. Show it to Peter. The sooner they started doing normal things like shopping, the sooner they might feel like normal people again.

She was at the bottom of the stairs when she remembered the ringing. Had it been the doorbell? There were a few envelopes on the floor beneath the letterbox and she bent down to pick them up, feeling the room tilt again as she stood. A wave of nausea slid up her throat, and she had to take a few long, slow breaths to beat it back down.

Why did they have mail? So far no one else knew who they were or where they lived. A quick glance told her that this was all for the previous occupants. She would mention it to Jasper later. She dropped the mail on the kitchen counter and set about exploring the fridge and the cupboards and was extremely pleased to find a pack of bacon and a loaf of bread. She hadn't noticed it last night, but she had only been interested in wine, beer and curry then. She'd have to get the number of that Indian from Ritchie later. She recalled the mountain of food and remembered it being lovely, even if it was coming back on her in spicy little burps right now.

She switched on the grill for the bacon, and filled the kettle with water. Should she just turn up at the door with the breakfast, or should she pop round and ask them if they wanted any first? They might not even be in. They might be those fitness types who like to run off a hangover first thing. She slid a tray out of the oven, and that's when she noticed the clock.

15.45.

What? She never slept during the day. Even after the biggest, craziest, latest nights out, back in the day. Even if she'd gone to bed at dawn, she'd be up again by nine at the latest. Those damn blinds. She had no idea when they went to bed, but it hadn't been daylight then. And now she'd slept away half the day. More than half. That damn sleeping pill. They'd been foisted on her prior to the court case, and she'd resisted them for as long as she could, but there was something tempting about oblivion – even if it did result in a fuzzy head the next day.

She decided that breakfast at nearly 4 p.m. might look a bit odd, even if the neighbours did like to party.

Her head was banging. She filled a pint glass with tap water and gulped it down. Her handbag was lying on the kitchen counter near the sink, the contents scattered. An empty blister pack of paracetamol on the drainer. Another flash of memory, raking around in the inside pockets of her bag in the middle of the night searching for the painkillers.

Maybe Lindsay might have some she could borrow.

Anna opened the back door and stepped out into the garden, which was a tip. Empty bottles and whatnot scattered across the grass. Another job for later. There was no one on the beach behind, despite the glorious sun. It was still hurting her eyes. She went out the back gate and hoped that Lindsay's was unlocked. She couldn't face going around the front.

It was locked. Damn it. Of course it was locked.

Head pounding even more, Anna hurried back into her garden, closing and locking the gate behind her, then through the house and out of the front door. Hopefully she could get the paracetamol and get back into her house before any of the neighbours saw her. Despite her interest in them the night before, all she wanted to do now was knock herself back into a deep sleep until this damn headache went away.

She stepped across the small patch of lawn to Lindsay and Ritchie's front door, and pressed on their doorbell. The ringing was harsh, even from outside. Same sound as hers. The sound that had made her brain rattle earlier and was making it rattle again now.

Come on!

She put her hands up against the glass pane and peered in, but there was no sign of anyone inside. Anna took a step back for a moment, confused. Then she leaned in again and pressed her face right up to the glass. That trickle of fear she'd felt last night was back, inching its way across her shoulder blades. The pounding head faded into the background.

Anna stepped away from the door and took a few more steps across to the front window. The blinds were open, and there was no need to peer in. It was all in full view. The living room was exactly the same layout as theirs. The furniture was the same too. Three-seat sofa facing out. Built-in bookshelves to the right. A coffee table. That was it. No scatter cushions or throws on the sofa. No magazines or coffee cups on the table. No books on the shelves. No ornaments.

Nothing at all, except the basic items that Anna and Peter had . . . and they had just moved in. The Walkers had been living in this house for six months, they'd said. Nothing about them that she had experienced last night would suggest that the couple were minimalist to the extent that they had nothing of their own in the living room.

Anna wanted to believe that the hangover and the after-effects of the sleeping pill were playing tricks on her mind, but it made no sense. Why was there nothing in that room?

She tried the doorbell again. Knocked too, but it didn't have much impact on the solid wood. Had they mentioned that they were going away? Maybe that's who'd rung the bell earlier – Lindsay, wanting to tell her they were leaving? Maybe their stuff was in boxes so they could redecorate? But why redecorate when they had only been there six months?

Anna opened the letterbox and crouched down to look inside. The air felt still. 'Hello?' she called, her voice echoing in the empty house.

No answer.

'What *are* you doing, dear?'

The voice came from behind her, making her jump. She turned to find a reed-thin woman with long dark hair shot through with streaks of grey. One of those women who could be anything from thirty-five to seventy. She was smiling at Anna, but it looked a little forced. Concerned. Suspicious, maybe.

'Oh . . . you gave me a fright! I'm Anna,' she said. 'I've just moved into Number Six.'

'Of course you have, dear. I saw you arrive last night.'

Anna blinked, tried to shake away that feeling again of people watching her. What if they knew who she really was?

The woman smiled. 'I'm Mary from Number Three. I wanted to bring you a cake, but I've left it at home now. I'll have to go and get it. I was just on my way back from my walk when I saw you.'

The cake. She remembered Lindsay mentioning Mad Mary and her terrible cakes. She tried to push away the 'mad' bit. She was trying her best not to have any preconceptions about her neighbours.

'Do you know if Lindsay and Ritchie were going away? I know we'd only just met, but I'm sure they'd have said . . .'

Mary's smile remained fixed. 'Who's that then, dear?'

'Lindsay and Ritchie! The Walkers? This is their house. We met them last night. They came round the back, and . . .'

She let the sentence trail off. Hadn't she thought that last night, just for a moment? They never actually saw where Lindsay and Ritchie came from. But they had been in the garden of Number Eight. She was sure of it. Wasn't she?

Mary shook her head. 'There's nobody living at Number Eight, dear. You must be mistaken.'

'No, I—'

'You get yourself back inside. I'll pop home and get the cake, then I'll be over to see you soon for a cuppa and a chat. How does that sound?'

Anna's heart was fluttering. Her chest felt tight. She recognised the first signs of a panic attack. Tried to breathe deeply. Balled her hands into fists and then stretched out her fingers. One . . . two . . . three . . .

'You don't understand,' Anna said. 'We met them. Last night. They were in our house and they were telling us about the other neighbours, and—'

Mary was frowning. 'Perhaps I'll leave you to it today. You definitely need a bit more rest. Sounds like you've had a bad dream or something?' She laughed a tiny laugh, like a bird twittering to its friend.

'No . . .' Anna was sure the woman was lying, but she couldn't work out why. She stared at her, helplessly. 'I don't understand.'

Mary's voice grew harder, but she kept the tight little smile pasted on her face. 'You are mistaken, dear. I can assure you, there is *no one* living in that house.'

Six

Eve: One Year Earlier

Eve had never liked walking home this way in the dark, but Casey insisted it would be fine. People walking across parks after sunset might be at risk, but not couples, right? Eve wasn't sure she agreed, but Casey was insistent. As usual.

Besides, it wasn't that dark, was it? It was a well-used park and there were a few streetlights. Although the light they gave off was a muted orange and it only shone on the path, leaving the normally bright shrubbery and bushes that split the grassed area from the wooded area in a shadowy darkness.

Casey wasn't really paying attention to her, either. Earbuds shoved in, listening to a podcast. As usual.

Eve marched on ahead, quickening her pace. The sooner they got out of this park, the better. She hoped the gate on the other side of the duck pond would still be open. She had a horrible feeling that it was closed at dusk, but she really hoped she was wrong, because the alternative was to cut through the lower part of the dog area, through the woods.

Moonlight bounced off the water, and there was barely a sound around them. A faint rustling in the reeds at the edge of the pond, which was probably ducks settling themselves in for the night. Or maybe those tiny moorhens. They were her favourite, with their small-bird syndrome and their aggressive little honks.

She was aware of Casey behind her, and that should've made her feel safer. Casey cast a fairly imposing presence, compared to her own slight frame. But Casey wasn't really aware of her discomfort because Casey was acting determinedly unscared.

As usual.

Eve hoped that her eyes were playing tricks on her when she saw the closed gate, the padlock hanging from the sliding lock. But she knew she was right. She was right when she'd thought the gates were locked at dusk. And now there was only one way to actually get there, unless they turned back to where they came in – and Casey wouldn't be happy about that. Not when it was almost time for *Naked Attraction*.

Shit.

'Casey . . . I think we need to turn back.' It was so frustrating, being so close to home but with no way out. She could almost see their front door from here. But it wasn't like they could climb over the fence to get out. It was two metres high with spikes all along it.

'Oh, for heaven's sake, Eve. We can cut through the dogging wood. It's no big deal.'

No one was really sure if the wood was mostly used by dog walkers or actual doggers, but the fact that they had the only means of access late at night probably suggested the latter. No cars, of course, on-foot doggers only. Casey reckoned they wore masks and carried out pagan rituals while also fucking whichever randoms happened to be hiding in the bushes, but Eve was a bit of a prude about these sorts of things and really didn't want to know if any of that was true. She liked to think it was late-night dog walkers who sneaked in through the broken gate – people who lived nearby and didn't like to let their dogs poo on the pavement. Naïve Eve wasn't her nickname for nothing, but she didn't mind it. Not really.

34

She turned left and took the fork in the path that led away from the tranquillity of the duck pond, towards the looming darkness of the woods. There could be anyone or anything in there, lurking.

Stop it, Eve!

While Casey was hooked on reality-TV trash like *Naked Attraction* and *Married At First Sight*, Eve was more inclined towards true-crime documentaries, and low-budget horror films on Shudder. There was something thrilling about scaring yourself silly and knowing it wasn't real. OK, well, the true crime was real. But the way they made those shows, dramatising the events, it made them seem unreal. There was a distance between what really happened and the glossy version on screen. There had to be. Or else no one would be able to stomach watching them. Even the glossy versions turned her stomach sometimes. As for the horror films, they were just fun. Especially as she usually watched them alone, late at night. Alone. And then afterwards, to dilute the fear and wash it away, she'd watch re-runs of quiz shows. *The Chase*, in particular, was a favourite. She'd often thought of applying to go on but was scared she would freeze when faced with the reality of it. The pressure. It was easier to watch from afar.

Another rustling sound, this time from the woods. Probably just a small animal, settling down for the night or waking up, ready to start its nocturnal life. She glanced around at Casey, who was still plugged into the earbuds. Oblivious.

Eve couldn't help but think that walking through a park at night, oblivious, was not a sensible option. Not at all. But then they were supposed to be looking out for one another, right? But would Casey even notice if someone grabbed her and dragged her into the bushes? Would Casey be spurred into action, the great white knight on a charger, ready to save the damsel in distress?

She could make out the opening ahead, dimly lit by one of the streetlights on the road outside. How far to go? A hundred metres?

She could run that. She wasn't fit, but anyone could run a hundred metres, right? She picked up her pace a little, swinging her arms to propel herself forward. Casey's footsteps faded a little as she raced on ahead.

That rustle again. Closer. The footsteps too. Had Casey speeded up to catch her?

Eve was turning her head to glance back at Casey once more when the hand went over her mouth. She didn't have time to work out was going on. Just felt the force of being yanked backwards into the darkness, breathing in the sour smell of the hand that did not belong to the person that she loved. The person who was oblivious, still, having fallen too far behind.

Eve kicked back, feeling her heels connect with bone.

A screech of pain. Sour breath on her face. 'You fucking bitch.'

Then she was on the ground, her face pushed into the dirt. Sticks and stones *can* hurt, you know. She managed to turn her head to the side, but the hand pressed down on her cheek, her mouth, stopping her cries. She caught a glimpse of her attacker's face, a horrible tattoo of an open-mouthed snake winding its way up his neck. She didn't want to see that. Didn't want him to know she'd seen him. So she closed her eyes, felt the weight on her back and the fight drain out of her. Fleeting thoughts of those horror movies, those true-crime dramas. Shouting at the TV: *fight back, you have to fight back* . . . But just like a quiz show, it's so much easier when you're watching at home.

Her eyes flew open as the pain ripped into her from behind. And she wasn't there any more. Her mind left her body. She was numb. And the last thing she saw before she passed out was Casey, standing too far away to help. Wide-eyed, watching.

Frozen.

Not so fearless, after all. Not at all.

Seven

ANNA: SATURDAY

Anna crept back into her own house and closed the door quietly. Her heart rate had slowed, but she still felt rattled by what had just happened.

Stay calm, Anna.

She leaned back against the front door, trying to regulate her breathing. She had to think. She didn't want to bother Peter with this. Not yet. Not until she had figured it out. If this had something to do with her, then she had to get things clear before she brought it up with him. She'd been stupid to get so panicked in front of that nosy crow from Number Three. Mary, wasn't it? The last thing she wanted was to attract the attention of the local busybody. She racked her brains for fragments of last night's conversation, worried that she'd revealed something to Lindsay and Ritchie that had put them in danger. Caused them to flee.

But it made no sense.

It was only last night that they'd spoken. How could anything she'd said even have raised an alarm? Lindsay and Ritchie had no idea who she was or why she had moved here.

She walked through to the kitchen, and almost jumped out of her skin. Peter was leaning against the counter, scrolling through his phone. The tray of uncooked bacon sat on the hob, the unopened loaf of bread beside it.

Peter lifted his head as she walked in. 'Ah, there you are. It's like the *Mary Celeste* in here. I was starting to think you weren't coming back.'

Anna walked over to the oven and turned the grill on. 'Needed some air.' She tried not to catch Peter's eye, but she could feel his gaze boring into her. She was pretty good at lying, but only when she planned it. She was caught off guard now and she had a feeling she wasn't going to get away with any bullshit. He had warned her last night, more than once, to watch what she was saying. They'd only been there five minutes and already she'd invited strangers into their house. Got drunk with them. And now they were gone.

Shit.

'Um, actually . . . I popped next door to see Lindsay. I couldn't find any paracetamol.' She paused, realising that she had forgotten about her pounding skull after the shock, and it didn't actually hurt any more.

Peter slid the tray under the grill. 'Did they sleep in half the day too? Jeez, we were wasted—'

'They're gone.'

Peter crossed his arms, and his brow settled into a frown. This was his usual response now, whenever she tried to tell him anything. Like he was struggling to trust a word she said. 'What do you mean? Gone out for the day? Gone on holiday?'

'No . . . *gone*, gone. Like they were never there.'

Peter rolled his eyes. 'Don't be ridiculous. They didn't mention anything about leaving when we spent most of last night with them, did they? Are you sure you're not making this up for some sort of drama? Haven't we had enough of that for a while?'

Anna bristled. She hated it when he did this. Acting like she was being hysterical. Making her feel stupid. 'No. I think they're actually gone. Moved out. All that's in their living room is the basic furniture, like ours. I rang the bell a few times. Their car is gone—'

'Maybe they just don't have any clutter?'

'I wondered that, but it just . . . it didn't look right. Anyway, then the woman from Number Three turned up. Mary?' Anna paused and let out a mirthless little laugh. 'She said no one lives in that house.'

Peter stared at her for what seemed like an age. 'What?'

'I know, I know. We saw them in the garden, right? Then they came to the gate . . .'

'We didn't see them in the garden. We heard them. Maybe they were further away. Over the other fence, in the side access?'

Anna shook her head. 'No, I swear. They were in that garden. They lived in that house. I know they did. I know it.' She grabbed a tea towel and pulled out the grill tray. The bacon was already quite done, but she liked it crispy. 'Can you butter the bread, please?'

'Anna . . .'

'Never mind, I'll do it.' She reached over for the bread and he grabbed her wrist. Not hard, but not gently. He pulled her towards him.

'Anna, we need to talk about this. We were warned about being discreet. I am sure this is just a weird misunderstanding somewhere, but I think we also need to consider that this is something to do with us. Well . . .' He let go of her wrist. 'With *you*, specifically.'

A sharp prick of annoyance threatened, but she pushed it away. 'But no one knows where we are,' she said quietly, laying the bread back on the counter and trying to ignore the burning in her wrist. This was his latest thing, grabbing and gripping just a little too tightly. 'We're safe here, right?'

Peter sighed and ran his hand over his chin. The day-old stubble made a scratching sound. 'Well, of course *someone* knows where we are.'

'Only Jasper—'

'And the rest of his team. The ones who followed us up here, for a start. It's not unfeasible that there could be a leak.'

She shook her head. 'No. He told us we were safe here.'

'He also told us not to get too close to the neighbours, not to ask too many questions, and to try to stay under the radar. We already blew it.'

'You don't know that.'

'It's witness protection, Anna. It's good, but it's not foolproof. Nothing is. Jasper told us this. He said even going abroad was no guarantee, but it would be the best bet . . . but we chose this instead. *You* chose this instead.'

He was trying his hardest to needle her, but she refused to bite. 'But I don't understand. If they know where we are, why not just come for us?'

'We need to call Jasper. Maybe they did come for us and got the wrong house. Maybe they had to take Lindsay and Ritchie somewhere safe? Maybe they had to warn the street to stay quiet?'

'While we slept through the whole thing?'

Peter took the butter out of the fridge and started scraping the hard block with a knife. 'I agree that it doesn't make a lot of sense.'

'Coincidence, then,' Anna said, handing him slices of bread. 'We'll check in with Jasper though, just in case. Then I'll ask the others about—'

Her sentence was cut off by the ringing doorbell. That awful shrill sound from before.

'Oh, great,' Peter said. 'Now what?'

Anna headed through to answer the door.

'Anna! Jeez . . . leave it.'

She ignored him, opening the door on the chain. She'd expected Mary again, but instead she was faced with a teenage girl. Muddy-blonde hair in a rough style that Anna couldn't decide was styled or just messy. The girl rolled her eyes, looked bored.

'Hey,' she said. 'I'm Donna. From Number Seven. Across the road? I saw you move in last night. My mum told me to come over and invite you round.' She bit her lip. Shrugged. 'Whatever. We're having a barbecue. Everyone's coming.'

'Oh, I . . . hang on, let me open the door properly.' Anna closed the door a little and took the chain off, then opened it fully.

Donna pushed her hair away from her face. She looked a little alarmed. 'That's it. That's the message. You don't have to invite me in or anything.' Despite her attempt at nonchalance, she leaned forward slightly, trying to get a look into the house.

Anna smiled. The girl was curious. It explained why she was watching them from the upstairs window last night. As Anna had suspected, there probably wasn't much to do around here.

'Do you *want* to come in? I mean, you're more than welcome. We haven't actually unpacked anything yet.'

Donna shrugged and took a step back. 'Nah, you're good. Maybe some other time. I'd better go.' She rolled her eyes again. 'Apparently I'm making the coleslaw.'

Anna sensed Peter behind her, and she moved aside to let him stand next to her.

'Hi,' he said. 'I'm Peter. I think I saw you last night . . . at the window?'

Donna flushed red. 'Sorry, it's just . . . well, no one new has moved in for a while.'

'No need to apologise,' Anna said. 'And sorry, I don't think I said . . . I'm Anna.'

Donna nodded. 'Right. Come over at six. Is that OK?' She turned to leave.

'Oh wait . . .' Anna said. Donna stopped and turned back, raised her eyebrows. 'Did you know the people at Number Eight? Lindsay and Ritchie?'

Something flashed in Donna's eyes. But whatever it was, she managed to hide it again quickly.

'No one lives there.' She turned away and hurried down the path and across the road, disappearing into her house without a backwards glance.

A low, churning feeling started in her gut as Anna watched the girl retreat. First Mary. Now Donna. Were they both lying?

Was everyone lying?

And if so, then the real question was: why?

Eight

'What about "Jasper"?'

Detective Sergeant Marcus Cole frowned. 'I don't know. Is it not a bit floppy-haired public schoolboy?' A loud sound of crisps being crunched travelled down the line, and he pulled the phone away from his ear. 'Sorry, am I interrupting your lunch, guv?'

'Marcus, it really doesn't matter. Just pick a name—'

'I know, but I've already—'

'Jasper sounds about right, if you ask me. I think your clients will feel at ease with a Jasper. It's memorable, but it's not that popular – hence they're unlikely to have any others in their contacts and therefore less likely to blurt your name out to the wrong people accidentally. Those other names—'

'Yeah, I know. But there's not a lot I can do about that now.'

'Fine then, that's settled. I'll get the file updated. Now, do you have everything you need for this one? You know the defendant's legal team are talking about an appeal. Something about new evidence, although I'm really not sure what. We all know our man is behind something much, much bigger – we just don't know exactly what yet. There's still a team on it. If I was him, I'd be biding my time and keeping my trap shut.'

'We all know that people like him think they're too clever for prison. He'll be in there boasting about how he'll be out in three months, once he's pulled the correct strings.'

His boss, Detective Inspector Lydia Mills, sighed down the phone. 'Thing is, without anything additional to pin on him, he's probably right. At the very least he'll be moved to a Cat D, and we all know what those places are like. Whatever it is he's up to, he'll be able to conduct it from there, swanning about like Jeffrey bloody Archer.'

'I hate the clever ones the most,' Marcus said, leaning back in his chair. 'Give me a good old-fashioned cat burglar any day.'

Lydia laughed. 'Are you saying cat burglars aren't clever? All that shimmying up drainpipes and opening windows with their swag bags over one shoulder? Their flexibility and co-ordination set them apart from all those non-cat burglars – you know, the scumbags who smash windows and steal bags from cars? Absolutely no class.'

Marcus heard the sound of a drink being sucked through a straw. 'I'm planning to come over and see you when I can. Have a proper face-to-face. Maybe you can buy me lunch and it won't be at your desk?'

'Good idea. It'd be nice to meet properly and put a face to the voice. This project is a big deal for us, Marcus. I'm sure I don't have to say the words.'

'No, guv. Message received loud and clear.'

He could hear her voice in his head, even after she'd hung up.

'Do *not* fuck this up.'

Nine

ANNA: SATURDAY

The back garden at Number Seven looked bigger than Anna and Peter's, but of course it didn't have the view. The back fence was just a fence, and they could see the tops of thin trees behind it – trees that had not long been planted and would take years to mature and fully shield the house from the road that ran along to the rear. But other than the garden, the downstairs of the house was exactly the same layout as theirs. The only other difference was the upstairs balcony with the sea view. Not that they had been given a tour of the place. They were standing in the kitchen, listening to the washing machine finish its spin cycle.

'We asked if we could have Number Four, didn't we, Kevin? But they said it was already taken. Such a shame. The children would've loved to have had direct access to the beach. You don't have any kids, do you?'

'No, we—'

'Must be weird rattling around, just your two selves.'

Anna forced a smile. Lorraine Whitelaw was smiling too, but it didn't quite reach her eyes. She looked to be around fifty, Anna thought, but she wore the years like someone carrying a very heavy chain around their neck. The husband, Kevin, was wiry and washed-out. He wearily took a tray of meat from the fridge and disappeared outside. Peter shrugged and followed in his wake, leaving the two women in the kitchen. Lorraine shook a bag of salad into a bowl, and didn't say anything else. Anna felt even more sorry for Donna after meeting her uninspiring parents. She wondered why they had volunteered to host this welcome party when they didn't seem particularly welcoming. It was definitely not the right time to ask about Lindsay and Ritchie – in fact, Anna was starting to wonder if she had hallucinated the whole of last night.

Without warning, Lorraine lifted her head from the bowl of salad leaves and shouted in the general direction of the stairs, making Anna flinch. 'Donna! Get Max and go outside. You're not sitting in your rooms all night.'

'I brought this,' Anna said, offering the bottle of wine. One of the nice ones from her case, because she hadn't had time to find a shop yet to buy anything else.

Lorraine sniffed. 'I like those boxes of Sauvignon Blanc from Lidl.' She took the bottle of red and glanced at the label, then shoved it to the back of the worktop. 'I'm sure someone will drink it. If not, I'll stick it in a spag bol.'

Anna wanted to ask why the woman was being so hostile after inviting them over, but she held her tongue. Lorraine, however, seemed to read her mind.

'This was all Mary's idea,' she said. 'Reckoned ours is the best house for a gathering, despite all of them being the bloody same. I said John at Number Four should do it, then at least we could spill out on to the beach. But he won't be back from work until later, apparently.'

The doorbell rang then, saving them both.

'You go outside,' Lorraine said. 'Kevin will sort you with a drink.'

The sound of footsteps clattered down the stairs and a young boy ran past her, followed closely by Donna, who threw a quick 'hi' as she passed, before disappearing outside after her brother. Anna followed, heading over to the barbecue, where Kevin was poking at already blackening sausages with tongs. He and Peter both held a bottle of beer.

'Ah, there you are.' Peter was wearing his patient smile. He was good at this sort of thing, where Anna was not. Despite all the events she had to attend for work, she did not like feeling out of place amongst strangers. Especially sober. The hangover was still barely a recent memory, but a beer would sort it out for sure. She took one from a bucket filled with ice and twisted off the cap, flicking it into the icy water. She took a long pull, and the cold, fizzy liquid made her feel instantly better.

She turned to the sound of laughing voices.

'Well, hello there!'

Two women stood in front of her. Thirty-something. One was as wide as she was tall, with ginger hair brushed into a quiff and a box of beer under her arm. The other was shorter, about Anna's height, but a bit curvier, with a pretty heart-shaped face and dark wavy hair pulled back in a ponytail. It was the bigger one who'd spoken, but the cuter one stepped forward and held out a hand. 'I'm Beth,' she said with a gentle smile. 'And this is my wife—'

'Finlay Wallace,' the other woman said, in a mid-Atlantic drawl that boomed across the grass. 'So awesome to meet you both.'

Anna and Peter introduced themselves, and the women helped themselves to beers, adding the bottles from the box into the ice bucket.

'Lorraine, I told ya last time. More ice, honey!' Finlay strode off, leaving Beth smiling shyly.

'Sorry about her,' she said. 'She's loud and quite annoying, but she's a sweetheart really.'

Anna, emboldened by the half-bottle of beer that had topped up her blood-alcohol level nicely, leaned in and whispered, 'To be honest, it's nice to hear a bit of *life*, after meeting Lorraine.'

Beth laughed quietly, and the two women chinked their bottles together. 'I can already see that we're going to get along.' Beth took a mouthful of beer. 'How are you settling in so far?'

'Oh, fine. Fine. It's just . . .' Anna let her sentence trail off. Was there any point in asking again about Lindsay and Ritchie?

Beth looked at her quizzically, but Anna just shrugged and took another drink. It was too early to try to confide in anyone else after the reception she'd had so far.

'Bit of a late one last night. I'm not sure I'm fully with it yet.' She glanced around, looking for Lorraine. Saw that she was still in the kitchen. 'Lorraine wasn't the friendliest . . .'

Beth rolled her eyes. 'She has appalling social skills, don't take any notice. Most people here keep themselves to themselves – I think we've only all met up about twice in the six months we've been here. I think it would be nice if we were a bit more of a cohesive community, but to be honest it's been hard. On the surface it's friendly enough, but everyone's pretty guarded . . .'

Beth seemed like someone Anna could get to know, and it seemed as if she needed someone to talk to too. But it was early days, and Anna had to keep her own situation in mind. Jasper had drilled it in repeatedly about not getting too involved, but it was hard to fight that instinct of wanting to fit in.

Anna wanted to keep talking, but their chat was interrupted as more people arrived in the garden – a glamorous couple in their mid-twenties whose names flashed back to Anna as soon as she saw the little dog the woman was carrying in a large pink bag. This must be Asya, and her husband, Brooklin. Anna tried to avoid making judgements on them before they'd said a word, but it was a diffi-cult task. These women with their fake hair and over-plumped lips confused her and made her a little uneasy. She'd always preferred a more natural look.

Beth caught her looking and smiled. 'She's really pretty under all the slap and hairspray but you'll rarely see her without it. Insecure, I suppose. I feel sorry for these young girls who don't realise what they've got.'

Anna nodded. She was about to launch into a diatribe about the damaging effects of social media on young people's self-image but then another couple arrived and she pushed it away. This wasn't a day for her soapbox.

Relax, Anna. Try to just enjoy yourself?

'Hi there, you must be Anna?' A well-built man who looked to be around her age held out a hand. 'I'm Bradley,' he said. 'Beckford. I live down the far end at Number One.' He turned and took the hand of a slim blonde who'd walked up beside him. 'And this is my fiancée, Lacy.'

'Hey,' Lacy said, leaning in to give Anna a hug. 'So nice to have you here!' She smiled at Beth, but she didn't say anything more. They stood smiling at each other until Anna began to feel uncomfortable.

Why were these people so awkward?

Lacy took a couple of beers from the ice bucket and handed one to Bradley, then she turned back to Anna. 'We can't stay long – left the dogs in the garden.' She nodded towards the furball in Asya's bag, who was looking over at them with suspicion. 'Ben and Jerry don't really get on well with BooBoo over there.' At that, the small dog yelped and Asya leaned in to its ear, talking to it like she was cooing to a baby.

Anna regretted coming to the party. Her head wasn't clear enough to interact with all of these new people. Not when she was trying so hard not to say the wrong thing and blow her own cover. She had to be so careful about what she could and could not say.

She couldn't shake the thought of Lindsay and Ritchie from her head. Both Mary and Donna claiming that there was no one in that house. But they *did* live there, Anna was sure of it. But how was she going to get to the bottom of it if her new neighbours were insistent about lying to her, and she herself had to be careful what she said about everything? This new life was already exhausting, and they'd only just arrived.

She glanced around the garden, looking for Peter. Needing to escape the attention for a while. She spotted him in the corner, talking to Mary, a plate of food on his lap.

A burger. That was as good a reason as any.

'Would you all excuse me for a bit? I am absolutely starving!'

Beth bent down to take another beer. 'Go for it. Just don't fill up on too many carcinogens.'

Bradley walked with her across the grass towards the barbecue. She didn't feel like she could get rid of him, but she really wanted to get rid of him. The headache from earlier was making a re-appearance, and she was small-talked out.

'I hope everything's OK with you in your new house. The whole street is pretty secure, but . . .' He lowered his voice and leaned in closer. 'The Street stands out a bit in this area. Bit too posh for some of the locals, you know what I mean? Best to be vigilant.'

Anna eyed the blackened burgers. Her appetite had gone. She was starting to feel quite creeped out. 'Everything's good so far,' she said. 'Thanks, though. I, er, I think I might head back home now, actually. I think the journey took it out of us a bit.'

She hurried away from him towards Peter, who looked up and clearly read the signs. He laid his plate on the table next to Mary and walked over to join Anna, who took his hand and led him into the kitchen, where thankfully no one was lurking. She practically dragged him through the house and out of the front door.

'I'm starting to wonder if we've made a mistake,' she said, as she closed the door to Number Seven behind them. 'I still don't understand what's gone on with Lindsay and Ritchie, and I don't feel like I can ask anyone else – not after the reactions from Mary and Donna. They are both obviously lying . . . and *I've* got to lie to everyone, and it's already feeling like it's just too much!' She felt tears pricking at her eyes.

Peter let go of her hand as they reached their own front door. 'We *both* have to lie, remember? It's your fault that we've ended up here. There's no point whinging about it now.'

His harsh words stung, and she blinked away her tears. 'But—'

'Go and get some sleep. We're both exhausted. Everything will be fine. Remember what Jasper said – take time to settle in. Don't draw attention to yourselves. This is *your* mess, Anna, but we're just going to have to get on with it.'

She watched him stomp up the stairs, and then the tears came again.

Anna had never felt more alone.

Ten

StreetChat WhatsApp Group

~Lorraine #7
So what did we all think of them?

~Beth #5
I only chatted to her for a bit but she seemed lovely. Hope to get to know her better. It really would be nice if we all met up a bit more, wouldn't it?

~Lorraine #7
Bit stuck up . . . did you see the fancy wine she brought?

~Brooklin #2
Too much quality for you, Lorraine? I'll drink it if you get stuck ☺

~Lorraine #7
He told Kev the wife's a writer . . . Bet it's all fancy stuff with big words that none of us can read.

~Asya #2

LOL speak for yersel! I can read perfectly well, thanks very much. Just bought myself that new book by Jordan actually, she's a great writer.

~Brooklin #2

actual LOL

~Mary #3

Well, I think we should give them a chance . . . and Beth's right, we should start making this more of a community – not just on here.

~Lorraine #7

Er, this group was set up to report security concerns, not for chit-chat . . . after that beach gate got vandalised right after we all moved in.

~Brooklin #2

Are you actually reading what you're typing, Lorraine? You're the biggest gossip on The Street . . .

~Asya #2

Aye. Maybe spend more time with your own lot instead of being all judgey about others, Lorraine #bekind

~John #4

Hi. Just wondering if anyone is going to mention the elephant in the room?

~Bradley #1 is typing . . .

~Brooklin #2
Elephant?! Jeez this chat is batshit most of the time but it's gone to a whole new level today – PMSL

~Beth #5
John . . . if you're talking about Number 8 . . .

~Bradley #1 is typing . . .

~John #4 is typing . . .

~Mary #3
Let's get back to the new neighbours, shall we? We should probably invite them in here. They're on the beach side so it makes sense that they're aware of the previous breach, even if we've been assured that the gate is now secure.

~Bradley #1
I think we should let them settle in. And stop the gossip. This is not what this place is meant to be about, is it? John – did you have anything you wanted to add?

~John #4 is typing . . .

~Bradley #1
John? FFS – stop teasing us with your non-messages. LOL

Eleven

Anna: Sunday

Anna woke early after a fitful night's sleep. The blinds weren't completely closed, and the sun had slid in like a laser across the bed. Peter was wearing an eye mask and didn't stir, so she'd left him to it, pulled on a pair of leggings and a light sweatshirt, finding her trainers squashed at the bottom of one of the cases. They needed to unpack, and she really needed to go shopping soon. She didn't even know what shops there were nearby. Since they'd arrived, they'd existed on what had been left in the fridge for them. She hadn't touched a thing at the barbecue.

That was for later, though. First, she needed to clear her head and stretch out her limbs. She needed to start thinking about getting into a routine of sorts, in this new life of hers. She had money in her brand-new savings account for now – but she didn't want to fritter that away. She would need it in the future, she hoped, if they eventually managed to get out of this programme and start again for real.

At some point she was going to have to decide what she was going to write next, and hope that she would be able to find a new agent for it, without her backlist as a lure. For the first time since her debut, it really was going to be all about the book. The thought excited her, even if it was a little daunting.

Anna left the house via the back gate. There was a set of wooden steps leading down to the beach, just past the house to the left. Number Eight.

Lindsay and Ritchie.

Stop it, Anna! Don't think about that right now.

She took a deep breath, inhaling the sea air.

The beach was glorious. The tide was out, and the honey-yellow sand seemed to stretch for miles towards the sparkling blue sea. At each end of the row of houses, tall groynes served as fences. Keeping the riffraff out, if what Bradley had said was true. Not that she had a problem with riffraff. You needed all walks of life, especially to fuel the imagination. And it had been very useful to know some of the 'wrong side of the tracks' types back in her old life. Best she avoided those sorts now. She climbed down the steps, jumping off the last one into the soft, thick sand.

She'd barely made it halfway to the shore when she heard loud barking behind her. Anna turned back towards the houses, and saw Bradley on the path. Speak of the devil. He waved, then unclipped the leads of the two German shepherds he was straining to keep hold of.

Anna remembered Lacy's quip from the barbecue. It was no wonder they didn't bring these two along when that powder puff of a handbag dog was there. They'd rip it apart faster than a chew toy.

Luckily Anna was OK with dogs, or she might have been alarmed at the two brown and blonde brutes that came hurtling towards her, and right past her into the sea.

Bradley jogged across the sand. 'Don't mind them,' he said. 'Timid as mice, the pair of them.' He grinned. 'Well, except when someone comes to the front door. As guard dogs, they're pretty effective, even if it just means deafening an intruder with their racket.'

'I can't imagine there are many intruders lurking around here. Not with gates at both ends of the street and the beach.'

Bradley frowned. 'You'd be surprised. Like I said – not everyone is happy with this development. It was all set to be a cruise-line terminal, with some shops and restaurants, but they pulled the plug at the last minute.'

Anna pushed her feet into the sand. 'Someone with deeper pockets?'

'Something like that.' He laid a hand on her arm. 'Anyway, I'm glad I caught you. Was there anything you wanted to know about the place? Maybe I can help . . .'

Anna sighed inwardly but kept a polite smile pasted on her face. She wasn't really up for company right now. 'I was about to go for a walk—'

He nudged her with his elbow. 'Ah, come on, you've got all day to walk. You're not writing anything at the moment, are you?'

Anna wondered how he knew what she did, and that he knew she wasn't doing it at the moment – she was sure she hadn't told anyone anything at the party. Perhaps Peter had, though – he usually liked an opportunity to tell people what a cushy job she had, despite it being far from the truth. She decided not to say anything. It would only provide an opportunity for her to accidentally reveal something she shouldn't. She was still very much getting used to living a constant lie. She might be able to sound Bradley out, though. Maybe he might be more willing to tell her what had happened to Lindsay and Ritchie?

She turned back to the sea, watched the dogs playing in the lapping waves. Tongues lolling and tails wagging with delight. Such a simple life. She was wrong to think of them as brutes. She wished she could be so carefree.

'Fine, walk with me, then.' She set off towards the shore, keeping an easy pace. He walked beside her for a bit, and the silence soon became awkward.

Anna opened her mouth to speak, just as the dogs came bounding across the sand, panting. They stopped in front of Bradley, then proceeded to shake the water off themselves, covering both Anna and Bradley with a torrent of sea spray.

'Oh shit, sorry! They must like you . . .'

Anna felt a stab of annoyance but she swallowed it back and smiled instead. 'No worries. I needed to buy a new top anyway. Talking of which, are there any shops nearby? Neither of us have left the street since we arrived and I have absolutely no idea where we are in relation to anything.'

Bradley laughed. Then pointed to the left. 'See that big bridge? That's the shiny new Forth Road Bridge. It's on the other side of Edinburgh. So if you go past it, you've gone too far.'

'Funny. I know Edinburgh is that way. About twelve miles, Peter said. He also said there's a train station but it looks a bit of a walk from here?'

'It's about twenty, twenty-five minutes' walk, along to the edge of Prestonpans then up the hill through the houses. Or you can get the bus from bottom road – that's what the locals call it – that's the road that runs along the front of The Street. The town itself has got a few shops and cafés. You'll get all your groceries there, a haircut, a pharmacy, takeaway food, most essentials. Don't think you'll find any clothes, mind. Nearest place is The Fort – on the outskirts of Edinburgh. You'll need to drive, unless you want a bus that winds through every estate on the way.'

'Noted. Thank you. Oh, and I think we've pretty much met all the neighbours now, except Number Four. John, is it? He's been mysteriously absent since we arrived.'

Bradley nodded. 'John likes to keep himself to himself.'

Was Anna mistaken, or had a small, dark cloud passed over Bradley's face at the mention of this neighbour? She'd been all set to ask about Number Eight, but changed her mind. She had a strong suspicion she'd be met with another blank response, and she wanted to dig around on that herself before asking anyone else. Mary and Donna had lied to her face. She had no doubt that Bradley would do the same.

'Anyway, I'll leave you to your walk. These two are after their mid-morning snacks.' He clipped a lead on to each of the two dogs. 'See you later, Anna. Pop round if you like. I'm sure Lacy would love to get to know you. It can be lonely working from home sometimes. She's just bought herself a new curry cookbook that she's dying to try out on someone other than me and the mutts.'

Curry . . . of course! Anna pushed her hands into her pockets. 'We'll take you up on that . . .' She paused, deciding to test him. 'Out of interest, though, is there a good Indian takeaway in the town?'

'I think the best one is along the other way, in Port Seton. Sorry, I can't remember the name of it. Lacy's doing her best to keep us away from takeaways and make everything herself – hence the latest cookbook fad.'

'Roger that.' Anna watched him walk away. Why had she not thought of this earlier? Because her head was too fried, that was why. They had no shopping in yet because they hadn't needed anything. Their first night had been the curry that Ritchie had ordered in. He'd said he would give her the number, but he hadn't. Maybe the receipt, or some packaging with the name of the restaurant, was with the rubbish. She could call them – or go in. That would be better. She could use the pretence of wanting to give them a tip. It was an excellent meal, after all. The restaurant could confirm that they sent that order. The restaurant could confirm that Lindsay and Ritchie existed, and that they lived at Number Eight.

Anna knew the couple existed, despite the other neighbours trying to convince her that they didn't.

She was going to get to the bottom of it, even if no one was willing to help her. People couldn't just disappear . . . not without help. Or something terrible happening to them – and whether it was good or bad, someone had to know something. She wasn't going to let them fob her off that easily.

She left the beach and headed back around to the front of the house. She wanted another look at Number Eight. She peered in through the window again, but it was just as before. No signs of life. No signs of anything. That familiar, fizzing feeling of anxiety started to blossom in her chest. Her throat. She swallowed hard, tried to regulate her breathing.

Was this her fault? Had someone come looking for her and found Lindsay instead? None of this made sense. She stole another glance through the neighbours' window before stepping over the boundary into her own front garden.

There was a box on the doorstep.

Anna stared at it for a moment as a carousel of possibilities spun around inside her head. A gun, left as a warning? A bag of drugs, left as a reminder? A severed finger, because she'd suddenly materialised inside a gangster movie? But no one was supposed to know that she was here. This place was meant to be safe . . . and she most definitely hadn't ordered anything to be sent here.

Get a grip, Anna!

She used the tip of her trainer to lift the edge of the lid.

Jesus, Anna, what are you doing?

The lid was still on, but slightly askew. She took a step back. There was no way of knowing what was in the box without look-ing. But maybe she shouldn't be looking. Maybe she should call Jasper . . .

Stop being ridiculous, Anna!

She took a deep breath and stepped forward again, then gently kicked the lid off the box, scurrying back and screwing her eyes shut, holding her hands over her ears as she waited for a bang.

Nothing happened.

She opened her eyes and peered inside.

She smiled at her own stupidity, shoulders sagging as the tension flooded out.

Of course. Mary said she was going to bring it round. Presumably Peter hadn't bothered to answer the door to her.

It was a cake. It was just a bloody cake.

Twelve

The Diary

It was my therapist who suggested I start writing a diary. Well, a journal, she called it. I'm still not sure I know the difference. I started off with one boring, three-for-a-pound reporter's notebook and a cheap blue biro, but fast-forward a few years and I'm kind of addicted to fancy Moleskines and Faber-Castell fine liners. Those pens are much smoother to write with. At least everyone knows what to buy me for Christmas and birthdays. I keep the whole lot – nineteen notebooks and counting – in an old brown luggage chest I found at a car-boot sale. I'd been bored to tears and ready to leave when I spotted it. But when I did, I knew I had to have it. I picked up a new padlock in the crap little shop in the village that sells plastic boxes and cheap clothes pegs. I didn't bother to pay. Sometimes it's the smallest things that bring the biggest thrills.

I keep other stuff in that chest too. Stuff that no one else knows about. Stuff that could get me into *big* trouble.

Not that anyone would dare to try to break into it anyway. They're all shit-scared of me, even though they pretend they aren't.

I'm 'rehabilitated', you know.

What a fucking joke.

I reckon that Lindsay might know the truth. Some of it, at least. Maybe that's why her and that knob-end husband left like that. Overnight, no notice, no tearful goodbyes.

Yeah, that's right.

The new woman at Number Six *isn't* going mad. She *did* have a neighbour called Lindsay who lived at Number Eight.

Briefly.

Not that I'll be letting on. It's best to keep yourself to yourself on this street.

We all know that no one likes a gossip.

Thirteen

It had been years since Anna had been to an out-of-town shopping centre. She mostly ordered what she needed online, or occasionally popped into one of the nicer shopping streets in London if she felt like treating herself. The very concept of spending time in the normal high-street chain stores filled her with dread. That slightly too loud piped music, the hordes of people dragging carrier bags and screaming children around, all just waiting for the moment they could sit down in Costa for a hot-chocolate treat. She loathed those coffee shops too, always preferring to support the small local places instead.

As she pulled her new ugly, functional car into a parking space, and looked around at all the concrete and glass and harassed-looking shoppers, she realised she was going to have a lot more adjustment to do than she'd thought. Apart from anything else, should she really be here? On her own?

Jasper had told her to try to live life as normally as she could, but there had to be limits. Could she really just go about her business and remain safe? What if someone recognised her? What if someone told the wrong person? What if they found her?

Stop it, Anna.

Some people liked shopping. Of course they did. It wasn't their fault that she found the whole experience exhausting and disheartening, as, no matter what size she thought she was, every single shop thought differently. Even within the same shop it was a lottery as to whether the size twelve in one type of jeans was equivalent to a twelve in another, or would she need a fourteen? As for tops, forget it – anything from an eight to a sixteen, depending on the style.

Maybe she should start a new career in clothing size standardisation.

She'd just stepped out of the car and put her bag over her shoulder when her phone beeped. It wasn't an alert from WhatsApp or Messenger, because she had the notifications turned off, and the only people in her contacts list were Peter and Jasper – and she knew that neither of them was likely to be messaging her right now. She pulled it out and held it up. The biometric unlock opened the screen and she clicked the notification banner.

> Hi Anna! Mr StreetMate, here – your friendly Security Bot! Remember to keep your notifications switched on because I'm going to be pinging you lots of really useful info! Did you know most burglaries occur due to occupier error? Did you lock all the doors today, Anna?

'Oh, fuck off.' She swiped the notification away and muted the volume. She'd forgotten about the app that had downloaded itself on to her phone when the Wi-Fi had connected at home. And why was it asking if she'd locked the doors? How did it know she wasn't at home? Did it have a GPS tracker on it or something? Urgh.

Creepy.

She'd have to ask Jasper about it, she supposed, but she would deal with it later. There were so many things to deal with later, including finding that Indian restaurant. A quick search of the bin when she'd got back from her beach walk had yielded nothing, and it occurred to her that maybe Lindsay had taken the rubbish home – but that was absurd. The house and garden had been strewn with empty bottles. It would have taken an age to clear up.

Anyway. That could wait. First she needed to sort herself out with the clothes she was going to need for beach walking and hanging around a tiny town with absolutely nothing resembling a wine bar or even a fancy café. Hopefully she'd settle in soon, make a few friends, get back to work. As much as Lindsay and Ritchie's disappearance intrigued her, she couldn't let it take over her life completely. Some weird thing happened, she might never know what – and now she had to move on. It had nothing to do with her and Peter. They had their own shit to deal with.

But . . .

She was struggling to shake off the thoughts whirring around in her head; that desperation to know what had happened to the neighbours.

This was her big weakness. Once something found itself in her brain, she really struggled to remove it until she had a satisfactory explanation. It drove Peter mad sometimes, the way she refused to let go. But in this instance, maybe she was right to be concerned. She had come here with a big, dangling skeleton in her closet – this huge secret about who she really was and why she was really here . . . and despite the assurances from Jasper that they were safe, were they? Really?

Had she inadvertently brought danger to Lindsay and Ritchie's door? She shoved her phone back into her bag and set off towards the shops.

Focus, Anna! This is not about you. This is NOT about you.

The more she repeated it, the more she tried to convince herself of it, but it was hard to shake off the feeling that whatever had happened to her neighbours was something bad, and that the something bad was all because of her. She took a deep breath, let it out slowly while counting backwards from ten. Closed her eyes for a moment, then opened them again.

Shops, Anna. Look at the shops!

She started off in New Look. It seemed like as good a place as any. Then she moved on to Next, M&S, H&M, and finally Skechers. By the time she made it to Costa – now fully understanding that concept of a hot-chocolate treat and wishing she had a little bottle of brandy to tip into it – she was exhausted. She savoured her drink – enjoying the extra indulgence of cream and marshmallows too – while scrolling through her phone. The news was the usual clusterfuck of awfulness, and she wasn't interested in celebrity gossip. She opened up Facebook, but then realised it was pointless now that she could no longer use her real identity. She'd set up a new account, but with no friends on there it was a waste of time – although she did have a couple of requests: Bradley and Mary. She clicked on both, accepting them. Nothing from Lindsay. Time to let that one go? Chalk it up to a crazy night?

Stop it, stop it, stop it!

The more time went on, the more she suspected that Lindsay and Ritchie didn't live next door and never had – just as the other neighbours had said. They'd clearly snuck along the back footpath after climbing over into the beach, and they had *pretended* to live next door. They hadn't lied. It was Anna's fault for making an assumption. Plus, what Lindsay had said about the other residents was vague enough that they could've found it out just by being local. Everyone on The Street must use the local shops, right? Small towns are always filled with gossip. Maybe that was why Ritchie kept trying to get his wife to shut up.

If she was even his wife.

If Lindsay was even her name.

Draining the dregs of her drink, Anna's eyes went to the window. She could see the back of her car. It had taken a moment for her to realise it was hers, so unfamiliar it was still. A blonde woman was hurrying away, glancing around as if checking that no one had seen her.

Anna's heart fluttered. That woman . . . No. It couldn't be . . . She put her mug down a little too hard, and a few nosy faces turned in her direction, looking away again when they realised there was no drama. Anna grabbed her bags and ran outside.

'Hey!'

The woman was too far away to hear her. She was almost at the road. She didn't turn back, but as Anna stared at her retreating form, she was even more convinced that she was right.

'Lindsay!'

The woman hesitated, before carrying on faster.

Anna was at her car now. She pressed the key to open the boot, tossing her bags inside. Through the car, she could see that there was something attached to her windscreen, a piece of paper held down by one of the wipers. Was she mistaken? Maybe the woman was leafleting. She turned back to see that the woman was about to cross the road.

Anna thought about calling again. Running over there. But what was the point? Whoever it was didn't want to talk to her.

She went around to the front of the car and lifted the wiper. It was a piece of folded A4 paper. She was unfolding it when the commotion started. Her eyes went to the source, across the road, where the blonde woman had run to. The brakes squealed and the screaming started simultaneously, but Anna barely had time to register it before the noise stopped again. She looked on, mouth open wide, as a car door slammed and a few people shouted random things, like 'hey' and 'what the fuck?' and 'did you see that?'

But Anna was rooted to the spot.

She had seen it. The blonde woman had been dragged into a black Range Rover, which then had to swerve and take off down the wrong side of the road before righting itself on the other side of the roundabout. The whole thing had lasted seconds, and not one person had been able to do anything other than watch it unfold with horror.

Like the letter she now held, also unfolded.

Her hand shook as she held it, and judging by the writing, Lindsay's hand had been shaking as she wrote it. It was just one line of text, written hurriedly, in smoky grey eyeliner.

YOU ARE NOT SAFE IN THAT HOUSE.

Fourteen

EVE: TEN MONTHS EARLIER

Eve found herself in the last place she'd ever expected to be. Two places, in fact: in court, and in a position where she was no longer sure if she could trust her partner. She had been with Casey for fifteen years, and had never imagined for a moment that Casey was the type of person to freeze when faced with danger.

She sat in the small anteroom, sipping a tepid cup of tea, trying to process what they were telling her. Casey sat opposite, head slightly bowed. In deep thought. No doubt thinking about what had brought them here, to this.

Yes, Eve thought to herself. *If you'd only done something, then maybe we wouldn't be in this bloody mess! This mess where we have to give up our lives, our friends. Start all over again.*

The female police officer had said something earlier that had made Eve think. 'You don't have to stay together, you know. Some couples just can't find a way back after an assault like this.'

The inspector, a kind but somewhat abrupt man, had told the nice officer to shut her trap. Which Eve thought was rude, but it had made her laugh and cut the tension. Even more so watching him try to back-pedal his outburst, and succeeding only in blushing bright red.

Eve had smiled at them both, to let them know she wasn't upset. Besides, there was no way she was leaving Casey. It would be bad enough having to start a new life without having to do it on her own.

Eve had never been alone. She'd gone straight from her parents' house in the suburbs to a shared flat in the city centre, to Casey's flat, which was somewhere in between – plenty of green space, but with transport links to take them into the action when they wanted it. Then Casey's flat became *their* flat, and that was where they lived now. It had become a haven for both of them, where they'd spent countless days choosing soft furnishings, antiques, art that spoke to them both. She would miss it. They both would.

'And you won't need to take a thing, except your clothes and your personal possessions. We can arrange for a clearance company to come along and deal with all your old things.'

Eve blinked, listening to the man who'd called himself their 'handler'. He would be their key contact in their new life. Handler. That had made Eve laugh because it was all so ridiculous. She felt like she was living inside a TV crime drama.

'Eve?' he said now, laying a hand on top of hers. 'Are you listening to me?'

She nodded. 'It's a lot to take in.'

He smiled sympathetically. 'I know. And as I said, I can run through it as many times as you like. I'll make sure you're clear on all the rules, and you know you can always contact me any time.' He ran a hand through his short, dark hair.

Eve smiled back, trying to read him. He'd given her his name, but she wasn't sure it was his real name. It didn't seem to quite fit. But then, could you really tell what anyone looked like by their name? Of course not. But she liked being Eve. Her mum had named her after Eve Arden, an old Hollywood actress who'd played the head teacher in *Grease* – her mum's favourite film; now Eve was responsible for choosing her own name. And her mum wasn't even going to be allowed to know what it was. Not at first. Maybe not ever. It would all depend on the outcome of multiple connected trials. Her testimony was only a small cog in a very complex set of wheels.

This new identity, new home – new life . . . it was all for her own safety. And Casey was just going to have to accept it too. It was Eve's eternal bad luck that not only had she been brutally attacked and had seen the attacker's face, but the suspect just happened to be part of a much, much bigger operation. Sex trafficking, modern slavery, class-A drugs – the works. And Eve's evidence was enough not only to put him away for what he had done to her, but had also blown the door open on everything else. She had been allowed to give her evidence remotely, her voice disguised, from behind a screen. But he would remember her, she was sure of it. He would tell someone to find her. And eventually, Eve had no doubt, someone would.

If only they hadn't taken that shortcut.

Casey looked up, caught Eve's gaze. *If only you hadn't frozen like that*, Eve thought, but she knew it was mean to blame Casey. Who knew what would have happened if Casey had actually intervened?

And who knew what would have happened if a dog hadn't started barking and running towards them in the woods. If her attacker hadn't been spooked. Eve could only imagine that he would have finished the job and smashed her head in with a rock, or strangled her. Because Eve had frozen too, in her attempt to stay alive. Perhaps, with continued therapy sessions, the nightmares would stop.

Maybe when they moved away to their new life, she might find a way to trust Casey again.

Fifteen

ANNA: SUNDAY

Anna had almost stopped shaking by the time she got off the phone. The conversation had been brief to the point of abrupt. He'd given her a postcode to type into the satnav and told her he would meet her there in thirty minutes.

She typed the numbers and letters into the console keyboard. It was a twenty-minute drive, hopefully. She had no idea if there would be traffic. She had no idea where she was meant to be going. The Street's postcode started with EH33, and she was already twenty minutes closer to Edinburgh. The postcode she'd been given was EH20. So, outside the city still – a different direction? But it meant nothing to her. He'd have chosen somewhere quiet, she assumed. She'd find out soon enough.

Anna turned the radio to Heart 80s, put the volume up high, then started the car. She'd considered calling Peter to update him, but then changed her mind. She knew what he would say. He wanted her to focus, he wanted them both to stay calm, to move on with their new lives. He wasn't at all sympathetic about her 'obsession' with the missing neighbours. He would not appreciate her loading him up with more panic. Peter had always been the calm one in their relationship. The one who could rationalise instead of catastrophise. The one who told her she was being ridiculous, often to the point that she felt like he didn't respect her thoughts and concerns at all. But perhaps he might not be so calm if he knew the truth.

The real truth. Not the version she'd acted out in court.

The music took her away from it all.

Madonna, singing about getting into the groove. Then Simple Minds, not wanting to be forgotten. Music always took her out of herself, transported her to another place. She loved eighties music in particular because it took her right back there, to simpler times when she had fun and no responsibilities. Where she could be who she wanted to be without having to hide.

Where she felt safe.

Unfamiliar scenery passed her by as she whizzed along the dual carriageway. Green fields with bright yellow rapeseed in the distance. High banking covered with thick shrubs; the occasional building, partially obscured. She was vaguely aware of seeing a sign for somewhere called Straiton, and then it was fields again, and the robotic satnav voice told her to keep right . . . in one hundred yards turn right . . . take the next right.

Anna slowed, then turned on to what looked like a farm track.

You have now reached your destination.

She pulled into the side, stopping next to what appeared to be an abandoned cottage. The land around it was gravel and weed, the small house all peeling paint. One of the upstairs windows was boarded up. Anna switched off the engine, and waited. She glanced around, but there was no sign of anyone nearby. No cars parked. The place felt deserted and that prickle of fear that had been goading her since they'd arrived in Scotland made a reappearance along her shoulder blades. Someone could be watching her. Someone who knew this area better than her.

What if this was a trap?

Stop it, Anna! Paranoia is not going to help you.

She picked up her phone to see if any further instructions had been sent. Nothing. But she did have a voicemail from Peter. She pressed 'Play'.

> *Hey, where are you? I connected to the Wi-Fi and some stupid app has downloaded on my phone. Have you got it too? I tried to uninstall it, but it seemed to be locked. A message popped up asking me what I was doing today! There's enough to think about without having this bloody thing monitoring our every move. I'm walking into the village to get something for dinner. See you later.*

Anna's hands shook as she typed out a hasty reply via text. She hesitated, wondering if she should tell Peter what she'd seen, where she was now . . . but it would be better to explain later, back at home over dinner. They needed a bit of time to themselves to start getting organised in the new house. To start fixing everything that had fallen apart.

> Let's look at it together later – thanks for getting some food in ☺

She hadn't really given the app another thought since she'd had the notification earlier, but thinking about it now, it was a bit intrusive. She would have expected it to be something that was mentioned when they were briefed about the move, but there were so many things going on then, it wouldn't be too odd to imagine that she might have missed it. Still, it was annoying.

She looked at her messages again, but there was nothing more from Jasper. She frowned, slid her phone into her pocket. The air was still, and she turned around slowly, taking in her surroundings

– clouds darkening over heather-clad hills to one side, the busy road somewhere to the other, although she couldn't see it now and couldn't hear it at all. No other cars had passed on the B-road she'd taken to the cottage, and she felt another stirring of unease, her stomach a tight knot.

She reached into her pocket to take out her phone, just as the front door of the cottage swung open with a creak and Jasper stuck his head outside.

'Oh, you're here – sorry. I was around the back.' He glanced over at the road, but there was nothing and nobody on it. A crow squawked somewhere above them, and, with a flap of wings, it was gone. Jasper beckoned her. 'Come in.'

Anna followed him into the cottage. It was furnished sparsely, but it was clean, and most definitely not as abandoned as it had appeared from the outside. A wooden table and chairs sat in the centre of the room, with a little kitchen area to one side. An open door on the other side revealed a small sitting room. An electric kettle flicked off in the corner of the kitchen area, steam belching out of the spout. Two mugs sat beside it, a teaspoon sticking out of one.

'What is this place?' Anna pulled out a chair and sat down.

Jasper poured water into the mugs. 'It's a safe house. Only for very temporary situations. Bit lacking on the facilities front. Tea OK? Milk?'

She nodded.

'It works fine as a rendezvous point,' he continued, pouring in milk. He set a mug in front of her then pulled out another chair, joining her at the table.

Safe house. She thought back to the note on her car.

YOU ARE NOT SAFE IN THAT HOUSE.

Jasper was watching her. 'So . . . what's up? Your voice message said it was urgent?'

She'd called the number that he'd programmed into her new phone. It had gone to an automated answer-service, and he'd called her back before she'd even started the car.

She took a mouthful of tea, almost scalding herself. 'It's about the neighbours. The ones on our right. Lindsay and Ritchie Walker.' She blew on her tea and took another sip.

'Go on.'

Anna flinched slightly. Everyone else had denied anyone even lived there. Was Jasper just humouring her? Waiting for her to say more? She took a breath and carried on. 'Well, the thing is, we met them on the first night, had a few drinks with them, blah blah—'

'Remember the rules, Anna. Discretion is key . . .'

She rolled her eyes. 'I know. We were discreet – we kept to the story. Fed them all we could about our new identities and didn't let anything slip about the old.' She paused, looked down at her tea. There was that one moment, when Lindsay had asked about her pseudonyms. Anna had almost given her the name of one of the books. She wasn't even supposed to mention them. But there was one that she was really proud of, and she would've loved for Lindsay to read it. There would have been no way to trace her back from that. Not quickly, anyway. Not without proper digging into Companies House and the names of directors, and maybe not even then. That pseudonym was on a contract between her and her publisher. It wasn't public. She'd wanted that book to be completely anonymous – for good reason, as it turned out.

'Anna?'

'They disappeared the next day. We haven't seen them since. Well, until now – when I saw Lindsay being dragged into a car right outside a shopping centre—'

He slammed his mug down on the table, making the whole thing shudder. Anna jumped. Stopped talking.

'Why didn't you say this before? I'm going to need a bit more detail, Anna.' He looked annoyed. Angry, even. His brow furrowed. His lips tight. Then, after a moment, his expression softened. 'Just run me through it, please. From the start.'

So she did, and Jasper did his best to reassure her that whatever had happened to Lindsay and Ritchie was nothing to do with her.

'You are safe, Anna,' he said.

She wasn't sure she believed him.

He'd told her he would look into it, though, just in case. But he'd seemed rattled by what she'd said, despite his best attempts to hide it. Anna had a feeling that he knew more about it, but that he had no intention of telling her anything.

But why?

Why was everyone being so bloody cagey?

She got the sense that she was going to have to deal with this by herself. And that she was going to have to tell Peter the truth about why she was so damn scared.

Sixteen

PATRICK: THREE YEARS AGO

It had been an accidental meeting, or at least, not something that he'd planned himself. His friend had been booked in to build a set of floor-to-ceiling wardrobes in one of the fancy detached houses on the edge of the common that Patrick could only ever dream of owning. Despite his wife's books selling in their droves, and his own business doing well enough, they were still in the terrace that they'd moved into right after they got married.

Fine, it was a very nice terrace, and it was on one of the desirable roads that led off the common. It wasn't like they were missing out on that lifestyle or anything. But when he found himself working in the bigger houses, the ones with the high-ceilinged reception rooms and all the ornate cornices, the perfect original tiled floors . . . the bloody wine cellars, for Christ's sake . . . well, then he felt inadequate.

Anyway, his friend had cut off one of his fingers at the weekend, using a circular saw without a guard because he'd wanted to finish the job fast and he'd been too impatient to pop down to the builders' merchants and get a replacement – so he'd spent the weekend in A&E instead. He reckoned he'd be back soon – optimism was always his forte – but in the meantime the client was getting antsy, so he pulled in Patrick as a favour. The framework was all done. It was mostly just the doors, and one final piece that had intrigued him when he'd read the plans – it was a hidden door type of thing, with space burrowed into the wall cavity behind.

Interesting.

Something was already in the cavity space, and he would have to remove it so he could finish off the little door. He crouched down and leaned in, but he couldn't get a proper grip on what it was that had been pushed into the wall. He then lay down flat, and shuffled forward, using a chisel to get some leverage and pull the thing out. This wasn't a good design. If the client wanted to store something in this cavity, it would be much better if there was a little platform underneath, with runners, so it could slide in and out. He wedged the chisel in to one side and gently manoeuvred it until he was able to get his fingers on the side and pull the box out. Then he shuffled himself back out of the wardrobe space, pulling the box with him.

He was nearly out when a door slammed downstairs and he flinched, causing the box to catch on the runner for the sliding doors and tip on to its side. The lid flipped off and the contents scattered across the carpet, just as the door to the bedroom opened and a tall, blond man marched in. Patrick had enough time to register his perfectly cut black suit and his incredible sculpted cheekbones, before both men's eyes were drawn to the scattered contents of the box.

Money. Lots of it. Rolled up neatly and secured with elastic bands. A gun. Patrick had no idea what type. He knew nothing about guns, having only ever seen them on TV. And a bag of something that looked like cocaine.

Fuck! Patrick almost laughed at the madness of it. *Who keeps all of this together in an unlocked box?*

'Well,' the man said, at last. 'This is rather unfortunate. I was using that box to test the size of the space. I have a new lockbox on order. I wasn't expecting anyone to crawl into my wardrobe and pull it out . . .'

Patrick stood up. 'I'm so sorry. I'm Patrick . . . I came because—'

The man held up a hand. 'It's OK. I know why you are here. I don't allow just anyone to have access to my property. I was told you were trustworthy, and as such I am sure I can trust you not to mention anything you've just pulled out of my wardrobe?'

Patrick nodded. 'Of course!' He shrugged, trying to move quickly back to the job at hand. 'I think a small platform on runners would help. Turn it into a drawer-base, and your box can sit on top. It'll make it a lot easier to get it in and out.'

The man put his hands into his pockets, clearly unfazed by the episode. 'That's a good idea. That wasn't suggested before, but then again, I didn't fully explain to your friend what I was putting in there.'

'I can get the parts. Do you have the exact dimensions of the lockbox?'

'Sure. How about you come down for a coffee and we can discuss this in the kitchen?' He held out a hand. 'I'm Lars. Lars Kristiansen.' He gave Patrick a wry smile. 'And you seem like a man who can solve problems – especially those types of problems that one does not even realise that they had? I like this in a man, very much.'

Patrick shook his hand, attempting to match Lars's firm grip. His hands were huge. Looked like they could snap a man's neck like a twig.

Yes, Patrick thought, *that's me. I can solve problems.* He was trying to convince himself.

'I also like your fast reaction time. And that you didn't bat an eye at the contents of that box. I've been looking for someone like you.'

Patrick swallowed and tried to look more confident than he felt. He'd thought quickly, yes, but it was as if some sort of survival instinct had kicked in. It wasn't a conscious thing. Patrick built wardrobes and shelving units. The occasional piece of furniture. Yes, he was a problem solver – he could work out the best use of an awkward space – but the inference here from this man was that these were skills that could be used elsewhere.

'Please,' Lars said, holding out an arm and gesturing to the open door. 'Let me make you coffee and you can tell me about your life as it is right now, and we can discuss how I might be able to make it even better for you.'

Patrick took in his surroundings as he descended the stairs. He'd like a place like this. He'd like something more in his life. Why should it only be his wife who got to do anything exciting with her life? He needed something. This was one of those moments of serendipity, and he was going to take full advantage of it. The implications of the drugs, and more importantly the gun, were pushed to the back of his mind – because the thing that had really jumped out of that box was the money.

Seventeen

ANNA: SUNDAY

She was barely paying attention as she drove back home. It was lucky the roads were quiet, and that the satnav was guiding her back to The Street. Anna knew she should pull over and take a break. Get her head straight. Jasper had told her to sit outside the cottage for as long as she needed, but she didn't like it there. The atmosphere was all wrong. Everything felt wrong now, after her fleeting moment of hope when they had arrived a couple of days ago. Was it really only two days ago? It already felt like a month and she hadn't even made it to the local shops.

She saw a sign for Rosslyn Chapel. She knew that name. It had been in a book she'd read, years before. Oh, of course – *The Da Vinci Code*! She took a right on the next roundabout and headed towards it.

The satnav lady started to recalculate the route, trying to get her to turn back, then as she carried on, the route reconfigured and Anna decided to go with it. She needed the distraction. As she drove along the winding country roads, passing signs for Penicuik, Bonnyrigg and Lasswade, her mind went back to a night in her old house. Her old life. A heated discussion between her and Lars about the works of Dan Brown.

Agneta, Lars's ridiculously beautiful blonde wife, had picked up the bottle of Chilean Cabernet and shaken it gently. 'I'll get us another, shall I? While you two bang on with your literary silliness?' She rolled her eyes and disappeared down the steps to their wine cellar.

Lars and Agneta had finished excavating the basement last summer, amidst much consternation from the neighbours on either side, who feared the entire street would collapse. Anna and Peter lived on one of the less salubrious streets nearby, and were smugly unfazed by the possibility of a sinkhole opening up beneath them as no one could afford to dig holes under their properties around there.

'I'll help you choose,' Peter said. He made a big show of kissing Anna on the head before following Agneta down the stairs. Peter had told Anna all about the wine cellar when he'd first met Lars after doing a small job in his home. He was envious, despite also finding it all a bit over-the-top ridiculous. They were well enough off, and Anna didn't want anything else, but Peter thought Lars was a show-off and often made fun of him, despite also becoming slightly obsessed with his lifestyle.

Anna looked across the table at Lars. He gave her a slow smile, then took a sip of his wine. 'You know, if I didn't know better, I'd say your Peter might quite fancy a bit of my Aggie.'

Anna laughed. She had nothing to worry about there. For all her Swedish model looks, Agneta was absolutely not Peter's type. He'd always hated women who tried too hard to be perfect, who were happy to be kept by their rich husbands. Who spent their time shopping for designer items they didn't really need. Despite all that, Agneta was good fun – she had a razor-sharp wit. Maybe Peter *did* like her, come to think of it. Anna knew that her own wit was one of her best features. But Agneta had the beauty to boot . . . Was wit enough on its own?

It was definitely what had drawn Lars to her.

'Anyway,' he was saying now, having finished his wine. The others were still in the cellar. 'Dan fucking Brown. Absolute trash.'

She shook her head. 'Fundamentally disagree. He might not be writing Booker Prize-winning prose, but you can't fault his storytelling abilities—'

'Oh, I think you'll find that I can – that whole nonsense about Mary Magdalene being married to Jesus, when we all know she was nothing more than a local prostitute—'

'Sex worker! But OK, I'm not sure I actually believe anything that he tried to present as fact, but it was put together in such a compelling way . . .' She let her sentence trail off. Lars was looking at her, a smile playing on his lips, which he then licked suggestively.

Anna almost laughed, but then she felt a stirring inside herself that she really hadn't expected.

'Come here,' he said, getting up from the table. He backed into the kitchen, beckoning her with a curled finger.

She glanced towards the cellar door. The others were still down there, choosing the wine. She heard Peter's muffled voice, then Agneta's tinkling laugh. She looked at Lars, and something shifted. That was the moment when she knew things were about to change, but she had no idea what it would lead to.

Lars took her wrist and pulled her close to him. Their faces were almost touching. She could smell the wine on his breath, the heady, herbal scent of his cologne rising up through the open neck of his shirt.

Sometimes, now, she tried to convince herself that it was he who moved in first. That it was his lips that first touched hers. But they both knew it was her who crossed the line. Yes, he had definitely instigated it, but she had several opportunities to stop it, and she chose not to.

The kiss was gentle at first. Soft. Shy, even. Then it was harder, and deeper, and then he had pulled away and stuck a finger into her mouth, rubbing it across her gums.

It tasted sharp. Acidic. And she realised what he had been luring her into the kitchen for. She felt an almost instant fizz at the back of her head as the coke kicked in.

'Well,' Lars said, turning away to chop a small white mound into several thin lines. 'I was only going to ask if you fancied a bump, but . . . that was pretty nice. Happy to continue down that route further if you like. Funny, I never thought you fancied me . . .'

She turned away. 'I don't, I—'

He whirled around and kissed her again, hard. 'Oh, I think you do, my dear. Anyway, let's see if the others fancy a bit of gear first, shall we? It's my last bag. Bloody dealer got himself arrested, and half of his gang with him, so I'm going to have to venture back out on to the bloody common to scope out some new possibilities.'

Her head was thumping now. She wasn't really someone who took drugs, at dinner parties or otherwise. Paracetamol for a headache, that was about her limit. The coke had emboldened her. 'Can't believe someone of your means has to resort to scratching around the bushes to find your next fix.'

He roared with laughter. 'You're right, of course. But maybe I like scratching around in bushes. You should come with me some time—'

'What's this, darling? I hope you're not boring our guest with work talk.' Agneta appeared in the kitchen doorway, wine bottle in hand. Peter stood behind her, rolling his eyes and trying to mouth something to her that she couldn't quite make out. Agneta swept past her, licked a finger, and ran it across the remnants of loose powder around Lars's perfectly manicured lines. She stuck her finger in her mouth, then grinned. 'He's such a bore sometimes.' She walked up to her husband and kissed him. 'I think I might turn in, actually,' she said, glancing over her shoulder at Anna. 'Early start in the morning. You three feel free to carry on without me.'

'I'm pretty done in too,' Peter said, giving Anna a hard stare. 'You stay, though. If you want?'

Anna took in his gaze and felt herself flush. Did he know? Had they been seen? She felt a knot of guilt deep in her stomach, but, above that, a butterfly-wings flutter of anticipation. She wasn't sure if it was the drugs or the thrill of what had just happened, but she knew it was only a matter of time before it happened again.

A car horn blared, slamming her back into the present. She was on the main road again, barely aware of where she was, or where she'd been – driving on autopilot, subliminally following the instructions from the satnav. The driver of the car that she'd almost swerved into gave her the finger, and she held up a hand, trying to placate.

Fifteen minutes later, she was back home.

Thirty minutes later, she had confessed all to Peter, who had been quietly sitting in the kitchen, gazing out of the window and eating a Pot Noodle he'd bought along with a few other random items in the garage he'd taken a wander to earlier.

Well, not *all* all. She'd got as far as telling him about the kiss, and had been ready to spill her guts about everything else that had happened between her and Lars. She wanted to explain it all, and the implications of it. Tell Peter that this was why she was so jittery and scared. But the kiss had been enough to set him off and he'd walked out of the kitchen without saying a word. This was worse than shouting, when it came to her husband. His silent treatment was unnerving and could go on for hours. She knew better than to try to talk to him now.

She picked up the discarded Pot Noodle and poured the remains of it into the food-waste bin on the windowsill, looking away for a moment as she scraped the last of the noodles into the compostable liner. When she looked up again, something caught her eye outside, just the other side of the back fence. A man, watching her. She gasped, dropping the fork she'd been using into the food bin. Her heart started to thud hard in her chest.

'Peter!'

But the man standing out there on the beach was not her husband.

Eighteen

THE DIARY

Isn't it interesting how easily you can find out things about people with just a little bit of digging online? Dear Diary – this is the *most* fun thing about living in a boring little backwater. It's almost like it's *expected*. All these small towners spend their days and nights endlessly scrolling through social media, bleating on about their tedious little lives, but what kind of lives are they really?

You've got the over-sharers. The ones who need to give the world a blow-by-blow account of every mundanity, shouting into the void and hoping that the replies will validate their own opinions. Then there's the vague-bookers. The ones who drop just the tiniest nugget, hoping to entice and intrigue their followers into their DMs, begging to be told the big secret. Then there's the experts. The ones who know the answer to every question ever posed. Sometimes they start their own thread, sharing their deep knowledge gleaned from Dr Google, or else they're happy to just scour the posts of all their friends, commenting with unwanted advice, whether it be right or wrong.

Then there's the arguers . . . If only they kept their views to themselves, the internet would be a far nicer place. And then you have the photo-sharers – from the daily selfie to the occasional holiday snap, these photos are carefully curated to maximise the wow potential for all the sad little friends and followers who couldn't take a decent photo if they tried.

There are all sorts in this town. The local Facebook group is a particular source of joy, with posts ranging from 'anyone know a good cleaner?' to 'what's happening on Shore Road? Two police cars been there for hours.' Oh, the comments! The idiocy. The smugness.

It's not so exciting amongst the residents of The Street. The whole lot of them have their security set high, sharing only the minimum. Lots of sunset pics, of course. I have to admit, this is a particularly nice stretch of coast for those.

But it's what they *don't* share that interests me.

I'm good at finding stuff. I suppose you could say that secrets are my speciality, and boy does this street have them in *spades*.

Nineteen

ANNA: SUNDAY

Anna stood there at the kitchen window, looking out at the stranger. Her heart was beating too fast, the adrenaline rush making her feel sick. The stranger stood still, and she felt as if he'd locked his gaze tightly on hers. But it wasn't possible. He couldn't see her. The Perspex fence only allowed you to see through it from one direction – from her house, out towards the sea. Not the other way. Definitely not. She'd checked. Peter had checked. Hadn't he? The man turned his head to the left, as if he'd heard a noise, or seen someone nearby. He took a step closer to the fence. Anna could just make out the shape of a tattoo, snaking out of his t-shirt and up his neck. She shivered.

'Peter? Quick! Come and see . . .' Her voice trailed off as she heard the sound of the front door slam shut.

She rushed out of the kitchen and into the lounge.

'Peter?'

She wasn't sure why she was still calling his name. He'd obviously left. She could hardly blame him, after she'd just confessed to an affair with one of their mutual friends. The fact that it was the biggest, stupidest mistake of her life was irrelevant. She had hurt him. Of course she had. And at this point, she had no idea if there was any coming back from it. Anna stood behind the front door, hand hovering over the latch. Pull it open, run out after him? Or leave him be, give him space . . . hope that he came back?

The doorbell rang, playing its annoying little tune, and she jumped. Her fast-beating heart seemed to have leaped into her mouth. She coughed, clearing her throat. She painted on a smile and pulled the door open. 'Darling, I'm—'

It wasn't him.

It was one of the women from the barbecue. Beth? Was that her name? She was standing on the path, a small potted cactus in one hand, a bottle of wine in the other. Beth shrugged, holding the plant towards her. 'Spiky,' she said. 'Perhaps not the most appropriate house-warming gift . . .' Anna looked past her, up and down the street.

'He took the car,' Beth said. 'He didn't look particularly happy.' She tried a smile. 'I'm sorry. This is clearly a bad time.' Anna looked at the bottle of white wine. She tried to avoid the stuff. She seemed to be able to tolerate red, even rosé, but white had never done her any good. But right now, oblivion was calling. Again. And white wine was a sure-fire way to get there. So much for the new, sensible 'Anna'. At least it wasn't drugs.

She nodded towards the bottle. 'Is that chilled?'

'More than you are, I'd say.' Beth smirked.

Anna stared for a moment, wanting to be offended. But then she saw the twinkle in Beth's eye, and she let out a small laugh.

'Touché.'

Beth took a step towards the door. 'Can I come in, then? Or are we going to swig it on the doorstep? I mean, either way is fine with me, but, honestly, unless you want Mary on your case . . .'

Anna stepped back and opened the door wider, letting Beth inside.

'You look a bit rattled,' Beth said, closing the door behind her. 'Is everything OK?' She laughed, then shook her head. 'I'm sorry. I must sound nosy as fuck. It's kind of dull around here, most of the time. It's normally only Lorraine who tries to stick her beak into people's business. Like I told you at the barbecue, that woman has no social skills. God! I'm babbling.'

Anna couldn't help but smile as she sat down hard on the couch, letting herself sag into the cushions as if the air had been let out of her. 'Glasses in the kitchen. Probably in the same cupboard as yours.'

Beth placed the cactus on the coffee table then disappeared into the kitchen.

Anna heard cupboards opening and closing. Maybe Beth had rearranged her own cupboards. She had been living there a few months. Plenty of time to get things how she liked them in her own kitchen.

Beth reappeared carrying two glasses in one hand, the wine bottle in the other. 'Screw top,' she said. 'Always be prepared. You never know who might be out there, in need—'

'Oh,' Anna said, remembering what she had wanted to ask. 'You didn't happen to see anyone outside, did you? On the beach?'

Beth poured the wine. 'One of the residents, you mean? No one else is meant to have access, although there is the other street behind us, who apparently do have access even though none of the houses have a sea view. I'd never have chosen one of those. I'd feel cheated.'

Anna sat up straighter, and took her glass of wine from Beth's hand. 'Did you get a choice of property then, when you moved? Or were the other places already snapped up?'

Beth's face clouded briefly, then she smiled again. 'We got the last one, as it happens. Couldn't quite believe we were able to move to a place like this. So very different from our old place. The whole set-up just suited us, actually.' She took a sip of her drink. 'We really needed a fresh start.'

'I know that feeling.'

Anna was pleased with herself, steering the conversation to Beth instead of her own reasons for being there. It was becoming a little easier as she settled in.

'Anyway, in answer to your question – no. No one on the beach. There rarely is, actually. It's often too windy out there. Perfect for Bradley's dogs, but not for most humans. I heard they spent a fortune making this part of the coastline into an accessible beach, but still no one uses it.'

'Oh?' Anna's interest was piqued. She didn't know much about the history of the development. Jasper told her what she needed to know, and with his 'discretion' rule, it seemed that digging around into the history of the development was frowned upon. Not that she'd been able to find much online. Because yes, despite his 'rules', she had searched anyway.

'Yeah, some bigshot developer bought it from the council. There was a power station here once – well, for a long time. Big, iconic chimneys that the locals wanted kept. Quite an omission now from this line of coast towards Edinburgh, if you look at old photos. Shame. Anyway, then they wanted to make it a cruise-liner terminal with shops and all sorts – the water is so deep here, and it's so windy, they thought it would never work for housing or coastal leisure. Or it was, until they scrapped that plan and the bigshot developer sorted out all those issues. Brought in mature trees to act as a windbreak. Tore down the old jetty and built up a slope to create an artificial beach. Designed a load of luxury housing . . . then just before they finalised it, it all went tits up.' She took a mouthful of wine.

'What happened?' Anna took a sip of her own wine, trying not to drink it too fast. She needed a clear head, her earlier plans for oblivion long gone.

'He got done for fraud. Banged up. The whole development turned into a ghost ship. Mothballed. And then, mysteriously, the council got hold of it again and finished the build.' She shrugged. 'Well, all according to John at Number Four, that is. He seems to know more than anyone else. The rest of us try to keep ourselves to ourselves.'

There was a loud ping, followed quickly by another. Beth took her phone out of her pocket and glanced at the screen, frowning. She threw her phone on to the table, seemingly without checking what the notification was for.

Anna lifted her own phone up and read the message, keeping the screen turned away from Beth.

> Hi Anna! Mr StreetMate here again! Thanks for keeping your notifications switched on! We hope you're settling in well and getting to know your neighbours, but remember – discretion is key! Be careful as you straddle that fine line between knowledge and gossip. We wouldn't want anyone's privacy to be compromised, would we?

Anna frowned. 'Stupid app.'

'What app's that?' Beth said. Her expression was innocent enough, but Anna wasn't quite sure what to say, so she tried to be vague. 'Oh, just something linked to our Wi-Fi, I think.'

Beth nodded, but she didn't quite catch Anna's eye. Was this more cagey behaviour, or was Anna imagining it? 'Finlay thinks I'm paranoid, but I'm actually convinced our phones are listening.

I mean, it's not hard, is it? Your phone *does* listen to everything – otherwise why would you get all these ridiculously specific targeted ads when you go on the internet?' She lowered her voice. 'I use a VPN at home and I try not to have my phone in the same room as me. I'm getting sick of it, to be honest. I say one thing, or I search for one thing, and then the internet thinks that's all I want from it, for ever.'

'But, um . . . what about social media?'

Beth looked at her again, her expression unreadable. 'I try to stay off it. I used to be on there all the time, but, well, it wasn't good for me. I closed down all my profiles before we moved.' She picked up her phone, frowning at the screen.

'Everything OK?' Anna's heart had started racing. Something about Beth's behaviour was flashing red.

'Oh, it's nothing . . .'

Anna pushed. 'Was it a message from Finlay? Is everything alright at home?'

Beth mouthed, almost silently. 'I shouldn't be showing you this, but . . .' She held her phone over so that Anna could see.

> Hi Beth! Mr StreetMate, here! Thought for the day: rumours and gossip are dangerous, Beth. You of all people should know that. You've been out for a while now, haven't you? Isn't it time you got back home to your wife?

'What the fuck?' Anna whispered. A chill crept over her. If Beth had this app too, did that mean . . . ? She didn't want to finish that thought.

Beth kept her voice low. 'I told you. It's listening, and it's tracking. And if you switch off notifications, or try to uninstall it, it just reinstalls itself again. What with this and the security cameras . . .

I'm not keen on the Orwellian Neighbourhood Watch set-up. If they'd told us before we moved here, I reckon we'd have had second thoughts.' She picked up her wine glass and drained the last drop. 'Anyway, I do have to go. I've got three cakes to bake this evening for a last-minute order so I'd better get cracking.'

'Literally.'

Beth laughed. 'Yep. Luckily we've got our own chickens. You'll need to come along and meet them sometime.'

'Thanks, I'd like that.'

Anna saw Beth out, then decided to have an early night. She'd probably imagined seeing the man on the beach. Her mind playing tricks on her.

Seemed like that was happening a lot lately.

Peter would return when he was ready, and she would continue their difficult conversation then. But, in the meantime, a sleeping tablet would deal with the residual gnawing anxiety in her gut. She'd made a friend, at least. Someone who she suspected was in the same boat. She hoped she would get the opportunity to get to know Beth better, to talk to her about things. But they would have to find a way to do it without the app listening in.

Anna thought she could suggest that they both throw their phones into the sea, but she had a feeling that would draw even more attention to them – because whatever Beth's situation, Anna was sure that she wasn't meant to know about it.

Twenty

ANNA: MONDAY

Yesterday's chat with Beth had done her good. Anna woke up refreshed after a twelve-hour sleep that had been badly needed. She was feeling a lot more positive about her new life, lying in bed thinking about her plans for getting on with work again. Maybe she'd write something set in Scotland. Move into something Gothic and creepy – she was sure there must be some ruined castles around for inspiration. Beth might know, or maybe one of the other neighbours. She still hadn't got to know any of them properly.

Her mood shifted as her brain fully awoke, and the initial thoughts of writing and new friends got jumbled around with the issues that a good sleep couldn't fix . . .

What happened to Lindsay?

Why did Beth have that app?

She rolled over on to her side, noting that Peter's half of the bed was uncreased, the duvet still neat. Peter had not slept there. The sleeping tablet had knocked her out cold and it was rare that she woke during the night after taking one.

He could've returned late, seen she was fast asleep, and slept in the spare room. But she knew him. He would disappear off to sulk, then he'd clear his head and come back when he was ready, and they'd talk about things and they'd work it out.

This was how it had always been with Peter. Even when he'd been the cause of the stress or arguments – not supporting her being one of the common complaints. He was good at being supportive on the surface, but now and then a resentment would find its way up from the depths and he would disengage from her. Luckily these episodes didn't usually last long, and they didn't happen often, but when they did she felt alone and let down, and it was times like these when bad things had happened.

And bad things were already happening – even if it didn't seem like anyone else was concerned or even believed her.

The reasons for the current argument – if you could even call it that, because so far he had said very little, choosing to stay silent then leave the house instead – were firmly down to her. She'd been ready to explain, about how her friend Gloria had had an affair and it had saved her stale marriage. An unconventional solution, and not one that would work for all . . . but she hadn't got that far. She'd only got as far as Lars kissing her in the kitchen on the night they took the coke. That was the *first* night – although she'd omitted the drugs part too. For now. Not that she supposed Peter would care much about that.

You can do so much better than him, you know . . .

She shook away Lars's words inside her head. There was no real excuse for what had happened. She hadn't been particularly unhappy at the time, but there was something about the thrill of it. Lars had been so complimentary, but she hadn't expected things to go so far. Men had their mid-life crises, didn't they? But Peter seemed to have passed through the danger zone without trading her or their car in for a younger model. In fact, their new car was the *opposite* of mid-life crisis – he'd moved straight on to future-proof mobility mode.

She smoothed her side of the bed to match Peter's, then showered quickly and dressed in some of her new clothes. Fitted navy joggers, a plain white tee and a pale grey hoody. She pulled on a pair of elastic-topped Nikes and appraised herself in the mirror while she pulled her hair back into a ponytail.

I look just like Beth, she thought. Their body shapes were different, of course, and Anna was taller. But the outfit she'd put on was almost identical to what Beth had been wearing yesterday. Had she inadvertently chosen the standard local 'uniform' when she'd gone to the shops? Maybe it was no bad thing. Jasper had made it clear that the best thing she could do here was blend in.

Pushing all dark thoughts from her mind, she smiled as she pulled the front door shut and headed along The Street, taking the winding path through the trees that led to the main road, rather than the other route via the beach. She hadn't been this way on foot yet, and as much as she loved to stroll along the seaside walkway, she knew she would only dawdle, and it was time to get to know the place properly. Not to mention do some food shopping.

Bradley cornered her just as she arrived at the gate.

'Anna! How are you? Fancy walking with us?'

He held the two dogs, straining on their leads. They both looked at her expectantly, their long tongues hanging out.

Why did he seem to pop up every time she wanted to be on her own? Irritation swiped away her good mood as she thought of the app, and those messages she'd received. She was probably being stupid, but she felt like Bradley was keeping tabs on her too.

'I'm in a bit of a hurry, actually. Maybe some other time?'

He looked crestfallen and she felt bad.

'Oh, sure,' he said. 'OK. Why don't you come round soon? Lacy would love to see you again, and—'

'Sure. I'll see you later.' Anna yanked open the gate and walked briskly through to the other side. She felt like she was escaping something – like she *needed* to escape. It was just coincidence that he'd appeared both times she'd gone out walking. It had to be. Because she wasn't at all comfortable with being monitored. She rushed off, leaving him standing there with the dogs. He called after her once, then she heard nothing but the dogs' excited barking. She took a few long, slow breaths, slightly regretting her spikiness. She knew she was distracted, and she had definitely come across as rude. She would have to make it up to him later.

She made it out on to the pavement of the main road. Opposite her was a steep man-made grass bank, which she supposed had been put there to shield the houses beyond from the sea winds. This end of the village was very exposed and it made sense now that the developers had brought in the trees to windbreak The Street – but she wondered if it would really be enough, if a big storm was to come in. So far the weather had been warm and sunny, but it *was* Scotland – and it was only a matter of time before that changed. She would need another shopping trip to buy wind- and waterproofs.

It didn't take long to walk into the town – or the village; she wasn't entirely sure which. From her brief time spent there, it seemed to be composed of rows of older houses – white-painted pebbledash – surrounded by huge new estates full of modern new-builds and patches of green. Somewhere amongst it all there was history. She'd read up on it. Witches and salt pans and sites of ancient battles. Plus the sea, of course. It was a shame about the high street, which, as she'd been warned, contained very little.

She passed an old pub, where a couple of men in plaster-dust-coated jeans stood outside smoking, holding pints of lager, watching with interest as she walked by. She passed a pharmacy, a supermarket, a barber's. She was about to turn back, thinking it was a waste of a walk – she wasn't interested in these quiet little shops and would have been better off walking along by the water – when she saw something that set a loud bell jangling inside her head.

The Taj Mahal.

Not the palace in Agra, of course. An Indian restaurant with one of the most common names of Indian restaurants in the whole of the UK. There was a chance it might not have been the same one, but she knew it had to be. Bradley had said the best Indian was in Port Seton, but Ritchie hadn't said anything like that. The burgundy paintwork and the white-line drawing of the famous landmark where an emperor buried his favourite wife. Not a palace at all, in fact – but a mausoleum. The wind picked up suddenly, making her shiver, and she wrapped her arms around herself as she stood there looking at the restaurant. There was no mistaking it – the logo had been on the carrier bags that they'd delivered the food in. This was the place she'd eaten the takeaway from the other night. The one that Ritchie had ordered.

Ritchie . . . husband of Lindsay. Both of whom everyone seemed to want to deny ever existed. Jasper hadn't got back to her since they'd met yesterday. She knew he was hoping she was going to drop it. But just because she hadn't done any more obvious digging, didn't mean she didn't want to know what was going on.

She took a deep breath and pushed the glass door, wedging it open against some sort of magnetic door stop. She tried to pull it away to close it, but it remained stuck. A beaded decoration that hung behind the glass rattled and tinkled, and within moments a kind-eyed man in burgundy trousers and a crisp white shirt appeared from a door to the rear of the bar.

'Don't worry. Please, it is fine to let in some fresh air.'

Her eyes took in the room. It wasn't a big restaurant. Six tables of four and four of two. A small wood-panelled bar with a well-stocked gantry, containing all the spirits you might need to wash down your meal. She wondered how many people drank spirits in an Indian. Wasn't it all about the beer?

'We start serving in thirty minutes,' the man said. 'I can keep a table for you?'

Anna smiled. She couldn't imagine the place filling up. Not at 6 p.m. on a sleepy Monday in a backwater town.

He read her mind. 'Lots of people coming tonight before football, but I can give you this table if you like?' He gestured to another table for two, slotted in beside the bar. She hadn't noticed it before, probably because it wasn't set but covered with several stacked dishes and a pile of unfolded cotton napkins.

'Actually, I'm not looking to eat right now. We're new to the area and we had friends order a takeaway for us the other night. I wanted to come in and tell you how much we enjoyed it.'

The man grinned. 'Oh, this is very lovely news, madam. Thank you!' He nodded his head, still smiling. 'And who are your friends? Maybe our regulars?'

'Yes, I think they are.' Anna mirrored the man's cheerful expression, hoping to keep him on side. 'Ritchie and Lindsay Walker? Number Eight, The Street? It's the new development along . . .' She let her sentence trail off as the man's face clouded.

'Sorry, madam. Don't recognise that name.' He was still smiling.

'Are you sure? My friend ordered us the party banquet, and he said he'd had it before . . .'

The man was still smiling. 'I can't give out customer names, madam.'

'No . . . of course. I mean, you don't have to. I just wanted to tell you how much we enjoyed the food. I wanted to leave a tip. Maybe you can check and see exactly what it was we had?'

He took a step back, turned towards the bar, then picked up a hard-backed ledger. 'You said Friday night? Party banquet, yes?' He ran a finger down the entries in the book, flicked back a page.

Anna was amazed that the orders were written on paper in this day and age. 'That's right.'

'OK, yes, I see it now – but it wasn't delivered to Number Eight – it was Number Six – to Mrs Anna.'

Anna blinked. Took a breath. 'You're right, yes. It was delivered to me. I'm Mrs . . . Yes, I'm Anna. Sorry for the confusion.'

He was grinning again. 'No problem, Anna. I'm very happy you enjoyed the food.' He was looking at her expectantly now, and she realised he was waiting for the tip she had promised. She pulled a twenty-pound note out of her purse and handed it over.

'Thank you,' she said, turning away and heading rapidly for the door. She felt like a fool. Her little mission hadn't achieved anything, apart from costing her twenty quid. She still had no evidence that Ritchie had ordered that food.

Damn it!

She closed the door behind her, then stood for a moment, watching through the glass as he bustled off behind the bar and through the door at the back without giving her a second glance. Then she let out a long, slow breath. It was no good. Whatever had happened to the Walkers, she wasn't going to find anything out using her own limited detective skills. Maybe she should take a hint and move on. Easier said than done when she was still convinced that there was something very, very dodgy about the whole situation.

Fed up now, she turned quickly and hurried down the steps, almost bumping straight into a woman on the pavement.

It was Mary – standing right outside the restaurant, a cloth shopping bag in each hand and a scowl on her face. 'Watch yourself there, you almost knocked me over.'

Anna took a step back, flustered. 'I'm so sorry, I didn't see you. I wasn't expecting anyone to be standing outside, so close to the door—'

What had she been doing standing there anyway?

'Last time I checked it was still a free country. I was merely walking by on my way home from picking up a few bits and pieces. You practically leaped on me from that doorway.'

Anna took a deep breath before apologising again. Not that she thought she had anything to apologise for. The woman had clearly been standing by the open door, listening to the conversation. She would have heard exactly what happened when Anna asked her question about Lindsay and Ritchie. It was obvious that Mary knew something about their disappearance, despite her previously telling Anna that she was mistaken about their even living in the house in the first place.

Mary's face was set hard, her jaw rigid. But as Anna stared, she noticed a slight pulsing in the woman's cheek. The flicker of an eyelid. As if the pressure of keeping things inside was making her head fit to burst. Anna was sure that Mary was desperate to blurt something out. People like her thrived on knowing more than anyone else. It was clear that she was torn between revealing her knowledge and maintaining the moral high ground by keeping her mouth firmly shut.

Mary had obviously been told to stay silent. Like Beth. Like Donna from across the road. Like everyone on The Street. Anna was certain that if she asked any of her neighbours, she would get exactly the same response.

They all thought they were being so clever, but all that they were doing was making her even more curious. More determined to uncover the truth. Beth was a weak link, perhaps. Someone else in the same position, too scared to put a foot out of line – but she might know something. Anna would have to try to push a bit harder.

Meanwhile, Mary continued to stare at her. They'd reached a stalemate.

'I need to get back,' Anna said, eventually. 'Have a lovely evening.' She hurried off, without waiting for a reply. But she was only a few steps away when she heard Mary's words behind her, uttered under her breath.

'*Please*. Just be careful.'

Twenty-One

Patrick: Three Years Ago

It didn't take Patrick long to realise that Lars was really not a very nice man. He wasn't sure why he was surprised by the revelation. He'd been finishing that first job on the wardrobe, and his genius idea for the secure, secret compartment, when he'd heard Lars and Agneta come home. Lars had given him a key when he'd agreed to finish the job, and he'd let himself in the following day – Lars having assured him that both he and his wife were out until the evening.

So why were they back?

Patrick had parked his van on a side street as there'd been no spaces outside. It was likely they didn't know he was there. The moment he'd heard the front door slam, he should've gone out to the landing and called down the stairs – let them know he was here. And he did go out to the landing . . . but he had his shoes off, and there were no creaky boards in this house – not like in his own. He'd been about to call down the stairs, announce his presence, but then he'd heard Lars speak and the tone had made him stop in his tracks.

'You *will* do this job for me, Agneta . . . is this not what I pay you for?'

A quiet sob, then Agneta's voice. 'You make me sound like a whore.'

Silence.

Then a loud slap. More sobbing.

'This house. Your jewellery. Your unlimited funds on the platinum card! What else are you, dear Aggie? It's not as if you can call yourself a mother.'

Patrick held his breath.

The sobbing faded as soft footsteps retreated on the downstairs wooden floor. Patrick stepped back into the bedroom as quickly and quietly as he could. He spun around, trying to work out how he could get out of there without being seen. Lars sounded furious. He didn't want to be found there. But he was on the top floor and it was a long, tall townhouse, and there was no way anyone was going to get away unscathed jumping from that window.

As it turned out, it didn't matter. Lars was already on his way up the stairs.

Patrick slid on to his knees and buried his head in the wardrobe, pretending to tighten the screws on the lockbox at the back. Hoping that Lars might buy the ruse that he hadn't heard the exchange. Hadn't even heard them come in. He would turn in a moment and look surprised to see Lars standing there, and then everything would go back to how it had been. He didn't want to piss Lars off. Despite the way he'd spoken to his wife – assuming she actually was his wife – Patrick wanted what this man had. Money. Power.

Lars cleared his throat.

Shit.

Patrick crawled out of the wardrobe.

'Lars—'

The other man waved a hand, dismissing him. 'Don't bother with the lie, Patrick. I know you heard everything.'

Patrick swallowed. Then he stood up tall to face Lars. 'None of my business.'

Lars gave him a slow smile that didn't quite meet his eyes. 'I knew I was right about you.' He stepped over to the wardrobe and crouched down to check Patrick's work. 'Good job,' he said, straightening up again.

He was standing very close, and Patrick had to resist the urge to take a step backwards in an attempt to regain a more reasonable personal space.

But he refused to show any weakness, any indication that he found Lars intimidating.

'Let's have a drink,' Lars said. 'I'd like to run a few things by you.'

Twenty-Two

EVE: SEVEN MONTHS AGO

It had been three months since the verdict. Three months since they'd left their lovely flat and moved into something much less lovely. *It's only temporary*, the handler had insisted. Bit of a delay with the proper place. The place that was apparently luxurious and fully furnished and where their new life would be so good they'd wonder why they ever cared about the old one.

It was also three months since she'd changed her name, but she still couldn't think of her and Casey as anything other than Eve and Casey.

She knew it would take time. She knew she would get used to the new identities, new jobs, new place to explore, new friends to be made – albeit cautiously, as per the new 'rules'.

But it was hard in this place, when she knew it was only temporary. What was the point of trying to move on, only to have to move on again? So they were stuck in this tedious limbo and neither of them was happy. Casey had threatened to leave more than once. Eve was beginning to no longer care. Maybe things would be better in her new life if she went it alone. So far, her thoughts had remained inside her, unvoiced. But it was only a matter of time before the tensions the two of them felt spilled into words that couldn't be taken back.

'I'm just going out for a walk,' Eve called into the small living room, where Casey was glued to some crap daytime TV. One of those shows where the couple had notions of buying a dream house in a Spanish town, only to realise their budget stretched to an apartment in a dingy suburb and the nearest beach was a thirty-minute drive away. Eve slammed the door without waiting for an answer. She'd long stopped asking if Casey wanted to come out with her for a walk.

She hurried across the communal square, where a bunch of teenage kids was sitting by the dried-up fountain, smoking and drinking. They eyed Eve with interest, and a prickle of fear crept over her shoulders, but then one of them said something she couldn't hear, and another laughed, and then she was out of the other side, through the piss-smelling alleyway, and out on to the street.

The street was filled with fried-chicken takeaways and charity shops and shady-looking solicitors. Further along, an Asian grocery bursting with fruit and veg, and next to that, a café-slash-kebab shop, with a mix of old locals smoking and various younger types vaping and talking loudly on phones. She hurried past it all, heading for what the area called a park – not the type of park she was used to, with grass and trees and flowers, just a sad concrete rectangle with a couple of graffitied metal benches. That aside, it was still the closest there was to tranquillity in this part of town, and she'd been going there daily since they moved. Casey had come once, proclaimed it a dump, and Eve hadn't bothered to extend the invitation again.

Eve liked the ugly park, as she'd come to know it. She recognised the regulars. The old man in the bright blue joggers and the faded grey suit jacket. He smoked a pipe and always had one can of beer in a faded M&S bag-for-life. He wasn't the chatty type, but he always said hello, showing off his rotten little pegs that were once functioning teeth. Then there were the two women in the matching cream tracksuits, hair scraped into ponytails that pulled their cheeks up to their eyes. They drank cans of energy drink and prattled away in a language she thought might be Russian or Polish, and they never as much as acknowledged Eve despite seeing her every day for months.

And of course there were the skateboarding teens, who blew vape smoke and called each other names and spat next to the overflowing bin.

None of them really paid attention to Eve, and Eve was more than happy to sit quietly, taking them in but not really caring too much about them either. It was that peculiar sort of loneliness cure – being somewhere where no one really cares, and yet just them being there makes you less alone.

The chattering women glanced up at the newcomer with mild interest, then looked away and continued their conversation. The old man had left. The skateboarders were too busy perfecting their jumps. The newcomer sat on the bench where Eve sat – not next to her, but it wasn't that long a bench and he wasn't really that far away either. She could smell him. She could hear the light wheeze in his chest as he breathed. She was still looking ahead, but out of her peripheral vision, she saw him turn towards her. And she could smell his stale breath.

Something squirmed inside her stomach. The knot that had been there since the attack gently tightening around her waist, pulling in. Squeezing beneath her rib cage and restricting her breath.

His breathing became louder, more laboured.

She refused to look at him. She wanted to stand up, to walk as fast as she could right out of that park and back to her horrible flat and her disinterested partner, who maybe, just maybe, might react if Eve was to project her fear and switch off that damn television.

But she was frozen. Just like before. And the knot pulled tighter and tighter, until she was scared she might pass out.

'Miss?'

Eve stayed still, staring straight ahead. Willing for one of the women, or even one of the teenagers, to notice her. To feel her discomfort. To come to her aid. All the sounds of the park seemed to have disappeared. The scrape of the skateboard wheels on the concrete. The chattering Eastern European voices, and their occasional shrieks of laughter. The rumble of cars behind her on the road.

'Miss, can you spare any change?'

She knew what he was saying. She knew he was homeless, maybe an addict. He just wanted some cash or some food or maybe something to drink, but he wasn't there to hurt her. Rationally, she knew this.

But the knot in her stomach became a hard ball of pain, and she heard someone cry out. A small, anguished screech. And then he was shuffling away from her, pushing himself into the far end of the bench, against the armrest, and he was saying, 'Sorry, sorry.'

And for a moment the skateboarders stopped skating and the women stopped talking. And for a moment everyone just stared at her. And then she was on her feet, and she was running out of the park, and along the street, and the sounds started up again as quickly as they'd left – car horns beeping, people shouting. The knot unfurled and the rope inside turned into a burning, writhing thing inside her chest as she ran all the way home. And she knew, as she reached the doorway of her flat, that she would never feel safe there again.

Twenty-Three

ANNA: MONDAY

Anna had just about calmed down by the time she got back home. After the encounter, she'd nipped into Lidl to try to take her mind off Mary's whispered warning. She was going to have to talk to Jasper as soon as possible. People were definitely keeping things from her, and she wanted to know why. She intended to mention the man on the beach, too. If she *hadn't* imagined him, it was something that Jasper should be aware of. She had just finished putting away her shopping and switched the kettle on when her phone pinged.

'Oh, please . . .' she muttered to herself, dropping a bunch of bananas into a wide-mouthed glass bowl. Not that bloody app again. Was it going to berate her for asking questions in the Indian restaurant now?

She was already sick of the constant surveillance. She really wished she'd paid more attention to Jasper when he'd run through the terms and conditions of their relocation. But staying annoyed about it was helping her ignore the cloying feeling that something very bad was going on. Also, she was starting to wonder where Peter had got to. She picked up her phone and was glad to see that it wasn't a message from the app-bot. It was a text.

> Fancy a walk along to Port Seton? The baker's
> is worth the trip. Best pineapple tarts in the
> country! Beth x

Port Seton was the village on the other side of The Street, further down the coast towards the tourist towns and beaches of Gullane and North Berwick. She hadn't been that way yet. Apparently, the car park at Longniddry Beach had a good chip van, and attracted doggers by night. Neither of these phenomena existed where she had lived before, and she was intrigued by both. The chips sounded good, and the doggers sounded like an excellent potential plot strand for whatever it was she was going to write next. She filed it away, wondering if it would fit into her plans for a creepy Gothic horror and suspected it was unlikely.

She replied quickly.

> Sounds perfect. Just freshening up. See you at
> the bottom gate in twenty. Ax

Beth replied instantly with a thumbs-up emoji.

Anna nipped into the downstairs loo to tidy up her face and hair, and she was bent down in the living room retying her laces when she heard the key in the lock. When she looked up, Peter was standing there with a bunch of pink gerberas in one hand and a paper bag in the other – something greasy had left an imprint on the side of the bag and a tempting meaty smell entered the room with her husband as he shut the door behind him and came in close, drawing her towards him.

'I'm sorry,' he said. 'I should've told you where I was. You must've been worried sick.'

Anna looked at him, took in his wounded expression, and decided not to mention that she hadn't actually noticed that he hadn't come home last night until she woke up. 'You're here now,' she said. 'Just a sec.'

She opened her messages app and quickly tapped out another message to Beth.

> Wanderer has returned. With food! Raincheck
> on the walk? I'll message later x

Beth replied with a sad face, a shrug, and a thumbs-up. Anna put her phone down and took the flowers from Peter. 'They're gorgeous. My favourites.' She kissed him on the cheek and headed towards the kitchen to find a vase.

He followed her in, still trailing the aroma of something greasy and baked.

'I got us something from the baker's in Port Seton. I heard it was good.' He opened the bag and slid the contents on to the worktop. 'Scotch pies. I can't believe we've never had these before.'

Anna looked at the pies. Round, with a hard crust. She'd seen these before in the chiller in one of the supermarkets back at home but couldn't imagine they actually tasted good. Apparently they were made from the offcuts and leftovers of everything else, mixed with spices. They sounded revolting, but she had to admit they smelled good.

Peter switched on the radio in the kitchen and took two small plates out of a cupboard. 'I just drove for a while, then I slept in the car. It was stupid. But I just wanted to clear my head.' He put the pies on the plates and handed one to Anna. 'You know, I never really liked Lars. I was actually pleased when they arrested him.'

Anna took a bite of the pie. The hard crust cracked easily, and then the taste of peppery, unidentified meat combined with

117

crisp, greasy pastry hit her. It was a perfect combination. She took another bite, stalling. Not wanting to comment on Lars's arrest, or anything else to do with Lars, for that matter. She was glad he was cheerful, but she really didn't want to talk about the past.

Peter took a bite of his own pie, then just stood there, waiting for her to speak.

'Can we just . . . leave it? I don't want to talk about Lars. It's all over now, and we're new people with new lives.' She grinned at him, trying to convey a contentedness that she didn't fully feel but was trying hard to achieve. 'I was actually planning to go to the baker's with Beth,' she said, at last. 'I said I'd pop round later.'

Peter looked hurt. He wiped a hand across his chin, which glistened with grease. 'Don't you think we should talk some more? I mean, we've only just got started . . . But I feel like there was more you wanted to say. Needed to say, I think. This is my life too, Anna.' He paused to take another bite, and his tone softened once more. 'You were stressed out when you came back from the shopping centre. You started saying something about Jasper, and then . . .'

'Wait . . .' Anna raised a hand, silencing him. She leaned over to the radio and turned the volume up.

. . . aged forty-seven, originally from Brixton, South London, has escaped from HMP Full Sutton near York after secure transport was compromised during an external medical visit. A possible sighting of him boarding a train to Edinburgh was provided by a member of the public. Yorkshire police say he has a distinctive tattoo on his neck of a black snake. Prison governor David McCarthy has advised that the public do not approach this man as he is considered to be a danger . . .

Anna's stomach lurched, her undigested lunch ready to make a reappearance. She ran into the living room and turned on the TV, flicking the channels through to the lunchtime news. Peter followed her through.

'Anna? What is it?'

'Lars,' she said under her breath. 'Lars is in that prison. He must've sent someone.' She turned to him. 'For me!'

Peter shook his head. 'Back up a bit, you've lost me.'

She caught the end of the news item, with the mugshot of the escaped prisoner onscreen briefly before the segment finished. It was only a couple of seconds, but she knew it was the man she'd seen on the beach.

Anna sat down on the couch. Her hands were shaking. Peter sat down beside her and tried to pull her close to him, but she shrugged him off.

'Anna . . . I don't understand. Why would Lars send someone after you? How would he have any idea where you are? What would he even want from you now?'

His voice had become a bit high-pitched, but she was no longer really listening to him. She was watching the next news item. A man had been found dead in a disused warehouse near Dundee, his body badly burned. A photograph was onscreen of the man – from when he was still alive – smiling. He had his arm wrapped around the shoulder of a pretty blonde woman. She was smiling too. Their names were Jonas and Kayleigh Grant, both from Dundee. They'd been missing for nearly a year, since Jonas testified against his boss in a high-profile financial services fraud case that had been linked to a huge money-laundering operation. The woman, Kayleigh, had still not been found.

Anna held out a hand, pointing at the TV. 'Look,' she said. 'Peter, look.'

Peter looked. Then he frowned, shuffling forward in his seat. 'Is that . . . ? Jeez. It is. It's them.'

'Yes.' Anna was shaking, trying hard to hold herself together. 'That's Lindsay and Ritchie.' This was no coincidence. The tattooed prisoner had escaped from the same prison as Lars, and now something bad had happened to Lindsay and Ritchie, or whatever they were really called. It didn't make sense. Not completely. Not yet. But it was all connected.

It was all connected to her.

Twenty-Four

StreetChat WhatsApp Group

~Mary #3
I bumped into Anna. I'm worried about her asking too many questions.

~Asya #2
Omg this is so ridiculous! Why are we shutting her out? She hasnae done anything wrong and she must feel like a leper. Some community we are.

~Lorraine #7
We don't need any more nosey parkers. Best keep her at arm's length. Lindsay went snooping around that house and look what happened to her.

~Bradley #1 is typing . . .

~Lorraine #7
Fucksake, Bradley, you need to stop typing stuff and deleting it. If you've got something to say, just say it?? Or leave???

~John #4
Glad to see we've finally acknowledged Lindsay. **eyeroll**

~Asya #2
I'm sick of this. It's like no one really wants to say anything about anything, so what's the actual point? I vote we invite Anna in and tell her that she's no' going mad – that there was a Lindsay next door . . . otherwise . . .

~Mary #3
Otherwise what, Asya? We're all just trying to keep safe here.

~Asya #2
OMG safe from what?! Either we invite Anna or I'm deleting this group. I'm the one that set it up, so I can do that, you know. It's up to yous . . .

~Lorraine #7 has left the group

~John #4 has left the group

Twenty-Five

ANNA: MONDAY

Anna didn't bother to text Beth. Instead she just left a confused Peter and hurried across the street to Beth's house. She rang the bell, noting it played the same annoying tune that hers did.

The door opened and there was Beth, wiping floury hands on her apron. She'd obviously run a hand across her forehead too, as flour streaked her hairline. She looked surprised for a moment, and then grinned.

'Anna! I thought you couldn't make it until later. I've just started on a bunch of last-minute cupcakes. The number of customers who want urgent deliveries is getting ridiculous, but at least this one says they'll come and collect . . .' She paused, clocking Anna's demeanour. 'What's wrong?' She glanced up and down the street as if trying to work out why Anna looked like she'd just run away from something – or someone. 'Do you want to come in?'

Anna nodded and followed her inside. Her heart was thumping hard, and she had to take a few breaths before she could speak.

'I didn't ask you this before, but I'm asking now because no one else is telling me anything, and I don't know if everyone thinks I'm just going to drop it, but I'm telling you, I'm not.' She blurted the words out between breaths as she followed Beth into the kitchen.

Beth handed her a glass of water. 'Slow down! Bloody hell, you're making me anxious here. What's happened?'

Anna gulped the water, then took a breath. She was too hot. She wasn't used to running, certainly not sprinting short distances, and she'd had one too many adrenaline spikes recently. She slowed her breathing and sipped at the last of the water while Beth looked on, her face pinched with confusion.

'My neighbours, at Number Eight. Did you know them?'

Beth bit her lip, then turned away. She started fussing with the wire cooling rack she had laid out on top of a cloth on the hob. The kitchen smelled of vanilla. 'No one lives at Number Eight.'

Anna's moment of calm evaporated again. She took a step over to where Beth stood, gripped her arm, trying to get her to turn around.

'Ow!' Beth pulled away, but she did face Anna now, staring her down, nostrils flaring and mouth pulled tight.

Anna looked into her eyes and saw the lie, but there was more to it. Beth looked sad underneath. Or something else. Scared?

This was such a mess. Anna knew she was handling it all wrong, but after seeing the news item – the actual proof that the couple existed . . . she wished now she'd snapped a photo of the TV on her phone, or taken a video.

Anna sagged. 'I'm sorry. I'm so sorry. I shouldn't have grabbed you like that.'

'No, you really shouldn't have. Maybe you should leave. Go home and calm down. I don't know what this obsession is with Number Eight, but you should—'

'Hang on . . .' Anna folded her arms. 'I never mentioned it to you before. I was going to, when you came round. But after the reactions I got from anyone else I asked, I decided to leave it until I had more evidence.'

Beth snorted. 'Evidence? What are you, a copper now? Although . . . didn't you say you were a writer? Overactive imagination seems to be getting to you, I reckon.'

Anna watched Beth's face as she tried to laugh it all off, but there was still something under her skin, something that she couldn't quite keep out of her expression. 'You're lying to me. I know you are. You and everyone else.'

'You sound paranoid now, Anna. I think maybe whatever it is that made you move here might be affecting you a bit. You need to chill out. Try to settle in.'

'They were on the lunchtime news. It wasn't the names they gave me, but it was definitely them. You'll see it again later, at teatime. Or you could google it – assuming that stupid app hasn't blocked the news we're not meant to see.'

Beth seemed to sag at the mention of the app. 'Now you sound like a conspiracy theorist. Christ, Anna. What's really going on with you?'

'I saw her get dragged into a car, Beth.'

Anna waited for a reaction. She knew she wasn't supposed to tell anyone this. Jasper had told her to keep it to herself and leave it to him to investigate, but she needed to see something from Beth. She'd hoped they were becoming friends and she was disappointed that she was just another person on the street and in this stupid town who wasn't willing to tell her the truth. She hadn't imagined Lindsay and Ritchie. None of this made any sense.

Eventually, Beth reacted. She opened her mouth to speak, but then closed it again, turning away, back to the worktop where the empty cooling rack sat, waiting for her to take the cupcakes out of the oven. As if it knew, the oven timer started emitting a high-pitched beeping sound.

'You should go,' Beth said, still facing away from her. She lowered her voice. 'And I shouldn't have mentioned anything about that thing on my phone, by the way, so keep that to yourself.'

Anna stared at Beth's back for a moment. The woman still hadn't moved to retrieve her cakes. The oven continued to beep. So much for her new friend and confidante.

'Fine.' Anna turned and marched out of the kitchen. She wasn't one hundred per cent sure, but just as she unlatched the door to leave she was convinced that she heard Beth say 'Sorry.'

Anna walked home, feeling dejected. Alone. A text pinged, and she took out her phone to look.

> I'll be out walking on the beach in the morning.
> Don't bring *anything* with you. Beth.

She dropped her phone back into her pocket. Well, that was interesting. Maybe Beth would come up with the goods after all. Presumably by 'anything' she meant phones . . . listening devices. Of course Beth wasn't going to answer her questions in the kitchen like that, because while Beth thought it was just the phone and the app that were an issue, Anna was already considering the possibility that the Wi-Fi had something to do with it too. She just wasn't entirely sure why anyone needed to listen to her, or to Beth for that matter.

It was only a theory that Beth was in witness protection too – there could be another explanation for her having the app and being so secretive . . . the other residents were every bit as cagey.

Anna felt bad now about her outburst. She thought back to Lindsay's warning . . . *the walls have ears*. Maybe Beth really *was* trying to tell her that the beach was the only place they could speak freely? Or maybe Anna really *was* just being ridiculous. Reading too much into things. She hadn't seen much of the others on the street lately. Maybe she never would. Maybe the others just hadn't been friendly with the couple at Number Eight. But even so, wouldn't they know who they were?

Her phone pinged again and she pulled it out of her pocket, wondering if Beth had changed her mind already.

But it wasn't Beth.

> Hi Anna! It's your friend, Mr StreetMate! Remember to keep your phone on you at all times. It's for your own safety!

Oh God. The app was reading her texts now, wasn't it? It had picked up on Beth's cryptic message.

Anna couldn't carry on like this. She was going to have to talk to Jasper.

She was fumbling with her phone, trying to switch it off, when a man hurried up the path to Number Four. Was this John? She still hadn't met him, and only now realised she had no idea what he might look like. She thought back to earlier . . . He'd been at a distance, but she was pretty sure this wasn't the man from the beach. But . . . it could be an associate. Could she trust anyone right now?

'Hi,' she called, walking a bit faster. But either he didn't hear her, or he chose not to. He disappeared into Number Four and slammed the door. It *was* John then. She breathed a sigh of relief. As she walked past, she could see that his blinds were already drawn tight, and she couldn't see anything inside. It was still daylight. Perhaps he was just a very private person.

Just another freak on the street.

I give up.

Back home, Peter was cooking dinner, but she had no appetite. She asked him to plate something up for her and leave it in the fridge. She knew he wanted to talk to her, and she knew she should continue the conversation from before, but there were just too many things swirling around in her head. She headed upstairs, pulled off her shoes and tossed them across the room. She lay back on the bed, fully clothed, and closed her eyes. It was still so damn bright in the room, and she felt a tension headache starting to pound behind her right eye.

Coming to Scotland had been a mistake. Running away from things wasn't going to fix what she did. She should've taken Jasper's advice to move abroad – at least being further away would make it more difficult for Lars to find her. Her mind went back to the other news story. The tattooed man. The man she was sure she'd seen on the beach yesterday. She should have told Jasper straight away, but she had been clutching at straws, hoping she'd imagined him. So much weird stuff had happened already he might not even listen to her concerns. Accuse her of being paranoid.

She *was* being paranoid though, about everything. She couldn't help it.

But it still made no sense. Why were they only reporting him as escaped and at large now? Had they tried to find him first, in an attempt to save face? But he was dangerous, they'd said. And he was heading to Edinburgh. And Lindsay had said they were from Dundee, hadn't she? And the couple on the news really did look like them . . . and the woman who left the note on her car had most definitely been Lindsay.

You are not safe in that house.

She was starting to think she was never going to be safe. That she'd never be happy again. That Lars was going to find her soon, and it would all be over.

Lars is in prison. He doesn't know where you are . . .
But what if he does?

The light was really affecting her now. She needed to take a pill and go to sleep. She needed to close that damn blackout blind, but she couldn't bear to lift her head from the pillow.

Outside, raised voices carried across from somewhere nearby. Both female. Lorraine and Donna? Donna's room was right across from hers.

'You need to stay away from him. It's not right.'

'Don't be so stupid, Mum. He's a friend. I've got no other fucking friends since you brought us to this shithole.'

'Don't swear at me, Donna. If your dad was to hear you . . .'

'Oh yeah, right, like he's going to give a shit about what I do. He doesn't want anything to do with me. I told you, as soon as I get some money together, I'm getting out of this dump.'

'Don't be ridiculous! Where are you going to get money? Where are you going to live? You can't just leave here – you know you're not allowed—'

'It's all going to shit here, Mum. Even you must've worked that out . . . That house over the road . . .'

Anna's ears pricked up at that. What were they talking about? Did she mean her house, or did she mean Number Eight? She'd been sure Donna knew something when she'd asked her the other day. It was almost like she wanted Anna to know that she was lying – unlike the adults, who were doing their utmost to win an Oscar for their own performances. She shuffled down the bed and sat closer to the window. She would pull the blind in a minute. Try to sleep off this headache. But she was intrigued.

She was also intrigued as to why they had stopped talking so abruptly.

Anna looked out of the window and saw that Lorraine and Donna were looking out of theirs. Staring straight at her. She flinched, then stepped back, out of their line of sight. Did they know she was there? Or had they merely been gazing out across the street? Had they just realised that their words were carrying out of the open window?

She sat there, frozen. She waited a few minutes, listening to her own heavy breathing, her eyes closed against the brightness of the early-evening sun. Then, when she could bear it no more, she stood up to pull the cord to close the blind. She opened her eyes, squinting as the pulsing pain increased in intensity as the light hit her retinas.

Donna was alone in her room now, and she was staring straight across the road at Anna.

Twenty-Six

A Police Station: Six Months Ago

Detective Sergeant Georgia Lawrence had just sat down to eat her very late lunch of a slightly crispy ham salad baguette when her phone rang. She thought about ignoring it, but the withheld caller ID piqued her interest. There was a rumour going around the station about one of her cases, and she had a feeling that this call might be confirmation. She pushed the baguette back into the plastic wrapper and slid her finger across the phone screen.

'DS Lawrence speaking. Is this who I think it is?'

The caller laughed. 'You know exactly who it is, love. Who else knows your personal number and calls from a place that never flashes up on the screen?'

It was true, then.

'Get on with it, Marcus. I'm trying to eat my lunch.'

'Two words that might interest you.' He paused for effect. 'Lars. Kristiansen.'

Georgia stood up from her seat and cupped the phone closer so that no one could hear, then she walked out of the office and into the grey-carpeted corridor, all thoughts of her lunch now forgotten. A couple of uniformed trainees walked past, chattering, and she waited until they were safely out of earshot before she spoke again. 'Go on.'

'You've heard the rumours, I assume? Our man is lodging another appeal.'

'I heard murmurings.' She walked down to the end of the corridor and turned left towards the small kitchenette. Thankfully there was no one in there, and she managed to wrangle a pod out of her pocket and into the coffee machine while keeping her phone wedged under her chin. The chief had treated them to the machine after a run of successful outcomes, but it was every man – or woman – for themselves when it came to procuring an actual pod. She kept a supply on her person at all times.

'You still there?'

'Yes, sorry. Getting a sneaky coffee before anyone comes and asks me to swap them a pod for something less valuable.'

Marcus laughed. 'Same old, same old. Bunch of children.'

The coffee machine whirred, doing its thing.

'Well?' Georgia said. 'What's the basis of his appeal this time? I didn't even think it was that long since the last one.'

'You're right, it's not. But as you know, if more evidence comes to light, they're going to push it.'

Georgia took the cup from under the machine's spout and laid it on the side. There was a packet of chocolate digestives lying there, unopened. She eyed them hungrily but, convinced it was a trap, left them alone.

Detective Sergeant Marcus Cole used to be her partner, but he'd moved on several months ago to another division. One that no one was supposed to know about, not without the right level of clearance. But she knew where he'd moved to. For someone who had to work covertly, he was shit at keeping secrets from his mates. Not that she'd seen much of him since he'd moved, but life goes on.

'Just spit it out, Marcus. I'm kind of busy here.'

She wasn't. But she didn't want him to think he was the only one with important things to do.

'He's saying that his fancy-piece is lying.'

Georgia sighed. 'He's always said that. No one believed him. She was a very convincing witness.'

'Agreed. But apparently someone else has come forward. Someone who saw what happened that night in the woods.'

She lifted up her coffee and took a sip. 'After all this time? They just happened to remember that they'd seen something critical to a high-profile case?'

'I know . . . when you put it like that, it sounds weak. But it's not just someone saying they saw something . . .' He let the sentence trail off again, clearly enjoying the suspense.

Normally she'd play along, but she didn't like the way this was going. Her instinct had told her from the start that there was more to this case, but her boss had been adamant that they had what they needed. They got their man. They blew open a lot more than just him and what he had done. It was a spectacular coup for the team, and instrumental in the events leading to the purchase of the coffee machine. She should be happy. She had done her job.

But it had never felt quite right. Something about the witness had sent her synapses firing like a fairground-stall rifle shoot. *Pop – pop – pop!*

Whatever Marcus said next was going to ruin her day, and most likely her weekend. Maybe even her career, depending on how the boss decided to lay the blame.

'What is it, Marcus?'

'There was someone else in the woods that night. They saw the whole thing. And guess what?'

She didn't answer. Took a mouthful of coffee.

'They filmed the whole thing on their phone.'

Georgia coughed, spluttering boiling black liquid all over the coffee machine. She would have to clean the damn thing now, on top of everything else.

'And they didn't come forward with this information before, because . . .'

She could actually hear his grin down the phone. He sounded triumphant. 'Because someone paid him off . . . someone who wanted the footage for themselves.'

'And who might that have been?'

'Her husband.'

Georgia stared at the mess of the coffee machine, then raised her eyes to the ceiling. She blew out a breath. Then she closed her eyes and shook her head gently. 'I've got four words for you, DS Cole. Fuck. You. Very. Much.'

He was laughing as she spoke. She hung up before he could respond.

Twenty-Seven

ANNA: TUESDAY

Anna woke feeling groggy, and it took her a few minutes to remember where she was. She was still getting used to waking up in total darkness. She had a vague memory of taking co-codamol for her headache, chased down with a sleeping tablet, and she had no idea if Peter had come up to bed or not. This was starting to become a habit. One that she knew she would need to nip in the bud as soon as possible, but everything just felt too hard right now. She would sort it out when she was ready. She left the blind down and shuffled through to the shower, setting it to tepid and lowering the temperature further when she'd acclimatised. It was brutal, but it worked. A few minutes later, her head felt much clearer, and she knew exactly what she had to do. She dressed quickly, throwing on the same clothes as the day before, and hurried downstairs.

'Peter? Are you here?'

The was no answer, but the back door was open, a gentle breeze drifting through to the kitchen. A teaspoon holding a teabag lay on the worktop. She touched the teabag and found it still warm. He must be in the garden. She called out of the back door. 'Peter?'

He appeared from the shed, mug in hand. 'Morning,' he said. 'Thought I'd make a start on this place at last. Get my tools set up and whatnot. It's about time I got back to work.'

She smiled, but it felt like an effort. He was right to be keeping busy, but she still had too much inside her racing mind. How could he be so calm about everything?

'I'm just popping out.' She tried to make her voice sound breezy, but she clearly didn't succeed. He started to walk up the path towards her, his face etched with concern.

'You OK? It's been a weird few days. I know you don't want to talk about it right now, but I promise you, when you do, I will listen.'

'I know.' She blew him a kiss and turned away, hoping he'd get the hint.

She picked up her phone and scrolled through her recent calls until she found Jasper's number. Her finger hovered over the screen, something stopping her from pressing it. It was odd that he hadn't got back to her already. Maybe things were progressing in his investigation into Lindsay. Maybe that's what had actually led to them finding Ritchie – or whatever his name actually was. She closed the recent calls screen and swiped through her apps. That StreetMate thing was still there, with its stupid little smile. The nosy little fucker. Perhaps it wasn't Jasper she needed to talk to, after all. Who seemed to keep popping up, knowing her business? If anyone knew the details about what had happened to Lindsay and Ritchie, it would be him.

Bradley.

Did he usually go out with the dogs at this time? She didn't know. She'd seen him at different times of the day, but those dogs clearly needed a lot of exercise. She pulled on a hoody and slid her phone into the pocket with her keys, and headed out, crossing the road and walking quickly past Beth's house, feeling a pang of regret about their argument and hoping they could resolve it soon. She'd slept too late for their morning meet-up on the beach, but she would text her and rearrange. She felt a stab of annoyance as she walked past Mary's, thinking about their strange confrontation in the village. Both of these things would have to be dealt with, but not right now.

Unsurprisingly, Bradley's doorbell played the same tune as the others. She wondered why no one had tried to change theirs to something suiting their own taste. The uniformity of The Street was beginning to creep her out.

The door was opened by a smiling Lacy, who immediately invited her in.

'I was wondering when you might pop by,' she said. 'Bradley said he bumped into you and you seemed a bit distracted. Hope you're settling in OK?' Lacy paused to lean in and hug her. 'It's so nice to see you. Tea? Coffee?' Lacy flapped her arms around the messy kitchen. 'I'm not the street's resident baker, but I can do you some toast?'

'Just a glass of water is fine,' Anna said. She felt even guiltier now about how she'd spoken to Bradley, when he and his fiancée were clearly nice people. 'I was hoping to see Bradley, actually. I think I was a bit rude to him . . .'

Lacy handed her a glass of water. 'Don't be silly. We all know what it's like when you're just moving in – even more so when it's a place like this. Bit weird, eh? All the houses being exactly the same. All the people keeping themselves behind closed doors. We can be a suspicious lot in the beginning, but you get used to it. There's actually a really nice community feel to the place, once you're settled in.'

Anna felt calmer now, in Lacy's company. She was bubbly and refreshing and Anna got the feeling that she might get a straight answer to a straight question from her. Something about her was authoritative but kind.

Lacy's laptop sat open on the worktop, amidst the mess. 'You work from home?' Anna asked her, peering at the screen but unable to work out what was on it. It was a dark background with small white writing, separated by vertical and horizontal lines.

'Yep, for my sins.' Lacy closed the laptop lid and pushed it out of the way. 'Time for a break now, though, I think.'

'What is it that you do?' Anna sipped her water.

'We're both in IT. Pretty dull but it pays the bills.' She glanced at a spot somewhere over Anna's left shoulder. Avoiding Anna's eyes. It was a marked shift from her earlier friendliness and it put Anna's hackles up. She'd researched plenty of tells for her thriller novels, and she knew what that one meant. Eyes to the right.

Liar.

Anna tried not to show her discomfort. Were these two in on it too? Whatever *it* was. 'I'm fine with internet browsers and Microsoft Word, but that's about my limit.' So much for her open and honest demeanour, Anna thought. She was disappointed. It seemed as if everyone on this street had an agenda. But she had no idea why. She sipped more water. 'Is Bradley around? I wanted to ask him something.'

Lacy smiled, but Anna felt nervous all of a sudden, as if the other woman was appraising her. Waiting for her to make a mistake. It was an odd sensation, a shift in the atmosphere that seemed to happen every time she spoke to one of the residents. It hadn't happened with Beth – not at first – but then last night in her kitchen, it had been there.

'Maybe *I* can help?' Lacy said. 'If it's something about the house or the village, or—'

'Well, actually, I wanted to ask if you knew anything about the couple at Number Eight?' She wondered if maybe she should also ask Lacy about the app. If she had it, and Beth had it . . . maybe it was something linked to everyone's Wi-Fi?

Lacy's grin was turning a bit Stepford Wife. 'Ah, yes, nice enough people. Moved in same time as us. She can be a bit of a moaner about some things, but I actually think she's quite shy—'

Anna's stomach lurched. That didn't sound much like the Lindsay she had met, but the Lindsay she had met had a lot to drink – maybe that was also to hide the shyness. Maybe the couple on TV just looked like them. Maybe Anna had got everything wrong? She cleared her throat. 'So there *was* a couple at Number Eight? The Walkers? Only there was that thing on the news yesterday about this couple from Dundee, who—'

'*Oh!* I'm so sorry.' Lacy was still grinning, but it looked pained now. Her eyes darted to the right again. Some people might say that tells are a myth, but Lacy definitely had some kind of non-verbal gesture that she couldn't seem to control. 'I get mixed up with the numbers sometimes,' she said. 'I thought you meant the Whitelaws, across the road from you.'

Anna shook her head and tried to bite back her annoyance. 'No, that's Number Seven. Odds on your side, evens on mine . . .'

'Right, of course. You know, I don't think I've had enough coffee this morning. Doesn't bode well for my work, does it?' She forced out a small laugh. 'Listen, why don't I get Brad to come and find you later? Maybe he can help?' She took the glass from Anna's hand. 'You should come back over one evening. Bring your other half. I'll cook us something.' She gestured again at the kitchen. 'It might look like a mess, but honestly it's organised chaos. A bit like my work. I really should get back . . .'

Anna knew she was being asked to leave. Dismissed. Just like at Beth's, although this time there was no argument. Just complete avoidance of the question. She hadn't read Lacy well at all.

'Sure. Absolutely. Need to get back to it myself. It's about time I cracked on with my own work.'

Lacy saw her out, giving her a small hug on the doorstep. The smile was still stuck on, but there was something very different behind her eyes.

Had that been another waste of time? Yes and no. It hadn't helped uncover any more information on the missing neighbours, but it had revealed that there was another cagey liar on the street: Lacy.

Feeling dejected, Anna took the cut-through at the far end of the street, past Brooklin and Asya's house. She hadn't seen them at all since the barbecue at Number Seven, but it hadn't really crossed her mind until now. She'd barely spoken to them in the Whitelaws' garden and, to her shame, had formed an instant impression of them both. In short, she had written them off with no good cause. Something else to be rectified. Or was there any point?

She was beginning to think that all the neighbours were the same. They were all in on something that they didn't want Anna or Peter to be part of. But she was no longer convinced that it was something to do with her. Maybe they were just really cliquey, and if that was how they wanted it, then fine. She wasn't going to force anyone to be her friend.

But she was still determined to find out what had happened to Lindsay.

The police report had said she was missing. It was only Ritchie who'd been confirmed as dead. She still couldn't get her head around that. He'd been in her house, full of life, only a few days ago. She would call Jasper and ask for an update. She wasn't going to be fobbed off again.

The beach was deserted, as usual. The tide was out, and there were a few ropey clumps of seaweed peppered across the dark sand. A couple of chunks of driftwood, one of which she'd noticed the last time she'd been down and had been thinking of dragging home and putting it in the garden. She needed to do something to make the place look less sterile, less like every other house and garden in this development that she was quickly starting to hate.

She should definitely call Jasper. Ask him if they could move somewhere else instead – bring up the idea of going overseas again. She was jumpy and unsettled here. It seemed like everyone was lying. Even Peter was acting weirdly, disappearing off then acting like nothing had happened. Why wasn't he pressing her for more information on Lars?

Clouds were gathering over the sea, turning it grey and murky. The breeze from earlier had whipped up too. After a few sunny days, it wouldn't be a surprise to have a storm rolling in. The few days of blue skies and sparkling seas had just added to the unreal feeling of the place. The perfect white cubes with their perfect green lawns. And yet it seemed that every family inside them was anything but perfect. Including her own.

Anna climbed down the steps to the beach and made her way across the sand. She might as well get that piece of wood now. It was probably too heavy for her to pull on her own, but she could at least drag it a bit further back, away from the shoreline – in case it got washed away if the waves started to crash in. She ran her fingers through her hair, attempting to detangle it as the wind started to whip it around her head, obscuring her vision. Why did no one use the beach? It was the most real part of the development, even if it was fake. She was surprised that the locals from the village didn't make more effort to get past the barriers.

Perhaps they knew something that she didn't.

Her mind flashed back to the man on the beach. She hadn't imagined him. She knew she hadn't. He was the man from the news. The escaped prisoner with the horrible tattoo. But where had he come from? How had he ended up on her beach? And where was he now?

She shivered.

The tide had started to turn. Foamy waves smashed against the shore. Tendrils of seaweed swirled like hair. She stood there, watching. It was too late to get that piece of driftwood now. The clouds had grown darker too. And that feeling she'd had before, that weird shift in the atmosphere, it started to creep over her skin. Goosebumps skittered, and the seaweed tendrils seemed to be reaching out towards the water, as if they were begging to be dragged back in.

It was the pale white lump that made her walk closer to the water. It looked like a small balloon, or a jellyfish, bulging out from under the seaweed. The water pushed and pulled, and then another one appeared, and the tendrils of seaweed revealed themselves to be more than just bladder wrack. It was actual hair. And the small pale lumps were hands.

A mannequin. Something dumped by kids to freak out the posh residents. She could imagine their glee when they did it. As pranks went, it was a good one.

Keep telling yourself this, Anna.

She walked closer to the shore, and as the sea drew closer, as much as she wanted to convince herself it was just a dummy, her churning stomach and the return of the pounding in her skull told her otherwise.

The water pulled back once more, revealing more of its quarry. Anna recognised the trainers. And the clothes – jogging bottoms so similar to the ones she was wearing right now. A crashing wave caused the thing to move, to roll on to its side, and another pale lump revealed itself, obscured by seaweed and hair.

A face.

Beth.

Twenty-Eight

THE DIARY

Well . . . there was something very interesting on the news earlier. That couple from Number Eight that no one is admitting to having ever seen before – well, except the new woman, Anna, who is absolutely *obsessed* with them – turns out they were missing persons. *Missing* before they came here.

Interesting.

Only, one of them isn't missing any more. They found him, charred like a burger that's been left too long on the barbecue.

They were using different names, of course. Kind of a given, if you don't want to be found. But the UK is really not that big. And they really didn't make much of an effort to get very far away.

Idiots.

Talking of idiots, Mad Mary has been on the rampage again. I heard her all the way from her house to mine. You can hear most things on this street from house to house, as long as the windows are open and the wind is blowing the right way. She's getting very upset about Anna and her search for the truth. I think she might be considering taking action. Campaigning to get rid of the newcomers.

I'm not sure why she's convinced that they're such a threat.

It's not their fault that they moved in just as the missing persons couple were about to do a runner. Something happened, and it was annoying me initially that I couldn't work it out. But then I remembered some of the advice my therapist gave me, and I took a step back. Stop trying to think all the time, she used to say. Sometimes you have to just *be*.

Be what?

She never really explained, but I think I got it anyway. Overthinking things is a curse. But when you bounce between that and a complete lack of impulse control, it's a bit of an issue. She tried to get to the root of it all, but I'm not sure she succeeded.

I'm not sure anyone could really understand me, and the things that I've said and done, and the things I want to do – or at least, the things that I think I want to do. I'm working on it. I think she'd be proud of me.

I've even stopped killing the flies.

I know that most people don't care about flies. You get those electric things in kitchens to fry them to death. Or those sticky strips to trap their wings. And there's that horrible toxic spray that's probably responsible for a lot more damage to humans than anyone has ever looked into. But that's all about pest control, I suppose. It's different if you kill them for fun.

No, don't – it's only a cliché because it's true.

I used to catch them in a jar, and leave it next to a light. I liked to watch them buzzing around manically, bashing against the glass, desperate to get to the light. It took quite a while for them to die, their small bodies twitching on the bottom of the jar for a while until the oxygen ran out.

Well, when I say the bottom of the jar, more like the bottom of the mound of fly corpses that lay piled there. It reached a point where I couldn't always see the last twitches of the latest catch, because they slid down amongst their dead friends. Sometimes if I wondered if they did that on purpose, like the innocent victims of mass shootings who're told to hide behind their dead schoolmates.

I doubt that flies are that intelligent. I could google it. But then I'd be as bad as those social media 'helpers' – finding the information needed to back up my own thoughts.

My window is open but I'm not getting much in the way of information from out there. Even Mad Mary has shut up. Maybe I'll go online, do a bit more digging on those missing persons from Number Eight. Maybe Anna isn't the only one with a bee in her bonnet about the mysteries of this street.

Mmm, *bees*. Their lovely, fuzzy, stripy little bodies.

Wouldn't *they* make a pretty death jar?

Twenty-Nine

PATRICK: THREE YEARS AGO

He'd become a bit of a gofer for Lars. He hoped that it was just the beginning, that soon he'd be trusted with more: less of the special delivery stuff and more of the strategy. Not that he was much of a businessman. He could admit that. But helping out with whatever Lars needed to do was a good start, and he'd take it.

For now.

Patrick didn't know too much about Lars and his business just yet, only that while he maintained a respectable job in the City, he was also fingering many dirty little pies. Drugs. Guns. Money. Lots of moving stuff around.

People too, it transpired.

It had been Agneta who had told him that part. Sure, Lars had let him in on this side of the business eventually, but little did Lars know that Patrick had been getting quite friendly with Agneta when her husband wasn't around.

She was a fascinating woman. She looked and sounded Swedish, like Lars, but she was actually Russian. She'd been taken to Finland as a child, and her family had attempted to get her a solid Scandinavian education. They wanted her to have a fresh start, away from their own shady backgrounds, and she had done well.

She'd moved to Sweden for work when she was twenty, but that was when things had fallen apart. Wrong people, bad decisions.

And then she met Lars.

He'd brought her to the UK with him, got her cleaned up in an expensive rehab facility, and she had never gone back. But she didn't have the correct paperwork to live in the UK. She was worried about her family's background being unearthed . . . and Lars had helped.

For a price.

He'd forced her to marry him. He'd demanded children. But it hadn't happened. He could have divorced her, left her to fend for herself – but she knew how to make him happy. And he liked the power.

So she stayed. And she played the part of the uber-rich glamorous Swedish wife better than any Oscar-winning actor could manage.

Patrick's relationship with her wasn't physical – at first. He was the friend she needed, and she was the same to him. He felt increasingly adrift from his wife, and there was something about the different reality of mixing with Lars and Agneta that kept Patrick transfixed. Lars paid him in cash, and he squirrelled it away, still taking the occasional regular job so that his wife didn't suspect.

She was too busy to care anyway, it seemed.

She had been reluctant to meet Lars and Agneta at first, but it didn't take long for Lars to charm her . . . and seduce her.

The plan had been simple. Lars had explained it all over coffee one day at his fancy gym, where Patrick had tried his best not to feel inadequate, as he usually did when pushed into the environment of posh people, like his wife's fancy writer friends. Patrick hadn't been much of a coffee drinker before he met Lars – always preferring the stereotypical 'builders' tea' – but Lars drank espresso, and dipped one of those little caramel-gingery biscuits in it, and so Patrick did the same. He got used to the taste after a while.

'Agneta is refusing to deal with my side business, but I think your wife will be amenable, if you allow me to persuade her.' Lars had sipped his espresso, little finger poking out to the side as he gripped the tiny handle. 'I trust this will be acceptable to you, Patrick? You are very loyal, and you know I reward loyalty.'

Patrick had taken a moment to answer, as if pondering the concept of pimping out his own wife. What he was actually wondering was: *does he know about me and Agneta?*

They had recently taken their friendship to the next level, and while he was sure they had been discreet, Lars made it his business to know exactly what was going on, always. There was a good chance that he knew all about it and didn't care – as long as everyone played along with his plans.

'Patrick?'

'Sorry, yes. Of course. Whatever you need, Lars. I'm sure we can make it work.'

'You won't need to do much, actually. Turn a blind eye where necessary. Continue your current state of indifference towards her. She's crying out for attention, Patrick. I'm more than happy to provide it.'

Patrick's stomach did a little flip. This was his *wife* that Lars was talking about. How had he let things get like this? But then he thought about Agneta . . . and her bruises. And how he helped to soothe her troubled life.

His wife was perfectly content, wasn't she? And maybe a bit of fun with Lars might not be a bad thing. She was always looking for inspiration for her stories, wasn't she? A fling with a people-trafficking drug baron might be just the thing.

He almost laughed at the absurdity. None of this felt real. And it probably wouldn't last for ever. Lars would get bored of him soon enough. Might as well get what he could from their 'working arrangement'.

Patrick knocked back his espresso, suppressing an involuntary grimace. This was not a good blend. He bit into the stupid little biscuit, chewed quickly.

'Fine,' he said. 'How much are we talking?'

Thirty

ANNA: TUESDAY

The Street was swarming with emergency response vehicles. Four police cars and two ambulances so far. One for Anna, one for Beth. But Anna didn't need hers, and really, Beth didn't either. But they put her on a stretcher in a bag and took her away, to the mortuary, presumably. This was after the police had cordoned off the beach and attempted to erect a tent, but they had soon given up when they realised that the priority was to get Beth away from the shore before the sea took her for them.

Anna let them give her some diazepam for the shock. There didn't seem to be any reason not to take it. The co-codamol and the sleeping pill would be long gone from her system, and she hadn't had any alcohol. But if the purpose of it was to numb her, she didn't really need it. Because from the moment she'd worked out that it was Beth that she'd found on the beach, her whole body and mind had gone into some sort of numbed paralysis, where all she could do was exist on autopilot. *Come over here with us, Anna. Sit here, Anna. Drink this sweet tea, Anna.*

Beth. Poor, lovely Beth.

Anna was suffocating in guilt. She had meant to tell Beth about the news of the escaped prisoner. Beth hadn't seemed worried when

Anna had mentioned seeing the man on the beach, but maybe Anna hadn't been specific enough. Maybe if she'd described him, then Beth would've known what to look for. She would've known to avoid him.

Because the police had already let it slip that this was no accident. Beth hadn't drowned. The back of her head had been smashed in with something heavy. Possibly a piece of driftwood. It seemed opportunist, they said. Anna had overheard all of this while sipping her sweet tea. They thought they were whispering, but they didn't realise they were in the presence of a writer – someone with a finely tuned ear for other people's conversations. Peter had always told her it was a skill – to be able to sit in a noisy restaurant and remain engaged in a chat with him, while simultaneously picking up juicy details from the couples sitting at the tables on either side.

Should she tell the police that this might be connected to her? That Lars had sent someone after her? She was still pondering this when a tall man in a smart navy suit started walking towards her. His shock of red hair and his friendly face were at odds with the official-looking clothing.

'Mrs Clarke? I'm Detective Sergeant Russel McLean. Is it OK if I ask you a few questions?'

Anna took a deep breath then returned his smile. 'Of course. Although I'm not sure what else I can tell you . . . I explained to the uniformed officer earlier—'

'Constable Wilson has filled me in. But it would be good if you could just tell me too? Helps us get things straight. Sometimes people remember something significant when they tell their story again.'

'Story?' Anna crossed her arms. 'I can assure you, Detective McLean, it's not a *story* . . .'

He held up a hand, his grin grew wider. 'Russel, please. I'm sorry. Anna, is it? OK if I call you that? Please feel free to call me Russel. One "L" if you need to note it down. This is just an informal chat so I can gather the information I need to start the investigation into Mrs Wallace's death.'

Anna felt a tear slide down her face and she wiped it away. She felt her body slump. 'No, I'm sorry. Beth was a friend. A new friend – we'd only just moved in and I was just getting to know her, but I felt she was going to be a friend.'

'This is a horrible situation, Anna. Anything you can do to help me find who did this would be really great. Take your time.'

Around them, the other residents were being gathered. A couple of uniformed officers – one of whom she'd spoken to earlier, Constable Jen Wilson – was shepherding everyone into Bradley and Lacy's house. Asya had her arm around Mary as she guided her away. There was no sign of Finlay, Beth's wife – but presumably she was being looked after. Anna took a deep breath and told the detective what she'd seen. She mentioned that she thought she might have seen the same man before, on the beach. She described the tattoo as best she could, but it had been from a distance.

When Russel asked if she thought Beth might've had any enemies, anyone who might want to hurt her, Anna said no. Thankfully, he didn't ask the same question about her. It was much easier to lie by omission than outright, especially to a trained investigator.

He'd seemed satisfied with her retelling of events and had said he would come back to her with anything further, then suggested that she join the others, who were being advised on best practices while the investigation was ongoing.

Peter was waiting for her outside Bradley's house.

'Hey. Are you alright?' He pulled her close and she let herself sink into his chest. She was far from OK, but it was only now that she realised how distant she felt from her husband. How she'd barely seen him the last few days, and how they seemed to be just rolling through the motions of living together, while living separate lives.

'I wish we'd never come here.' She spoke into his t-shirt, which was already soaked with her tears.

He took her shoulders and moved her gently away from him, looked into her eyes. 'We will get through this. We've already been through so much, and we made it, didn't we?' He took one hand away from her shoulder and used it to wipe her tears. 'Let's talk to Jasper about moving somewhere else. Maybe abroad, like he first suggested. I'd hoped it might work out here, but I can see how jumpy you are. After what happened with the neighbours—'

She shrugged herself away from him. 'That's just it. We don't even know what happened to the neighbours. Everyone is being cagey as fuck. And now this! It all has to be connected, surely? At the moment it feels like we're in a bloody soap opera, waiting for the next dramatic storyline to unfold . . .' She stopped talking when she saw Bradley on his doorstep.

'Ah, great, you're both here. Everyone's sitting out the back. One of the officers is chatting to us all together. Talking us through everything.'

I wonder what Mr StreetMate is going to think of this.

Anna let Peter take her hand and lead her through the house. Out in the back garden, the residents of The Street were waiting. Mary was sitting on a fold-up chair, sobbing quietly. Asya was behind her, rubbing her back and looking pale and worried, despite the fake tan and Botox. The Whitelaws were huddled together near the shed, Lorraine with her arms around both of her children, and Kevin staring straight ahead, his brow furrowed. Brooklin was chatting to John – the man she'd only seen briefly before, entering his house. Neither of them noticed Anna and Peter's arrival. There was no sign of Lacy or Finlay.

Bradley was talking to two uniformed police officers – the pretty one with the kind smile that she had spoken to earlier, Constable Wilson, and a heavy-set dark-haired man she'd seen before, setting up the cordon. Two fold-up seats were sitting empty, near Mary and Asya, and Anna let Peter check that it was OK for them to sit there. She couldn't face Mary at the moment, and she could see that Asya was doing her best to look after the older woman.

It was the second gathering of the residents in a week – the first being the barbecue at the Whitelaws that seemed to have been held under duress. And now this – a group of people bound by one thing: the death of their neighbour.

It was clear from her individual chats with some of them that they were holding back on something, if not outright lying. However, it wasn't the time to bring that up, because this was about Beth, and Anna had liked Beth a lot – but there was still the situation of the missing neighbours that they all claimed not to know.

Well, someone had to know. They probably all knew. The ones she'd spoken to so far were terrible actors, but the others – John, maybe, or Asya and Brooklin, who she'd barely seen and judged to be stupid – seemed like they might be better at keeping whatever this secret was. Maybe they all knew who she was. Maybe they all knew she was in witness protection, and they'd all been told not to tell her anything about anyone.

This might be the most plausible explanation she'd come up with so far.

Peter leaned over and whispered into her ear. 'What do you think happens now?'

Anna glanced around. The police and Bradley were still deep in conversation. 'Whatever it is, they're not ready for us yet. I'm going to call Jasper.'

'What the . . . ? This is not about *you* right now, Anna. Let the police do their jobs first.'

Anna opened her mouth to speak, then closed it again. He was right. She was making it about herself, and she had no actual proof – not yet, anyway – that the man on the beach was the escaped prisoner, or that he was looking for her and found Beth. How stupid would he have to be, to mix them up? They looked nothing alike, apart from the clothes – and if his instruction was to find a woman in her thirties wearing joggers, then there were plenty to choose from around here. Besides, how would Lars have any idea what she might be wearing? He hadn't seen her for over a year, and on *that* day she had been dressed in a dark skirt-suit and pale yellow blouse, looking every inch the innocent, demure victim. A friend who'd been lured into destructive ways by a charming manipulator.

Anna hoped, yet again, that she was wrong about her connection to the unfolding events on The Street – but in her heart of hearts, she knew that Peter was wrong, because it actually *was* all about her.

She sat back in her chair and tried to stay calm.

Thirty-One

ANNA: TUESDAY

It was the male uniformed officer who spoke. He introduced himself as Constable Harry Thomas, and asked if everyone could just remain calm, and stay together, while they sorted a few things out. Then the doorbell rang out its annoying tune, and Bradley went to answer it, returning shortly afterwards with Detective Russel McLean in tow.

Anna had started to relax a bit earlier, but seeing him again caused her heart to race. She felt like his bright blue eyes were boring into her. Like he could see inside and read the lies that she was keeping wrapped up somewhere in her brain.

It's not about you, Anna.

No . . . it actually is!

Peter squeezed her hand, as if sensing her discomfort. Anna squeezed back, grateful to have him here with her. Maybe when all of this was over, they might think about rebuilding things between them. There was no denying that their relationship had felt the strain recently, despite them both attempting to embrace their new start and move on from the past. She didn't like the way he behaved towards her some-times, but he loved her, didn't he? He'd do anything to protect her?

Detective McLean's gaze travelled away from Anna, taking in the rest of the group. Then he raised his eyes skyward for a moment, before taking a breath. 'None of this is easy. For any of us,' he said, scanning the garden again before coming to rest on Bradley, who was leaning against the fence to Anna's left. Then he turned back to face the centre, not catching anyone's eye as he continued. 'A neighbour – a friend – has been found dead, as you know. And not only are you suffering this loss, you're facing the reality that this has happened on your doorstep. In an area that is supposed to be safe and secure.' He gestured to the two uniformed officers. 'Constables Wilson and Thomas will be staying with you all while we commence our investigation. Bradley here has kindly agreed to put them up for as long as is needed. There will be a family liaison officer assigned too, in due course, and if one of you could offer them a room, it would be much appreciated.'

Murmurs around the chairs, until finally Mary spoke. 'I'd be happy to have them, Detective McLean. In fact, I'd feel safer having someone in my house.' She sniffed. Her voice was choked with tears. 'Not that I think I'll feel safe again any time soon.'

'She's right,' Asya piped up from behind her. 'We all moved here because it was meant to be state-of-the-art security, and look what's happened. It could have been any one of us who was killed. How do we know he's not coming back to pick us off one by one?'

Anna felt a wave of nervous laughter threaten to escape. They were all in shock, of course. But the perpetrator of this was long gone, surely? It's not like they had a serial killer in their midst. Asya was making it sound like the plot of an Agatha Christie novel. Not that she was likely to have ever read one. Anna pinched herself hard on her inner arm in an attempt to bring her mounting hysteria under control. This whole situation – after everything else she'd been through – was making her feel like she was living in another reality. There was that crazy theory about parallel universes, wasn't there? Or was it a simulation, like in the *Matrix* movies?

Drugs bust, court case, witness protection and now a murder outside her house. These were the things that happened to other people. Not to her. She wrote about these things in her books. They weren't supposed to be real. She heard someone sobbing, and she sucked in a ragged breath, realising it was her.

She had zoned out of what the detective was saying, but then realised he had stopped talking and was staring at her, not unkindly. 'Anna? Are you OK? I know it must have been a terrible shock for you to find Beth like that, and we will do all we can to support you through it. Maybe you should head back home now and get some rest? There will be lots of officers and support staff in the area for some time, and they'll likely want to come and see you again at home – but in the meantime . . . ?'

'Come on.' Peter stood up and took her hand, tugging gently. Urging her to her feet. Asya came around to the other side of her chair and offered her a tissue.

'You go and rest, babes. We'll come and let you know if there's any news.'

Anna took the tissue and crunched it up in her hand. 'Thank you.' Then she let Peter lead her back through the house and back on to The Street.

They crossed the road, and she walked unsteadily along the pavement towards home. Past Brooklin and Asya's house and then John's. Mary's opposite. All of them empty, because all of the inhabitants were in the garden of Number One, which they'd just left. As Peter unlocked the door to Number Six, Anna turned and leaned back against the house, looking across the road at Number Five.

Beth's house.

It looked to be in darkness too. Anna assumed that Finlay had followed the ambulance to the hospital. To the mortuary.

She shuddered, imagining poor Finlay having to identify the body. Beth hadn't been dead long – they all knew that, because of when she'd last been in contact. But still, lying there on the shore, being whipped by the waves, had already changed her from the bubbly, bright, full-of-life Beth to the grey, waxy body that had been wrapped in floating seaweed and had already attracted a smattering of small, curious crustaceans. It wasn't Beth now. It was 'the body' – and Anna suddenly felt sick.

A light blinked on at the back of Number Five, visible through the living-room window. Someone was in the kitchen.

'I need to see Finlay.' Anna stepped away from the wall. Peter had already opened the door and stepped inside their house, but she didn't want to follow him in. Her head had cleared, and she knew she needed to talk to Beth's wife. She had to explain.

'Anna, come back. You need to rest. Just leave it!'

She ignored him. A couple of white-suit-clad CSIs, who were huddled over what looked like an iPad at the end of the cut-through lane to the beach, turned at the sound of Peter's voice, one of them catching Anna's eye briefly before she looked away from them and fixed her gaze towards Beth's house.

Beth is dead.

She rang the doorbell, half-expecting there to be no answer. She wasn't sure that she would answer, if it were her in this position, but she was filled with a dogged determination that she couldn't shake. She lifted her hand to press the bell again, just as the door opened and Finlay peered out.

'Oh, hi.' Dark shadows hung beneath Finlay's eyes, but the rest of her face was pale. She appeared to have aged ten years in ten minutes. She didn't say anything else, just vanished back inside, leaving the door open. Anna took this as an invitation to enter.

Inside, as Anna had already noted, most of the house was in darkness. It was still daylight, but shadows had fallen on this side of The Street, as if in mourning for what they knew they had lost. The kitchen light was on, casting a too bright artificial shine across everything, making Finlay look even worse. Anna switched it off and pulled out a chair.

'Finlay . . .' She paused. She'd been so certain of herself, marching over here with a purpose, but now that she was here, the reality of the situation kicked in. This woman had just lost her wife. Her life partner. Her love. Anna barely knew Beth – although she had liked her a lot – and she didn't know Finlay at all. She wanted to stand up, to run back out to the other side of The Street, where the sun still shone and partners still lived, and where, eventually, things would get better. But Finlay needed something, as she sat here in the darkness. She needed to know what had happened to Beth. She was staring at Anna now, her gaze hard but the wobble of her bottom lip giving her away.

'You were meant to be out walking with her—'

'Yes,' Anna cut in. 'I know, and I wasn't there, and I will feel forever guilty about that – and I should've warned her . . . about the man—'

'You saw him? The one who attacked her?'

Anna shook her head. Nausea was rising in her again. She hadn't meant to blurt that out. 'I saw a man the other night on the beach. He just . . . I had a bad feeling about him.'

'You're supposed to report that sort of thing to the management,' Finlay said. The corner of her mouth twitched. 'Don't worry. I hate the stupid app too. Big Bloody Brother. Fat lot of good it's done us now.'

'I'm so sorry,' Anna said. Thinking that it was all coming out now, about the app . . . it wasn't just Anna and Beth who had it. Finlay had it too. Did everyone have it? Was it just part of the security of the street? Perhaps her paranoia about it had been unjustified. Anna was more confused than ever.

Finlay shrugged. 'It's not your fault. She told me you hadn't replied to confirm you could make it, and I said I'd go with her. But then I started watching this stupid fucking programme on TV. That one where people want to move abroad but they don't understand that it's not exactly the same as where they are now but with more sun?' She shook her head. 'I watch so much shit. Beth was always telling me off for it.' A sob escaped then, and her shoulders shook. 'Guess I can watch what I like now.'

Anna leaned across the table and laid a hand over Finlay's. 'Look, I'm sorry. I shouldn't have come. I just . . .'

'I get it. I know. If it's any consolation, she walked on that beach all the time by herself. This is a safe place. I don't know what happened, but I think the police will do their best. They did last time . . . It's the whole reason why we're here.' She looked Anna in the eye, bit her lip. She looked like she wanted to say more, but stopped herself. 'I let her down before, Anna. If I hadn't, we wouldn't even be living here.' She let out a long, slow sigh. 'All of this? It's on me.'

Anna shook her head. 'No. You mustn't blame yourself. You can't. You didn't make this happen. Whoever made their way on to our private beach made this happen. I don't know who else has the stupid app, but I'm going to ignore it from now on, because it's done nothing to protect us here. It's watching and it's listening, but what does it actually do, when it comes down to it?'

Finlay looked again like she wanted to say something more, but she just shook her head instead. Sadness radiated across the table like waves.

Beth. Poor Beth.

'Go home, Anna. Hug your husband tight. Don't take him for granted. Don't take anything for granted.' Tears streamed down Finlay's face, as Anna watched. Helpless. She wanted to believe that going home to Peter would be enough to stay safe – but what if someone had found Beth. Someone from Beth's old life – whatever that had been. And if someone had found Beth here, and she was supposed to be hiding from them too, then this place wasn't safe. At all.

Thirty-Two

ANNA: TUESDAY

Finlay's words were ringing in Anna's ears as she walked down the path away from her house. She knew she should go straight home to Peter. Rest, like the police had told her to. There was still so much activity going on with the police and their support staff, so many things for them to do. But how would it help? It wasn't going to bring Beth back and it wasn't going to stop Anna feeling like it was all her fault.

She understood Finlay blaming himself. There couldn't be a loved one alive who didn't blame themselves for the death of their partner, even if there was nothing they could have done about it, and had no influence on it. Survivor's guilt – that was what it was called. Anna felt that too, but for different reasons.

It had to be something to do with her. Anna was the one who'd had to go into witness protection. She was the one who had testified against someone who thought they were in it together. More fool him. And more fool her for thinking she'd be safe because he was in prison. It was too much of a coincidence. The man on the beach had matched the description of the escaped prisoner on the news. He'd found his way to the right beach, the right street – but he'd found the wrong woman. Whatever it was that Finlay thought had happened – whatever it was from their old life . . . that hadn't been the cause of Beth's death. Anna was sure of it.

She really needed to speak to Jasper. But something was holding her back.

Maybe she should just tell the police. Detective McLean seemed nice. Understanding. But Jasper had told her not to talk to anyone else. Just him. No one except Jasper's team was supposed to know she was being protected.

Besides, she needed to clear her head. Stretch her legs. All that adrenaline had taken its toll, and even though by rights she should be passed out with exhaustion, aided by another diazepam that the paramedics had given her for later, she felt more alert than ever.

Anna cut down the lane to the beach and realised that she wasn't going to be able to get out that way. Of course she wasn't. The cordon ran along the fence to the edge of the promenade, and there was a uniformed officer guarding it. She had a feeling she wasn't meant to be going anywhere at all – they'd told her to return to her house, hadn't they? She turned back. Then started walking the other way, towards the trees. It would be cordoned off too, but maybe not guarded. The police presence around the wide gates for the cars was probably enough to deter most people – and it wasn't like she was breaking in . . . she wanted to break out.

There was something about walking through wooded areas that did things to your senses. The light changed. Shadows appeared. Different sounds crept in; the crunch of the forest floor, animals scurrying in the undergrowth. The rustle of leaves. It wasn't a huge area. The trees had not been there long enough to become fully established – you could see through to the other side, to the open parkland that separated the promenade from the main road and the shops, another privacy buffer for The Street . . . and yet that feeling was already there.

Anna stopped for a moment, closing her eyes.

She was back on the common, over a year ago. It had seemed like the right thing to do then. But she'd had too many drinks, and she was buzzing from a pill that Lars had given her. She didn't even know what it was. Ecstasy, maybe? Most people took that in their youth but she never had – she'd been far too risk averse back then. Those media campaigns showing ravers overheating and ending up on life support had been enough to deter her. She felt fuzzy, yet awake. She wanted to do things that she never did – like dance and run and smile so widely it made her face hurt. She had left Lars on the bench at the edge of the wide grassy area, skipping off towards the darkness of the woods, despite his cries behind her to 'come back', 'don't be so stupid', 'there could be anyone in there' . . .

She'd bumped into him almost straight away. Literally bumped into him, as she danced and spun and fizzed through the trees.

'Oi, watch it, love.' He'd grabbed her shoulders and pushed her away. Not hard, just away.

She'd spun around and grinned at him. He was young. White. Twenties? Black tracksuit. He smelled of sweat and citrus after-shave, with the greasy undertones of fried food. Smoke curled from a thin roll-up into his shiny black hair, which was cut so straight across the front the barber must've used a ruler.

'You look like a Lego man,' Anna said, giggling, stumbling backwards a little.

He leaned over and grabbed her arm, stopped her from falling. She giggled again and he frowned. He looked her up and down, taking in her floaty chiffon dress, her bare feet – she'd kicked her heels off at the bench where she left Lars. Peter was away all weekend, seeing old school friends. She'd said she'd amuse herself. She knew she would sleep with Lars. They'd both been waiting for the opportunity. Anna blinked, trying to re-focus. This wasn't Lars. What was she doing here?

'You shouldn't be in here, missus,' the Lego man said. 'You never know who you might bump into.'

She laughed. 'That's what Lars said!'

He stared at her, considering.

Anna had a brief moment where she felt like she was in terrible danger, but then it passed, and another wave of euphoria enveloped her. 'I need to buy some drugs,' she said to the man, stage whispering, with a finger up to her mouth. *Shhh!* 'Do you know where I might find some?'

His mouth dropped open, revealing surprisingly neat white teeth. Then he threw his head back and laughed. But when he returned his gaze to her, there was no trace of mirth.

'You fucking rich cunts.' His nostrils flared. 'You think you can just do whatever the fuck you want and that no harm will come to you, don't you?'

Anna felt the change in him, took a step back.

But then as quickly as the rage had clouded him, it cleared. Moonlight bounced through the trees, illuminating his face.

'What're you looking for?'

Anna stood up straight, pushed her shoulders back. Tried to show him that she wasn't intimidated. 'Coke,' she said, tilting her chin to look him in the eye. He was a foot taller than her, at least. She could've done with her heels.

'I can do you a bag—'

'I'll need it regular,' she said, feeling fierce now. 'We've lost our . . . supplier.' This is how Lars had described it to her when she'd asked him earlier that night, after Agneta had called to say she wasn't coming home, she was staying at her friend's in Maidstone because she'd missed the last train.

That first night at their dinner party several weeks before had been the start of something that had turned into something that Anna really hadn't expected.

165

The Lego man stared at her with a mixture of interest and contempt. 'Well then,' he said. 'Let's see if we can come to an arrangement.'

Anna opened her eyes and drew in a long, slow breath. She was back in the woods by The Street again. The night that she'd just recalled had led her here, and to everything that had happened since. Somewhere behind her, she could hear voices. She walked through the last row of trees and found the gate. As she'd suspected, it wasn't being guarded by anyone. They hadn't even run the crime-scene tape up this far. She tapped the security code into the keypad and pulled the gate open, glancing back quickly before she hurried out. There was no one behind following her.

She walked briskly around the edge of the grassed area, towards the road. Somewhere to the right she could hear the hiss and crackle of a radio. The police were focusing their resources down by the vehicle gates, and the beach gate. She couldn't quite see them, because of the gradient of the grassy slope, and the way the road access was hidden behind.

There was a café on the other side that she hadn't noticed before. She'd previously walked along the promenade, or taken a left on to the road and walked along the pavement, but both times she'd clearly been looking at other things. There were a couple of small shops hidden down the back of the small apartment block at the junction, and she headed over that way now. A coffee would be nice. When had she last eaten? Maybe a sandwich, or even a piece of cake. It was a small independent place, painted pale green and with a couple of yellow-painted metal chairs and tables outside in front of the wide window. Flower baskets hung from hooks above the door and at the other side of the painted front, where the wooden sign stretched across. *Blossom.*

It was a pretty name. It definitely looked the kind of place that would do its own baking. A gentle wind blew across the rough path between the grass and the café, turning the air slightly cooler. Maybe this was why there was no one sitting outside. But there were people inside, deep in conversation at a table by the window. As she got closer she thought she recognised one of them. The woman. Hair pulled back into a neat bun, she was resting her chin on her hand as she listened to the man. He was gesturing with his hands as he spoke. His head was turned away slightly, but something about his movements was familiar. She stopped walking, and stared. She knew him alright. It was *Jasper*. But what the hell was he doing with Lacy?

Thirty-Three

PATRICK: SIX MONTHS AGO

The visitors' room in the prison was pretty much as Patrick had expected. He'd seen all those crime dramas. What he hadn't expected was the airport-style security scanners, but luckily he hadn't brought anything with him other than his phone, and he'd been allowed to leave that in a locker.

He didn't have to wait long for Lars to arrive.

Even dressed in standard-issue grey joggers and top, he retained that air of confident intimidation that seemed to come naturally to him. Patrick watched as he walked across the room, nodding at the other prisoners who were already seated with their visitors.

It was clear that Lars still wielded some power, even locked up.

Patrick had spent a bit of time online since Lars had been arrested. Once it was clear that his wife wasn't getting locked up too. She had handled the whole thing well – calm and unruffled – repeating her story to the police and then the court, over and over, not a hint of nerves . . . or lies . . . and sometimes Patrick had found himself staring at her, wondering if he actually knew her.

Patrick pushed the black coffee in the beige cup across the table. 'Sorry, I don't think it's a decent blend.'

The corners of Lars's mouth curled slightly. He didn't pick up the drink. 'Thank you for coming,' he said, pushing the cup away. 'How is everything at home?'

Patrick sighed. 'She wants to continue with the witness-protection thing. The police think it's necessary, but I keep trying to tell her it's not.'

Lars looked amused. 'It's not?'

Patrick shifted in his seat. The round plastic stool was attached to the table, which was attached to the floor, and it was incredibly uncomfortable but there wasn't a lot he could do about it.

'Well . . .' Patrick said, trying to ignore the uneasy feeling spreading up his back, inching across his shoulders. 'It's not like you're going to send someone after her, is it?'

Lars stared. 'Why shouldn't I? She's stitched me right up, that wife of yours.'

Patrick swallowed. He wished he'd bought himself a bottle of water. His mouth was desert dry but there was no way he was drinking that murk that they were trying to pass off as coffee. He never touched the stuff now. He'd gone back to tea as soon as Lars had been forcibly removed from his life.

Cut all ties.

'I—'

Lars laughed. It was not a pleasant sound. 'I'm fucking with you, Patrick. Is that still your name? I suppose they are making you change it . . .'

'Yes, I—'

Lars held up a hand. 'Your wife has done me a favour, actually. I have a lot of business to attend to. This is a good place for me to do it.'

Patrick's face must have shown his surprise, because Lars laughed again.

He really didn't like to hear Lars laugh.

169

He'd had a message after Lars was arrested. Someone claiming to be one of Lars's associates. Warning him to keep his mouth firmly shut. The 'or else' was clearly implied.

'So, you're going to tell me the address of this place you are being moved to, yes?'

'I—'

'This is not negotiable, Patrick. I will need to pay your wife a visit at some point. When I'm out.' He grinned. 'Thank her for her services.'

'You're not . . . you're not going to hurt her, are you?'

Lars sighed. 'You know what, Patrick? Your wife has shown far bigger balls than you during this whole debacle. I have no problem with her. At. All. Also . . .' He paused. Sighed. 'I have other issues to deal with here. One of my delivery boys got himself entangled in something he shouldn't have. Couldn't keep his hands to himself in the park. Attacked a woman. A bloody lesbian, if can you believe it. Absolute idiot. He owes me for this. I will have to look after him in here, but it won't be easy. Surprising statistic for you: most of the men inside don't like rapists, you know.'

Patrick wondered why Lars was telling him this. He didn't want anything to do with Lars's gang. Lars's life. He would do what he asked, then he would go – and he would never come back.

'Anyway,' Lars said, waving a hand in front of his face. 'I need your help. One last job, as it were.'

Patrick said nothing.

'I had your wife filmed when she set up that drug deal. Insurance, you know? Someone will send you a file. I need you to take it to the police. Say it was you who filmed it.'

'But, I—'

'You'll work it out, Patrick. You must have realised your wife was collateral damage? A decoy? You were happy to have her involved. I'm sure you can sort out this final little part of the operation for me?' He lowered his voice. 'They're only holding me here on the drugs charge. They don't have any evidence for the wider implications of my business . . . If I can throw in some reasonable doubt, I can get my appeal . . . I can get downgraded to some better digs at the very least . . . They won't do anything to her. Not if she cooperates. It'll all blow over and we can all get on with our business. What do you say?'

He knew he had no choice.

'OK,' he said. 'I'll do it.'

Thirty-Four

ANNA: TUESDAY

Anna turned and hurried towards home. She would have to go back in the same way she had left. She hoped the keypad hadn't been disabled on this side. She was shaking, her breath catching in her throat as if she'd run a 10k race instead of jogged a few metres across the grass.

Jasper . . . and Lacy. What the hell was going on?

She stabbed at the buttons on the keypad entry gate. It beeped. *Error – code not recognised.* She tried again, her fingers fumbling. Got it right this time. She sucked in a breath, tried to calm down. The gate opened and she glanced around again before entering. She should tell the police about this entrance. It was a little disconcerting that they didn't know about it. Maybe this was how the man on the beach got in? They were focusing all their efforts on assuming a breach down there, but maybe he was cleverer than that.

Maybe he had this code.

Anna walked briskly through the trees and back out on to The Street. The place was deserted, and she could only assume that the residents had been told to stay indoors. She stopped walking, straining to hear the sounds of voices down the beach-access lane. They would still be there. A radio squawked and she looked across to the vehicle-access gate. There were still a couple of officers there, currently not looking her way. She could see the female officer from before, her back to Anna on the other side of the gate. She was leaning against an open car door, where a pair of booted feet were visible. Someone sitting in the car. The voices from the lane grew closer, and she hurried across the road and up the path to her house, jamming the key in and shoving the door open. She didn't look back to see if anyone had seen her.

In the living room, the TV was playing quietly but there was no one watching it. That antiques show with the man with the orange face.

'Peter? Are you there?'

He appeared from the kitchen, mug in hand. He rolled his eyes when he saw her. 'Christ, Anna. Don't you read your messages? I texted to say that the police had asked everyone to stay indoors. They wanted to talk to you but I said you were asleep.' He frowned, laid his mug on the bookshelf. 'You don't half like to make things difficult for yourself. Come here.'

She walked towards him and let him embrace her. She tried to hug him back, but her arms felt heavy – her whole body felt heavy. She was spent. And yet again, Peter was far too calm. Was he in on it too?

Whatever *it* was – she still hadn't worked it out.

'Anna? What is it?' He stiffened, pulling away.

She slumped down on to the sofa.

'I just saw Lacy in the café over behind Lidl. She was with Jasper.' She leaned forward on her elbows, head in her hands. 'I don't know what the hell is going on any more.'

She felt the weight as Peter sat down beside her. 'Anna . . . you're not making any sense. You've had a big shock today, we all have. You must've made a mistake. It must've been someone who looks like him—'

Anna lifted her head, shook it. 'I did not make a mistake! What was she even doing there? You just said – everyone is supposed to be in their houses. I know I wasn't meant to be out, but she wasn't there when we were at Bradley's, though, was she?'

Peter took her hand and squeezed it. 'She was probably upstairs. I think her and Beth were friends. Maybe she just needed a moment.'

Anna pulled away. 'It was her. At the café. And it was Jasper too. I'm not blind, Peter. I know what I saw. She's a cop. Maybe Bradley is too.'

'OK.' Peter stood up, and his voice changed from the slightly patronising, cajoling tone of a minute ago to something more serious. 'Suppose you're right. Suppose it was Jasper. There could be an innocent explanation. She and Bradley work in IT, right? Maybe it's some sort of police admin. Part of the security system. Maybe it's actually something to do with *our* situation. Maybe they're protecting us?'

Anna sighed. 'Interesting theory, but I'm not buying it. Jasper is our handler, Peter. He's supposedly the only person who knows that we're here. Who we really are. I hardly think this was the best time to have a meeting to discuss the pros and cons of IT systems in the protected persons programme.' She paused. 'And if Beth *was* Lacy's friend, like you say, then there's even less reason for her to go out and have this meeting right now.'

'I agree. The timing is a bit odd.'

Anna stood up. 'I don't think this is a coincidence, Peter.' She looked away, not sure she could hold his gaze while she said the rest of what she wanted to say. 'I think this is something to do with us. I think Beth was killed by accident. I think it was meant to be me.'

He put his hands on her shoulders, urging her to lift her head. 'Anna, this is madness. Why would anyone be trying to kill you? All you did was tell the truth!'

She was about to reply, to tell him he had that part wrong – very wrong – when something on the TV caught her attention. She moved away from him and picked up the remote, turning the volume up just as the picture of a woman she recognised filled the screen.

> *. . . after an extensive search of woodland close to where Jonas Grant was found only one day ago, the body of a female, thought to be his wife, Kayleigh, has been found. Kayleigh had also been missing for several months. As was reported previously, Jonas Grant was the whistle-blower for a large-scale money-laundering scheme that is believed to be linked to a trafficking operation that specialist police teams had been investigating for eighteen months. We can now reveal that the Grants had been placed in hiding under the UK witness protection service and were thought to have been living in East Lothian prior to their abduction and subsequent murders. A spokesman from the National Crime Agency has stated that there is no threat to the public, that the killers were known to the victims, and that the operation to apprehend those responsible is fully underway. In other news . . .*

Anna and Peter stared at one another. Peter had been so sure of himself earlier, full of possibilities and explanations, but now he was silent – and from the shine in his eyes, Anna knew he was just as scared as she was.

'None of this makes sense.' Anna picked up her phone and started scrolling through her contacts. 'That's Lindsay. I told you I saw her on Sunday. I told Jasper too, and he said he would dig into it – and now look.' She dropped the phone and balled her hands into fists, trying to stop them from shaking. Then she let out a low roar of pure frustration. A deep, almost silent scream that made the inside of her throat vibrate. She snatched up her phone again. 'There is something going on. Jasper was meant to get back to me, and there's been nothing. And now Beth is dead, and Lindsay is dead . . . and what the fuck happens next, hmm? We are not safe here.' She found the name she was looking for and pressed it hard. It rang once then clicked into voicemail.

I'm afraid I can't come to the phone right now, but if you leave a message, I will get back to you as soon as possible . . .

'Jasper, it's Amanda Barton. I need you to call me back immediately, and I need you to come and meet me, and I need you to tell me what the fuck is going on.'

Anna tapped out a text message too, for good measure, then threw her phone on to the couch.

Peter was staring at her, the shine of fear in his eyes brighter. His skin seemed to have blanched two shades paler.

'Anna . . .'

'What?' She snapped at him, fed up with his pathetic attempts at assurances. If he didn't realise there was something very wrong with this whole situation, then there was no hope for him. None at all. She might as well . . . and then she realised.

Anna. Anna. Anna!

Her name was Anna now. It was no longer Amanda. She was never supposed to reveal herself via her real name now, not even on Jasper's secure line. The voicemail should have reminded her. The small click on the line when it started recording before the message was even finished. The fact that Jasper himself didn't say his name. Again, she was struck by how little he actually seemed to be a Jasper. He was as much undercover as they were, for everyone's sake. He'd told her to take nothing for granted. To be discreet. To not ask questions of the other residents that she wouldn't be comfortable being asked about herself.

Shit. Shit. Shit!

Her phone beeped. That familiar sound of her new best friend – Mr StreetMate. The one who was never, ever going to leave her alone. She picked up her phone and looked at the notification, but instead of reading it, she hurled the phone hard against the wall. Peter ducked, swore under his breath, even though the missile was nowhere near him. A small flurry of plaster dust slid down the wall, landing on the smashed phone as it lay on the wooden floor. She took in the mess – the small hole in the once pristine wall, and the resultant cracks around it, creeping away like spiderwebs. Then she looked down at her phone on the floor, and stamped on it hard, several times, until she was sure it was cracked beyond repair. Then she kicked it under the TV unit. Finally, she remembered to breathe.

'Fuck all of this shit,' she said. 'I'm going to bed.'

Thirty-Five

THE DIARY

So they're dead, then. Mr and Mrs Number Eight. Lindsay and Ritchie Walker, aka Jonas and Kayleigh Grant. I suppose it was inevitable. There was something going on and it wasn't good. Shame they had to bring their messy lives to our dull little enclave, where nothing ever happens.

Oh, wait.

Oops. I forgot one. Poor Beth. She was actually quite decent, as far as the losers on this street go. She was always kind to me, although I had a feeling she wanted me to 'open up' to her. Maybe someone had put her up to it. Come to think of it, maybe she was a fake, like all the others.

Yes, I have trust issues. You would too if you were me.

Bloody Mary's been snivelling outside half the day, making her way up and down to everyone's house, trying to get them to snivel with her. It's not that hard a task to be fair – everyone's pretty cut up about poor old Beth. Thing is . . . I don't believe in that whole wrong place, wrong time bullshit that the others are spouting. Maybe Beth wasn't just that nice squeaky-clean lady who liked baking and beach walks. Someone clearly wanted her dead.

Is it really so bad to kill someone if they deserve it?

Fucking *Kevin*, going on and on to that Brooklin idiot right below my bedroom window. The two of them talking like they're the world's best investigators. Columbo and Jessica Fletcher don't have a patch on these two stars.

You know what? I love those shows. Luckily they're on repeat on one of the shitty Freesat channels so I can always rely on at least one of them. And if not, there's usually *Diagnosis Murder* instead. Dick Van Dyke versus Peter Falk in a fight – now that would be entertaining. Angela Lansbury as the referee, but she just lets both of them keep going, on and on and on, until they're both a pulpy mess on the floor.

I wonder what my therapist would make of *that* little fantasy?

I managed to trap a couple of bees since I last wrote. It was easier than I thought, and the jar is definitely going to look great once I can get enough of them in there to layer it up. I wonder if they lose colour from their bodies as they decompose? How long do they even take to decompose? Maybe I should put the jar under my bed, or in my wardrobe – keep them out of the sun. Maybe they'll fade, like a cheap conservatory rug.

I'll tell you what . . . this dump has turned out to be a lot less boring than I originally thought. Sure, it's taken a few months to get going, but two missing residents kidnapped, tortured and killed and one current resident suspiciously dead on the beach – that's pretty good going.

I wonder if anyone else has sussed out what's going on here on our wonderful street? Our high-security, fully monitored and tracked residential masterpiece of full-on dodgy business? The developer of which mysteriously disappeared . . .

It's obvious, really. But I'm not going to write down my suspicions just yet. I need to do a little more investigating of my own first. I wonder which one of the daytime TV investigators I'm most like?

One thing's for sure . . . we're all going to need a lot of popcorn as events slowly unfold.

Thirty-Six

StreetChat WhatsApp Group

~Asya #2
I'm scared, Mary.

~Bradley #1 is typing . . .

~ Bradley #1 has left the group

~Mary #3
Me too, dear.

~Mary #3 has left the group

~Brooklin #2 has been removed from the group

~Finlay #5 has been removed from the group

~Beth #5 has been removed from the group

THIS GROUP HAS BEEN DELETED

Thirty-Seven

ANNA: WEDNESDAY

The phone rang when Anna and Peter were sitting together in the kitchen. Peter's phone, given that Anna's had been smashed to pieces – and half of the living-room wall destroyed with it.

It was 6 a.m. and the sun was already high and bright. They both had cups of black coffee in front of them, and neither of them had anything to say. Although Anna had slept well, she'd woken up a couple of times to find Peter lying flat on his back, staring at the ceiling. They'd stopped closing the blackout blinds as they were both freaked out with the absolute darkness, but without them, the room barely got dark at all.

Anna stared at the phone, the withheld number, and knew who it was. Part of her didn't want to answer. She wanted to ask Peter to pack up the car, and drive them off somewhere – anywhere – as far away from this place as possible. As far away from her old life as possible. They didn't have passports in their new names yet, but they would be arriving soon – and then . . . well, then they would go.

She slid her finger across the screen and tapped the phone on to speaker.

'Anna, it's me – are you there? I tried your number, but it's going to voicemail.' He sounded a little breathless.

'We're here.' She caught Peter's eye, and he nodded. 'My phone is broken. I'll need a new one.'

'Right, OK, I'll keep this brief. We need to meet. I've been away for a bit, but I've had people following up on the couple at Number Eight for you, and I'm afraid—'

'It's too late, Jasper. We saw it on the news. What we're kind of concerned about now is why we were put in a protected house right next to theirs – assuming this is what happened? Has this got anything to do with Beth, because—'

'No, no. Of course not.' His voice became muffled as he covered the mic and spoke to someone else. 'Look, I can't explain on the phone. I'm snowed under here, to be honest.'

'Up a mountain, are you? Cold, is it? Only I'm pretty sure I saw you yesterday in a blue t-shirt, having coffee at my local café . . .'

'I must have a doppelganger.'

He laughed, but none of this was funny. He hadn't said anything about her name slip-up, though, which was both comforting and alarming. Either he hadn't noticed, or there were bigger issues to worry about. She suspected the latter.

When she didn't say anything else, he continued, 'Look, we'll talk tomorrow, OK? I can't do today, I'm sorry. I'll text you a postcode for the satnav. Come together. We'll sort all of this out.'

Anna sighed. Platitudes, just like the ones Peter was fond of. 'Just one question, Jasper . . .'

The line crackled. 'Go on . . .'

'Are we actually safe here?'

The line crackled once more, then three beeps signalled that the connection had been lost. Perhaps he *was* up a mountain. But one thing was for sure: he was avoiding her questions.

Anna was about to call him back when there was a knock at the door. She opened it, expecting it to be the police, but it was Asya. Anna felt a pang of guilt that she hadn't been round to see her since they'd moved in. She'd been so busy avoiding Mary and the Whitelaws, and trying to befriend Beth, that she'd forgotten there was another woman living on The Street.

She remembered the barbecue on their second day, and how she'd instantly judged Asya based on the spelling of her name, her fake tan, and the ridiculousness of her eyebrows. But the woman on her doorstep looked washed out, her hair extensions tied back in a stringy ponytail that hung limply over one shoulder. Her eyes were puffy and she looked much younger. Vulnerable.

'I'm sorry.' Asya sniffed, wiping her nose with her sleeve, which was pulled over her hand. 'I hate these stupid doorbells. Is it OK if I come in?'

'Of course, of course.' Anna stepped out of the way to let the younger woman in. 'Can I get you something to drink? Tea? Coffee?'

Asya bit her lip. 'Have you got anything stronger? I know it's early. But, well, I haven't even slept. It's still last night for me.'

As she walked past, Anna caught a whiff of alcohol on her. Not just her breath, but that sort of ingrained alcohol that leaches out of the pores of the heavy drinker. She wasn't judging. It might just have been from an all-night session. Anna couldn't blame her. She looked across at Peter, who was hovering half in, half out of the kitchen.

'I could, um, how about I chuck a bit of brandy into the coffees?'

Asya smiled at him and sat down on an armchair. Anna wasn't sure where the brandy had come from, but it probably wasn't a good idea.

'I'm sorry just to barge in like this,' Asya said. She pushed herself deep into the chair and pulled her knees up, twisting to fit her long legs on to the seat. She shuffled back further, cocooning herself. Trying to make herself smaller. 'I'm just so tired.' She closed her eyes and let her head flop on to the cushioned seat.

There was a hint of a slur in her voice, Anna realised.

'It's absolutely fine,' Anna said, thinking now that the offer of brandy was definitely a mistake. 'I'm sorry I haven't come round yet to see you. I wanted to get to know everyone but, well . . . it's all been a bit *intense* since we moved in.'

'Tell me about it.' Asya's eyes were still closed.

'Just, um . . . does Brooklin know you're here? Will he be worried that you've gone off out this early, what with everything—'

Asya sat up, opening her eyes. 'He's passed out on the couch. I didn't want to be on my own.'

'No, of course . . .'

Peter saved Anna from more pointless wittering by appearing with a tray, carrying three mugs. She secretly hoped he'd realised they had no brandy after all. Judging by the state of her, it was unlikely Asya would even notice.

Peter handed a mug over to her, and she sniffed it, then took a sip. She looked at him questioningly, then shrugged. 'You're probably right. I don't really need any more alcohol.'

Anna took a sip of her own drink. Definitely just coffee. 'You know, if you don't want to be on your own, you could stay here? Have a sleep upstairs. We're up now and more than happy to have you . . .'

'Nah, you're alright. I should get back. If he wakes up and I'm not there . . .'

She didn't finish her sentence, and Anna decided not to read too much into it. She probably just meant that he would be concerned. Not that he would be angry. It was hard not to let her mind drift to the darkest corners right now, but she had to try. Asya twisted herself back around and dropped her feet to the floor. She pushed herself up using the arms of the chair, and when she stood fully, she wobbled a little before righting herself.

'Thanks,' she said. 'For being kind.'

Anna glanced at Peter, who shrugged. They really hadn't done anything.

'Let us walk you back home.' Anna picked up her keys.

Asya didn't say anything, so Anna took her arm while Peter opened the front door. The Street was quiet. Anna glanced up and down the empty road. The crime-scene tape that covered the vehicle gates fluttered in the breeze. A police car was stationed outside, and she could make out the silhouettes of the two officers who were sitting inside.

They walked together down the path, just as someone came hurrying towards them from the path on the other side – the one that led to the trees and the top gate. It was John from Number Four. Anna still hadn't spoken to him. He'd hurried into his house one day, and she'd seen him at Bradley's gathering yesterday, but he hadn't spoken then either. She raised a hand in greeting, but he shifted his gaze, pretending not to see her, or the stumbling Asya at her side.

'Hey,' Peter said, closing the door behind them. 'It's John, isn't it? We haven't really met . . .'

Anna watched John's reaction. He slowed a little, raised his head slightly. Then he lowered his gaze again and upped his pace, practically running past them towards his house and disappearing inside, slamming the front door behind him.

'Fucking weirdo,' Asya muttered under her breath. She pulled away from Anna. 'Thanks for looking after me. I can manage from here.'

'Is he always like that?' Peter said, catching them up. He took Anna's hand.

185

Asya rolled her eyes. 'Yeah. He doesn't speak. Well, not to me. Not to Brooklin. Not really sure about anyone else. He's hardly ever here. Works for some charity in town, apparently. Although he's never struck me as a do-gooder type.' She paused. 'There was a WhatsApp group, you know. A sort of residents' thing. I wanted you to join it, but the others were all being fucking weird about it. We've deleted it now, though. I just wanted you to know . . .'

Anna watched as Asya meandered along the pavement. When she reached John's house she stopped, stuck her fingers up, and cut across the grass to her own house. Anna's eyes were drawn to John's front window, where he stood.

Watching.

Thirty-Eight

ANNA: WEDNESDAY

It was nearly 8 a.m. and Anna was considering going back to bed. After the weird visit from Asya, and the even weirder staring contest with John, she and Peter had gone back home and locked the door, closed all the blinds, and just sat on the couch, saying nothing.

What was there to say? They'd only been living there a short time and already it was a total disaster. Nobody was acting normally on the street, and that was before anyone had been found dead. And what had Asya meant about a WhatsApp group? Just something else that Anna had been excluded from? Why did the residents have such an issue with newcomers?

It didn't matter now.

Anna thought back to that first night – the fun they had with Lindsay and Ritchie – the high hopes she had for a new start with new friends. She'd been excited about starting work again, in this fresh environment where she'd hoped she would be inspired to write something different.

She'd thought *she* would be different.

But as soon as Lindsay and Ritchie had disappeared, everything began to unravel. All the anxiety she'd fought to keep at bay since the court case. Those racing thoughts about what might happen if Lars was to somehow track her down. It was meant to be a new beginning for her, and Peter too. Even if he hadn't known about the affair before, he must've suspected it. But he didn't push. He accepted it when she said that her and Lars's friendship had been all about the crazy moments of drug taking that had made her feel alive again. She wasn't even sure why it had started. She looked at Peter out of the corner of her eye, his expression of someone tired, who'd tried to make things right and failed, who felt betrayed and let down – and yet despite all of those things, chose to stay with her – to move away with her . . . to give up his life for her.

Unless he had some other agenda.

'Why?' She twisted around in the seat, folding one knee up, nudging into him.

He sighed. 'Why what?'

'Why did you agree to all this? You didn't have to. You could've let me disappear on my own. It was me who testified against Lars. It was me who was scared of the repercussions. Of the gang. It was me who—'

'Shut up, for fuck's sake.' He cut her off, his voice strained. 'I'm here because I love you. And as I told you already, whatever happens, we will deal with it. OK?'

She wasn't sure what to say to that. Anything she said felt like a deliberate attempt to push him away, and she didn't know why. He'd been inconsistent, to say the least, for a long time. She was no longer sure she trusted him. But who else did she have? Was she trying to punish herself? Punish him? When was she going to stop?

Her mind swirled with words, phrases, put-downs. Things she could say to try to hurt him. Provoke him. But she left them where they were – in her head.

The letterbox snapped, making her jump.

Peter pushed himself up from the couch and went over to see what it was. He picked it up and walked back over to the couch, handing it to her without giving it more than a cursory glance.

Anna took the piece of paper. It wasn't in an envelope. It was handwritten. Her hands shook slightly as she read it, imagination immediately going into overdrive. *It's a death threat. They know they got the wrong woman and they're going to come back and finish the job.*

Eventually she read it. Then she threw it on the ground and let out a small, mirthless laugh. 'It's from Mary. She's calling a street meeting. Her house in thirty minutes. She's made cake.'

'Seriously?' Peter took the note from her hand and read it himself. He shook his head. 'You were serious. Fuck. Me.'

'This is the street that keeps on giving,' Anna said, pondering the note. To be quite honest, things couldn't really get any weirder and so she was just going to have to embrace it for now, until they got a chance to talk to Jasper properly – and then got the hell out of there. 'I'm going to have a quick shower.'

Peter nodded. 'I'll come with you.'

Anna almost fobbed him off. She wasn't really in the mood, but maybe this was him making an effort? Some intimate time together might be what they both needed. All they'd done lately was bicker, and it *had* been one of her intentions to try to get closer to him again.

They took their time, even though Anna knew it would make them late.

Mary could wait. She hadn't given them much notice, but then what else were they going to do? They were meant to be staying at home. The police would be back later to talk to them again.

There were two officers patrolling the street when they stepped outside. They both nodded at Anna and Peter, but didn't speak. They seemed to be running an eye along the edges of the lawns, at the narrow planting borders. Anna was sure the CSI people had scoured everything in detail already, but maybe these two were trying to make themselves useful. There didn't seem to be a lot more that anyone could do. As far as they were all aware, the man on the beach had never even been on The Street. It seemed likely that he had got in via the beach gate and left the same way.

Mary's front door had been left ajar, and Anna and Peter walked straight in, not really sure what to expect. They were the last to arrive, and there was a charged, chatty atmosphere in Mary's living room.

The group fell silent for a moment as they clocked the new arrivals before resuming their conversations. Anna scanned the room. The Whitelaws were standing in the corner by the bookshelves, huddled in their own family conversation and paying no attention to the others. As she watched, the youngest one – Max – looked around furtively, then, realising that Anna had seen him, he glared briefly before turning back towards his family. Donna, clearly sensing this, glanced over and gave Anna a tiny smile. They were an odd bunch. The mother, Lorraine, had clearly taken an instant dislike to Anna. They'd really had nothing to do with Kevin or Max, and Donna was a teenager – they could hardly expect her to be interested in them, or anything else for that matter.

On the other side of the bookcase, near the kitchen, Finlay – eyes red-rimmed and cradling a mug in both hands – nodded as Lacy leaned in to talk to her. Near the window, Asya sat on the chair – exactly as she had in Anna and Peter's room earlier – she still looked washed out and was no doubt dealing with a murderous hangover. She clutched a glass of water like it was keeping her alive. Brooklin was sitting on the arm of the chair. His eyes were closed, and he looked equally, if not more, worse for wear.

Anna walked over to Asya and patted her hand. 'Don't worry,' she whispered. 'Let's get this over with and then you two can get yourselves off to bed.'

The younger woman gave her an almost imperceptible nod. Anna felt her pain. She probably felt like her head would detach if she made any sudden moves.

'I could really do with another coffee,' Peter said in her ear. 'I'm fading fast here.'

'I think we all are,' Anna muttered, heading towards the kitchen.

At that, Mary appeared in the doorway. Behind her, at the kitchen table, Bradley and John were sitting. Bradley was talking and John was doing his best attempt at pretending to listen. He glanced up at Anna then looked away again. Another odd fish. This street really was full of them.

'Oh, you made it,' Mary said. Her voice was warmer than usual, and Anna wondered at the change before dismissing it. It didn't really matter what any of these people thought. She would be gone from here as soon as it was feasible. There had been no official word yet, but surely Jasper wasn't going to make them stay on The Street after this.

Anna pasted on a smile so thick it hurt her face. 'Sorry if we're late.' She glanced around the kitchen. 'Is there anything we can do?'

Mary shrugged. 'Help yourselves to coffee and cake. It's fruit and almond. I baked it this morning so it's still warm. Need to find things to do with myself, you know.' Anna took in the older woman and realised she looked exhausted. Maybe she'd been a bit harsh on her. She seemed like someone who lived a life of order, and that had been taken away from her and she wasn't sure how to deal with it.

Anna was about to turn it down, remembering Lindsay's warnings about Mary's baking, when her stomach growled and she realised it had been a while since she'd eaten. She cut a slice for herself and Peter, and he poured them coffee. Mary ushered Bradley and John out of the kitchen into the living room, and Anna and Peter followed. Anna had to admit, she was impressed by Mary now

191

– rounding everyone up so quickly. She clearly wanted answers. Didn't they all?

'Right then!' Mary clapped her hands together twice and Anna was transported back to school. She'd had a teacher just like Mary. She'd probably been a teacher before she retired and moved here. Glancing around her house, at the various crocheted items and other trinkets, it was clear how she spent her time now. Anna took a bite of her cake and decided that Lindsay had been a bit harsh. Poor Lindsay. Anna's memories of her were already fading. It would have been interesting to see how their friendship might have developed. She chewed slowly, and her mind drifted to Beth. Two lovely women who'd been friendly to her. Both now dead. Suddenly the cake felt like wool stuffed down her throat, and she grabbed her drink from Peter and took a long swig. She tried to suppress the inevitable cough, and almost got away with it.

Mary raised her eyebrows. 'If you could keep it down, please. We have important business to discuss.'

The room fell silent, and Anna quietly willed her throat to keep doing what it needed to do to stop her from choking.

'Bradley . . . I think we'd all like to hear from you?' A murmur travelled around the room. Anna caught a glance between Bradley and Lacy. Lacy looked worried, biting her lip and turning away. 'I believe you're the contact for the security system—'

'Not really, Mary. I just know how to reset the cameras when they go offline.' He shrugged. 'Anyone could do it themselves . . .'

Mary waved a hand, dismissing him. 'I think I speak for us all when I say we've had just about enough of this so-called security.'

A ripple of laughter that stopped itself dead as Mary's eyes scanned the room. Anna had definitely underestimated her. This was not a woman to be messed with.

'We put up with the cameras and the intrusive app notifica-tions, and the gates, and the rules . . . Look after each other. Be discreet. Be careful. Blah, blah, blah.' Mary turned and pointed at

Bradley. 'We do all that, and what good has it done? One of our neighbours . . . our community . . . is dead!'

Anna looked around at the others, taking in their expressions. Shock quickly became neutral, as everyone realised that Mary was revealing things that no one was meant to discuss.

So, did they all have the app, then? What was Bradley's part in all of this? Was he in charge of the security system or not?

She was about to start asking these questions when Finlay cleared her throat. 'This is good, Mary. But I think we need to address the elephant in the room too.'

Another bout of muttering ebbed and flowed around like a Mexican wave.

Anna looked at Peter, who shrugged and took a sip of his coffee.

Finlay let out an exasperated sigh. 'Beth wasn't the first, was she? Is no one going to talk about the couple at Number Eight? I mean, jeez . . .' She pushed a flick of hair back from her face. Then she turned to Anna and Peter. 'I, for one, am so fucking sorry. You two must've been going out of your minds over that nonsense. Everyone telling you there was no one in that house? All of us having to lie to your face?' She looked around the room, at all the scared faces. 'I mean, didn't you think it was weird that most people were actively avoiding you?'

'Well, now that you say it—' Anna started, but Finlay cut her off.

'We all got a fucking notification. Didn't we?' She looked around at everyone again. 'I know none of you have talked about it with anyone else, but come on. Cards on the table now – we all have that secret app . . . You all got the messages, right? *Do not mention Lindsay and Ritchie Walker. Deny all knowledge of anyone living at Number Eight. This is for your own safety.* Seems like we're all being told to keep quiet about stuff, and we're all too scared to ask why . . . Am I *right*?'

Mary started a slow hand clap. 'And blah . . . blah . . . blah. Thank you, Finlay. Now, while we're at this – does anyone have anything else to add? Bradley? Lacy? Do you want to tell us what the hell is going on with this so-called security, because it seems pretty clear now that none of us is actually safe . . . and all of us want to know why.'

Murmurs of ascent mushroomed like clouds, and Bradley's face drained entirely of colour. Lacy held on to his arm. 'Tell them,' she said.

Anna wasn't sure if it was meant to be a whisper, or if Lacy wanted them all to hear. But either way, they all did. Everyone's gaze was glued to Bradley and Lacy now, like they'd just turned out to be the biggest stars in the most exciting reality TV show ever made.

'Tell us what, Bradley?'

It was the first time Anna had heard John speak. Judging by the others' reactions, it wasn't something he did often. Not to anyone other than Bradley, anyway. There was an odd expression on his face that, if the circumstances hadn't been so horribly serious, Anna would have read as a smirk.

In the corner of the room, the Whitelaws were looking on with interest. The four of them had their arms crossed over their chests, the same steely expressions.

Finlay and Mary had both gone red. Finlay, especially, looked fit to explode.

Even the dangerously hungover Asya and Brooklin seemed to have woken up now.

Peter moved in closer and took Anna's hand. She welcomed another step towards some renewed intimacy between them.

'Yeah, Bradley. Tell us what?' It was Max, the Whitelaw kid. He giggled, and his dad yanked him backwards by the shoulder, hissing 'Shut up' into his ear.

Bradley nodded towards Lacy. 'Can you hold the fort for a few minutes? I think I need to make a call.'

Thirty-Nine

A Police Station: Two Weeks Ago

Six months. That's how long it had taken to mess up her carefully cut-and-dried case. But DS Georgia Lawrence was happy, despite the fact that it was going to make her look more than a little inept. She had questioned Barton several times about his wife's involvement with Lars Kristiansen and he had sworn blind that he hadn't known anything about it. She picked up the printout of his last statement.

> I absolutely trust my wife and do not believe that she had anything to do with the drugs racket that was funded by Lars Kristiansen. As I stated previously, we were all friends – my wife and I, and Lars and Agneta. There was only one incident of drug taking, to my knowledge, at a party at their house one night. Lars said a friend from work had given it to him, and we all took it. It was cocaine. I didn't like it. It gave me a headache and made me feel sick. My wife did enjoy it – she was dancing more than usual and became very talkative and very risqué – but as I said before, we were all friends, and it was just a bit of fun. I absolutely

do not believe that she was the one who set up the drugs deal with that gang. She's a respected writer. Something like that could harm her career, especially with her children's book publishers. Lars Kristiansen is a liar and a manipulator who will do whatever it takes to save his own marriage and reputation, even if that can only be achieved by throwing my wife under the bus. I don't have anything else to say on this matter.

Well. *He* was a damn good liar, she had to give him that. He'd played an excellent role as the confused and innocent husband. And it seemed that his wife had played her role pretty damn well too. The pair of them should win a Bafta. To be fair, Georgia had been hugely suspicious of the wife from the start. A novelist? Literally paid to make things up? She was worse than a bloody tabloid journalist. To give Amanda Barton her due, if she was that good at creating a character, her books deserved to be bestsellers.

Why now, though, was the question. Patrick Barton had contacted them out of the blue to explain the 'change' to his story and to provide his new evidence. He said he'd thought he'd deleted it. Said he wanted to support his wife. But not any more? There were some discussions to be had there. Not just in the interview room, but also with his wife.

But not yet, Georgia thought. It wasn't like they were going anywhere. DS Marcus Cole was keeping a close eye on them.

Georgia leaned back in her chair and clicked 'Play' on the video again. The footage was still a little grainy, but it had been enhanced as well as it could be by the techs and it was clear who was on the screen, if you knew who you were looking for.

Amanda Barton.

She's running across the grass, then she enters the wooded area of the common. The footage is a bit wobbly, because whoever was filming this was walking fast to keep up with her and to stay out of sight. She reaches the trees, then cuts through a thicket. The camera pans out, then back in, as the person filming stays back, then zooms in. A bit of resolution is lost with the zoom, and the low lighting in the trees. There is a streetlamp, which has the effect of making everything a little more golden, a little more fuzzy. She turns as she runs and she smacks into someone – male, young, tracksuit, shifty-looking.

Georgia recognised him as Pete Langham, the low-level dealer who connected Kristiansen to the upper echelons of a much bigger racket – the operation that Georgia and her team were still trying hard to connect to him.

Except . . . it wasn't Lars who made the first contact, was it? It was Amanda.

The phone camera was too far away to capture any decent audio. As evidence went, it was not conclusive. Kristiansen could've set all this up to make sure his mistress was implicated.

Georgia wasn't sure where the husband fitted in – other than the fact that he was spying on his wife.

Georgia sighed. It wasn't enough, and yet it was. Kristiansen's expensive lawyer had this, and a few other technicalities that he'd taken great pleasure in pointing out, and he'd used it to get Kristiansen's risk assessment re-examined. And he'd got his client a rather cushy little transfer to HMP Castle Huntly – Scotland's only open prison. It wasn't usual to get inmates moved into another prison service, but the lawyer had argued that Kristiansen was in danger where he was. HMP Full Sutton might be two hundred miles from Clapham Common, but the gang's reach was wide and all-encompassing. Across England, at least.

Someone, somewhere had taken a back-hander to push all this through, Georgia was sure of it. But there was nothing she could do.

Well, there was one thing.

She picked up her phone and called her old colleague DS Marcus Cole. She still had his number in her phone under his real name. She let it ring three times, then hung up.

Georgia clicked on the timer app on her phone. One . . . two . . . three . . . Her phone rang as it hit four.

'Lawrence,' he said. She could hear the smile in his voice, and a snap of gum – which was very non-regulation for coppers on duty. But then Marcus had never been one for regulations. 'Always a pleasure.'

Georgia jumped right in. 'Kristiansen's being moved.' She had no idea where Marcus was keeping tabs on his witnesses, but she hoped it wasn't anywhere in Scotland. Open prisons had never made any sense to her. They were far too . . . open. She fully expected Kristiansen to abscond after his first breakfast.

'I heard. It's kind of unfortunate timing, actually. There's a bit of shit going down here that we are trying to dig our way out of without leaving a bad smell.'

'Has Amanda Barton been informed? I mean, this is just the first step towards that weasel being released.'

Another snap of gum. 'Not yet. But don't worry, she couldn't be safer at the moment.'

Georgia sighed. 'OK. Well, I imagine you'll be asked to bring her in soon. There are some questions we need answers for.'

'Roger that. Later, though. Like I said . . . there are a few things going on at the moment. Talk soon.'

He hung up before she could say anything more.

Forty

ANNA: WEDNESDAY

Anna felt a little sorry for Lacy as she tried to field the barrage of angry questions that were levelled at her from the moment Bradley stepped out of the house. Everyone seemed to be talking at once. It was as if a dam had burst, and the tensions that had been slowly building over the six months since the residents had moved in had finally exploded out of them in a torrent of anger and frustration. Anna couldn't help but feel, yet again, it was all her fault. Somehow on that night they moved in, the tiny stone that had been plugging the hole in the dam wall had come loose, water trickling in bit by bit, until the whole thing had collapsed.

Lindsay and Ritchie had vanished.

The residents had been forced to lie.

She'd seen the tattooed man on the beach.

Beth was dead.

Lindsay and Ritchie were dead.

Anna turned to Peter. 'Maybe we should go back home for a while, until everyone calms down?'

Lacy had gone through to the kitchen and Mary had followed. Anna could hear them from the living room. She thought about going through, but held back, listening.

'Well?' Mary said. 'Are you going to tell us what's going on here?'

'Please, Mary. Why don't you sit down? I'll make some tea—'

'You can't placate me with tea, *dear*.' The emphasis on the last word made an innocent sentence sound like a threat.

Mary was definitely not the mousy little woman Anna had taken her for – or perhaps it was just that everyone had their limits, and she had reached hers.

Anna tried to zone out their argument as it went back and forth, suspecting that there would be no resolution until Bradley returned. She wanted answers too, but there was no point in adding any more pressure to the situation in the kitchen.

Anna turned her attention back to the living room. Only the Whitelaws seemed to be keeping out of it. Finlay and John were arguing about something with Brooklin. Asya had curled into a ball on the chair.

Peter walked over to the window and pushed the net curtain to the side. Mary was the only one with a net curtain. The living rooms of the other houses were mostly bare. If they were staying, which was unlikely, Anna had already decided to get blinds fitted. 'I think we should stay here for now,' Peter said, raising his eyebrows at her. 'I think things are about to get interesting.'

'Oh?' Anna started to walk towards the window, but he held up a hand.

'Give it a minute.'

She was intrigued. Whatever Peter had seen outside must have been significant. She was itching to go and look, but then Asya called from her almost foetal position on the chair.

'Anna, have you got any more of those pills?'

That gave Anna a jolt. It took her a moment to understand that Asya was asking for painkillers for her hangover. Nothing else. Any mention of pills and she was thrown back into a darker place full of things she wanted to forget. Lars. The very thought of drugs

200

made her stomach turn now. What had she been thinking? She hadn't been, that was the problem – and it had all led to this. She rummaged in her handbag and found two Panadol in a foil blister pack, snapped off from the rest of the packet. She always kept two in her bag like this for emergencies, and Asya's need was greater than hers. She handed them over.

'Thank you.' Asya looked miserable. 'Do you think I can go home to bed? Whatever shit is going on, I'm sure it can wait.'

Anna shrugged. 'I'm tempted to agree, but I think Bradley's on his way back so maybe just wait a bit longer?' She leaned down and squeezed Asya's arm. 'Try to drink some more water.'

She stood and turned just as the front door opened and Bradley walked in, followed by a very familiar face. So he *had* been in that café then. Someone else trying to make her think she was going mad, seeing people who didn't exist. She'd had more than enough of people and their lies – and these people in particular. But it was good that he was here. She had plenty of questions for him, that was for sure. She took a step towards the doorway.

'Jasper . . .'

The dark-haired man walked into the house and all of the noise and chatter stopped immediately.

John's head flicked around towards her, whiplash quick. 'Er, this is Robert . . .' he said. 'Who the fuck is Jasper?'

Mary walked through from the kitchen, followed by Lacy, whose face had drained of colour. 'Oh!' Mary said. 'Gary? What on earth are you doing here?'

Finlay puffed out a mirthless laugh. 'Colin, you mean. Colin Scott?'

'No . . .' said Asya. 'His name is Brian Blackie.'

The man that Anna knew as Jasper stood there in the doorway, stony-faced. He refused to meet her eye. He refused to meet anyone's eye. For someone who was usually so completely assured about what he was doing, he actually looked a little nervous. He shifted his weight slightly, folded his arms.

Lorraine Whitelaw broke away from her family group and walked over to the doorway. She pointed a finger at Jasper, while addressing the rest of the room. 'You're all mistaken,' she said. 'This chap here is called Alistair Harper. I'm afraid I can't tell you how I know him, because me, and the whole family, are sworn to absolute secrecy. For our own safety, you see.' She prodded the air in front of his face and he flinched slightly.

'That's enough, Lorraine,' Jasper said. He uncrossed his arms.

Bradley took a step away. 'Should I—'

Jasper – or whatever his name was – shook his head. 'I'll handle this, Bradley. Cheers, mate.' He addressed the room, where everyone stood staring, either slack-jawed or tight with anger.

What the hell was going on?

Jasper cleared his throat, and looked towards Finlay. 'Firstly . . . again, I am very sorry for your loss.' His eyes travelled around the room, making sure he made brief contact with everyone, before refocusing on Finlay. 'Beth was a special person, and I am deeply sorry for what happened to her. I know you feel let down. You all do. And I feel like I've let you down.' He gestured to Bradley, who was now standing by the entrance to the kitchen with Lacy. 'I know I speak for my colleagues here too, when I say that—'

'Hang on . . .' Kevin Whitelaw pushed himself to the front, finally making his presence felt. 'When you say "my *colleagues*"?'

Jasper closed his eyes. Shook his head. 'I really hoped that this wouldn't happen.' He glanced at Bradley again, who looked like he wanted a sinkhole to open up and put them all out of their misery.

Anna thought that might be quite a neat solution, really. Being where they were, it would probably suck them all out to sea, and that would be the end of it.

'Hoped what wouldn't happen?' Mary said quietly. Her earlier bluster had all blown out, and she was back to the nervy, meek-looking woman from before.

'Do you want to tell everyone why you're here, Mary? Why you moved to The Street?'

Mary wrung her hands. Colour popped up on her cheeks. 'Well, no, Gary. Of course not.' She looked around the room nervously. 'I've told everyone that I wanted to spend my retirement by the sea.' She looked down at her hands. 'But that's only half the truth, of course.'

'Christ, Mary,' Brooklin piped up. 'Don't leave us on a cliff-hanger here.'

Jasper turned to him. 'What about you, Brooklin? Why did you and Asya really come here?'

Brooklin's eyes widened. 'Jesus, Brian. What are you playing at?'

Jasper raised his palms. 'I thought you might have worked it out by now . . . I had a feeling that some of you were getting close, with some of the things you'd been asking me. But I thought me coming in here . . . you all calling me by different names . . .' He let his sentence trail off. Then he shrugged and pushed his hands into his pockets.

'Anna? You're uncharacteristically quiet . . . Yes, I know I said I'd arrange to meet tomorrow, but you're right – I *was* in the area. You *did* spot me in that café.' He nodded towards Lacy. 'We were looking at some attempts at damage limitation, but I think we can all agree that it's too late for that.'

Anna swallowed. It was obvious, really. It should have been obvious from the start, when Lindsay and Ritchie vanished like that. There was only one way to vanish like that – and you couldn't do it by yourself. The app was part of it. That's why they weren't supposed to mention it to one another. This explained all the cagey behaviour, the lies, the secrecy. The gaslighting.

This explained why Anna had started to think she was going mad.

'Witness protection,' Anna said, her voice low. She was almost too scared to say it any louder. Scared of what it all meant.

'You can speak up a bit, Anna. I think everyone needs to hear it, and then we can deal with it.'

Anna looked around the room, at the faces that had morphed through the phases of anger and confusion to something else: fear. 'Witness protection,' she repeated, trying to keep her voice steady. 'I think we're all in witness protection, and Jasper – or whoever you know him as – is everyone's handler.'

Forty-One

ANNA: WEDNESDAY

A cloud of silence hung over the room.

Mary was the first to speak. Her voice wobbled. 'Is this true?' She turned around slowly, arms outstretched, gesturing towards the residents. 'Are you all in witness protection?'

'Are *you*, Mary?' Lorraine said, as she crossed her arms tightly over her chest, then uncrossed them again, balling her hands into fists. She was flushed in the face, and her jerky movements showed her growing agitation. Her eyes darted around the room, as if she was hoping for some reassurance that this wasn't all utterly, inevitably true.

Everyone looked at Jasper. Anna had always thought that he didn't look like a Jasper, and it seemed there was probably good reason for that. She had no idea if any of the names that they knew him by was his actual name. She suspected not. Maybe he used a random name generator. She did that sometimes for coming up with characters in her books.

The more she thought about things, the more she saw the parallels with her fictional worlds. It seemed that everyone on The Street was merely a character in someone's invented world. Herself included. It would be funny if it wasn't so completely terrifying.

Who were these people in this room right now? New identities weren't just given to witnesses, were they? It was actually the *protected persons* service. Sometimes the ones who had to be protected were the ones who did the bad things. A tingle of fear spread over her shoulders. She took a deep breath, waiting for Jasper to speak. For once in her life, she hoped that her theory about this place was totally and utterly wrong.

Jasper looked at her and frowned, then he faced the others. 'OK, I'll level with you all. Yes, I'm afraid it's completely true.' He raised a hand to silence the flurry of voices. 'But first, let me assure you that none of you has been compromised.'

'Hang on, though . . .' Brooklin stood up from where he'd been perched on the arm of a chair. He was a lot more alert than he had been when Anna and Peter arrived. 'Were the Walkers compromised? Is that why they disappeared into a puff of smoke?'

Asya took hold of his arm. 'They *died*, babe. Didn't you see the news?'

'And what about Beth?' Finlay cut in. 'Do you actually know who killed her? Have you been keeping this from me while you tried to mop up your mess? What is all this, anyway? Some sort of mad experiment to keep us all in one place so you can keep an eye on us more easily? Or was it all about saving money? One street, one handler?'

Brooklin carried on. 'That story about the council buying The Street off the dodgy developer never really rang true . . .'

'That part actually is true,' Jasper said. 'Not that it matters now—'

'You told us to be careful because our neighbours were all normal!' Asya cut in. 'You've lied about everything!'

Anna sighed. 'This place did seem a bit high spec for the protected persons service. We were more than happy to move here, though – I mean, who wouldn't be? I'm sure we've all heard horror stories about some of the places that people end up in witness protection.'

'Our temporary place *was* a total dump,' said Finlay. 'Beth was totally freaked out there. This place was a bit of a dream come true.' She sniffed. 'Too good to be true, obviously. Should've bloody known.'

Jasper raised his hands, palms out in an attempt to encourage calm. 'Please, everyone. I know you have questions, and I will answer as best as I can, but I'll also be setting up individual meetings with you all to go through everything in detail and discuss next steps . . .'

'Next steps? Well, presumably we're going to have to bloody move again, aren't we? Now that everyone knows that none of us are who they say they are.' Finlay shook her head. 'Are you going to tell me how that arsehole found Beth? Please don't try to deny it. It was Raymond White, wasn't it? The man who was put away for raping her in the park outside our home? The man who you incompetent fools allowed to escape from prison? How the hell did he find her? So much for us not being compromised!'

John stood up and cleared his throat. 'This is probably a good time for me to tell you that you've all been compromised. Well, you could be, at least. If I was to do anything about it. I know who every single one of you really is.'

The room erupted with noise. Lorraine Whitelaw seemed to burst from the corner of the room as if she'd been released from a catapult. She had John by the throat before anyone could react. And then Bradley was on her, pulling her away, twisting her arm behind her back, and she was bucking against him like a wild animal, until Jasper stepped in and took her by the shoulders and held on to her tightly.

Bradley loosened his grip on Lorraine, and she seemed to fold into Jasper's arms, like someone had let all the air out of her. She started to cry.

'We came here for a fresh start,' she sobbed. 'Wherever we go, we're never going to forget . . . but we thought here, at least . . .' She let her sentence trail off.

The smug look that John had been wearing when he made his revelation had slid off his face now. Anna watched him as he looked around at everyone's expressions. Stunned silence was sitting hand in hand with fear.

'What is it you wanted to tell us, John?' Lacy tried to bring things back down to a manageable level, but the air felt charged with angry particles that swirled around them all like an unexpected sandstorm.

John deflated, slumped against the wall by the window. 'I recognised Ritchie Walker about six weeks ago. There was a documentary on TV about the big fraud case in Dundee, and I spotted him in the footage. He was in the background at an office party scene. I think they showed it because the boss was there having fun and they were painting a picture of him – and, well . . . I know they're meant to get clearance to use stuff like this, from all the people in it. But I think someone messed up.' He shrugged. 'Maybe they couldn't find him, because he was already in protection when they started their checks.'

Jasper sat down on one of the kitchen chairs that Lacy had brought through to the living room. 'Go on.'

John nodded. 'Well, obviously it was odd – I mean, I'm here because I'm in protection and then one of my neighbours shows up on TV, connected to this criminal and case, and I'm thinking: he's in protection too? A bit of a leap, maybe? But then I started thinking about . . . the app. The rules about privacy.' He nodded towards Bradley. 'The reminders to be vigilant.' He made his hands into fists and gently pressed them together. 'It all seemed a bit Big Brother. But then I wasn't really in a position to complain or ask questions. I don't want anyone finding me, and maybe Ritchie was in the same boat.'

'You're not explaining how you know about the rest of us, though?' Brooklin looked confused. He caught Anna's eye and she nodded at him, urging him to carry on. 'You didn't even know for sure with Ritchie . . . although, to be fair, you were right . . .'

'I started reverse image searching everyone,' John said. 'Most people are all over the internet, you know. Almost everyone here has a profile on Facebook set up with their new name – but even if you've changed your appearance a bit, you're still using your own photos. We were all told to stay away from social media, right? But who's going to listen to that? VPNs, private groups, restricting who you accept as friends. It's good, but it's not going to keep you hidden for ever. As for your old identities . . .' He paused to take a breath, 'Well, whoever was in charge of cleaning them up didn't get *everything*.

'Sometimes it takes a while, I guess. And there are lots of hidden sources. Being tagged in other people's social media photos is one of the worst. Not everyone is good at locking down their content to friends only. You wonder why people get scammed and hacked all the time and then you see how easily they give up their private information . . .' He shook his head. 'Those stupid things on Facebook where they ask you to answer all these questions and then share with your friends to find out their answers? First pet's name? What's your favourite colour? What was number one on the day you were born?' He raised his palms, turned his head slowly to look at everyone in turn. 'Don't you see? You're giving people everything they need to work out your passwords and steal your identity!'

Asya let out a small squeak that let everyone know that she had definitely been guilty of this. 'I just thought they were fun ways to get to know your friends,' she said. She looked crestfallen, like this was the biggest betrayal of her life. Like this was more important than the reason she was here and who she was being protected from.

Anna pressed her fingers into her eye sockets. *What. A. Mess.*

'Don't worry,' John said at last. 'I'm not going to tell anyone what I know. Why do you think I mostly keep my distance from you all? I'm actually trying to help protect you . . . protect all of us.'

'Wait, though,' Finlay said, pointing at Jasper. 'You said Bradley and Lacy were your colleagues. Did I hear that part correctly?'

Everyone turned to face Bradley and Lacy, who were together now by the kitchen doorway. Both were standing straight, hands clasped and held down in front of them. There was no hint of a smile on either of their faces. An official-looking stance – like they were awaiting permission to move.

Jasper went to stand beside them. 'DS Bradley Beckford and DS Lacy Nelson have been part of an undercover operation that has been used in collaboration with the protected persons service, while we trial this new set-up.' He paused, waiting for a reaction from the room. But everyone stayed silent. 'They've been protecting you.'

Kevin Whitelaw let out a small bark of laughter. 'Tell that to Finlay over there.'

Finlay nodded. 'Don't worry, Kevin. I'll be pushing for an investigation into all this. I'm not going to let them get away with covering it up. My Beth . . . my Eve. She was too important for this to be swept under the carpet like the failed government experiment that it is.' She turned to Jasper. 'You might think you can keep this hushed up, but I am more than willing to forgo my so-called protected status to get this information out there. I used to be a journalist, you know. You can look up some of my stuff. It's under Casey Bell. I've been silenced while I've been here, trying to find a way to move on with a life that I never wanted. I came here because I loved Eve. I will always love Eve. She was my rock, and I never told her that enough. I never appreciated her enough. And now she's gone, and I am telling you all now: I will not rest until I get justice for her. I failed her in life, but I will not fail her now. I will not.' She buried her face in her hands as huge wracking sobs shook her whole body.

Mary moved in close and put an arm around Finlay's shoulders. Mary looked over at Jasper, her eyes gleaming.

'Shame on you,' she practically spat. 'And for what? Some sort of cost-cutting measures? These are our *lives*.'

Jasper, to give him credit, looked suitably shaken by the outburst. Bradley and Lacy were still standing like sentries, staring straight ahead. Anna could see that Lacy's hands were shaking, and she was holding them together tightly, trying to make it stop. 'I think you should all go back to your homes now,' Jasper said quietly. 'There's a lot to take in, and things will be put in motion to have you all safely moved and given new identities again – should you want them – as soon as is feasible.'

He patted Bradley on the shoulder, and then he opened the front door and walked out of the house without another word.

Anna looked around the room, from one person to the next, taking them all in. So, they were all protected persons . . . She wondered what it was that everyone was being protected from. And why they were all being kept so close together.

Forty-Two

The Diary

What was I saying about this place being dull?

WELL!! It's certainly livened up now! Tell you what, though, that was an interesting meeting. That 'Jasper' turning up like that. I should feel betrayed, like everyone else does, but actually it's pretty impressive. This little experiment in group protection that they cooked up – it was never going to work, was it? It makes so much sense now, though, why everyone in this stupid street has been so cagey – me included. It was drummed in the minute I arrived – don't talk about your past. Don't ask others about theirs. Be friendly but don't be too open. Be careful. Be vigilant. Stay safe. Ha ha. Well, I've managed to do all of those things pretty successfully, I think. I've even managed to contravene one of the rules and get away with it so far – yeah, I forgot that one: don't dig into other people's business.

I should've sussed it all out from the start by looking at everyone's social media profiles. Of course it was suspicious that everyone I added from The Street seemed to have a recently created account.

I am such an idiot!

Certainly no Columbo or Jessica Fletcher, that's for sure. I'm not even as smart as John!

I wonder what will happen now. I suppose we'll all have to move again, won't we? More new names. More new locations – not all in the same place next time, eh? So much for their surveillance app and the not-so-hidden cameras. I really don't want to move again. I've finally felt like I was settling in here – building up my collections of things that I need, and couldn't bring.

The jar of bees is taking a lot longer than I thought it would. Maybe I need a window box with some bee-friendly flowers out there, so I can lure them in. My luggage chest is starting to look good, though. I like to take everything out and unwrap them. Look at them. Think about what I could do with them.

People wonder where I go when I go out, but I never tell them.

I'll tell you, though, Dear Diary. I go out and I find the things I need and I bring them back. I'm preparing. I'm keeping safe.

I'm looking at everything now, all nicely laid out on the floor between the bed and the window. No one ever comes in this room but me, but just in case – it's better to be able to hide things if necessary.

I was planning to draw everything, start a sort of inventory book. Then I could see what I still need to get, without having to take everything out all the time. Maybe I've still got time . . .

I'll start with the rocks.

Then the knives.

I wonder if my drawing skills will do them justice?

Forty-Three

Peter had barely said a word in Mary's house. Back home, in their own kitchen, he still seemed to have nothing to say. Anna watched him as he made them both tea and toast, bustling away with butter and jam, dunking tea bags and pouring milk. He was probably in shock. Anna thought that she probably was too.

'Well . . .' she said, when he sat down opposite her, pushing her plate across the table.

'Indeed.' He took a bite of his toast, slurped his tea.

Anna stared at him, taking in his blasé attitude. Any hints of their earlier intimacy were gone in a flash. 'Don't you have anything to say?' she snapped. 'You quite happily agreed to give up your life for me. You barely reacted to what I told you about Lars. We've been brought here to this bloody mental government *trial*, for fuck's sake. We need to leave!'

He took another bite of his toast. 'Jasper said he was going to move us as soon as possible. The whole thing will be a logistical nightmare for them now. Having to find new safe places for the whole street? Even the police couple will have to move. I wonder what they'll do with this place after that.' He took another slurp of tea. 'Sell it, I expect. Poisoned chalice.'

'Why are you so bloody calm?' She tried to temper her anger, but it was a struggle. She couldn't understand why he seemed to be so unbothered by what had just been revealed. 'Did you not listen to what John said? He knows everyone's real identities. Didn't even sound like it was much of an effort to find them.' She blew out a hard breath. 'Why the hell didn't they think of this? Whoever it was who came up with this stupid idea of bringing us all here and keeping us in one little plot like a bunch of battery chickens. It stands to reason that if you're keeping secrets about your life, you're going to be a bit suspicious about everyone else. At least if there's only one family in protection, they're going to be pretty safe from people snooping around. But putting us all together . . . it's a wonder that John is the only one to have worked it out.' She picked up her toast and took an angry bite, chewing as she spoke. 'I should've worked it out myself straight away, when Lindsay and Ritchie disappeared. When she tried to bloody warn me at the shopping centre. If I'd done more, then maybe she'd still be alive.' She dropped the half-eaten toast back on the plate. 'If I'd said more to Beth about the man on the beach, maybe she'd still be alive too!'

Peter gave her a hard look. 'You don't know that. The people who killed the neighbours are bad people. They tracked them down, and they got to them. It's got nothing to do with you, and what you may or may not have worked out with your super-sleuth "I'm a writer so I know things" hat on.'

Her mouth dropped open. 'What has got into you? You're acting completely insane.'

He shook his head. 'No, *dear*. You're the one who's been acting ridiculously since we arrived. I told you I was happy to support you, and leave my home and my friends and my job – because I love you. And I thought . . . well, maybe if we had a fresh start, we might actually find each other again. Because I lost you in London, Anna. I don't know what happened to you, but getting mixed up with Lars

215

and his bloody drugs parties . . . that's not you. What the hell was it all about? Just some crazy thrill-seeking moment? I've tried to understand, I really have . . . but then this place. Well, I thought it might be good for us, but you've caused nothing but drama since we arrived.' He sat back in his chair and crossed his arms.

Anna wanted to shout at him, to fight back, but she bit her tongue. He was venting his frustration, that was all. And besides, a lot of what he'd said wasn't far from the truth. She swallowed. In fact, maybe now was the right time to tell him the truth. The real truth.

She took a sip of her tea. 'The reason I've been acting like I have is because I have not felt safe here since we arrived, and I feel even less safe after finding out where it is we've actually moved to.'

'What are you so scared of? Lars is in prison. The gang members are in prison. None of them are getting out any time soon. It's not like anyone knows where you are—'

'Finlay thought that no one knew where they were, but someone clearly did because they found Beth, and they killed her. Lindsay and Ritchie ran away because someone found out where they were . . .' She stopped, realising she didn't know that for sure. Jasper had not actually said what had happened, but it had to have been that. They were moved, but they weren't moved far enough. Beth didn't even get that chance. 'Given that this whole street experiment is such a failure, it's only a matter of time before word gets out. Prisons are worse than being outside – they have networks. They have ways of getting to people—'

Peter laughed. 'Would you listen to yourself? You're nothing in that whole situation. So you told them stuff about Lars that helped get him put away? Well, he must've told them all plenty about the gang. No one said anything about you. No one cares about you.' He sneered. 'It's really not all about you.'

'I don't know where this aggression is coming from but if you just listen to me for a minute, I will explain!'

'I don't need you to explain, Anna. We're going to have to start afresh *again*, and there's nothing either of us can do about it. As for Lars . . . I'd really rather not talk about him any more, if it's all the same to you, OK?'

'Peter! Just listen to me for a minute. Please?'

He took another bite of toast, chewed noisily. 'Go on, then.'

She almost didn't say anything. She was starting to think that there was no point in this. His hostile behaviour was giving her a lot to think about. It was telling her that when she moved on from here, to wherever that might be, that maybe she was going to have to do it by herself. He should go back to London. Make up some bullshit about where he'd been for the last few months, in that horrible temporary accommodation in East London before they'd come up here.

But it wasn't fair to keep him in the dark any more. The guilt was eating her up. She had to tell Peter, and then at some point soon, when she was ready, she was going to have to tell the police. As much as she tried to convince herself she could live like this, she knew it would always be at the back of her mind.

She couldn't spend the rest of her life jumping at shadows.

'It wasn't Lars who set up the deal,' she blurted, looking him straight in the eye. 'It was me.' She paused, seeing if he would react, and when he just continued to stare at her with that stony expression, she carried on. 'He agreed that we would share the responsibility. He thought it would be better for us both. That it would reduce our sentence if we co-operated fully. And, well . . . he wanted to protect me.'

'Because you were fucking him.'

Anna looked away. He'd worked that out then. There was no point in denying it. She spoke quietly. 'Not just because of that.

I told you. We were friends. It was a moment of madness.' She brought her gaze back to his and he was still glaring at her, but he'd cocked his head slightly. Interested now. 'We had a story. We'd always had a story. We cooked it up right at the start, repeated it to each other now and then, to make sure it was all fixed in our heads. Just in case.'

'Just in case the police got wind of your little deal that had shifted very quickly from a personal-use situation to an intent to supply?'

Anna nodded. 'That was kind of Lars's idea. I wasn't keen. But he tried to tell me that if we didn't do it, then someone else would just come in and make money from this gang. I think he thought it was glamorous, being some sort of drug baron. I don't think he would've done it for much longer . . . if there hadn't been the raid . . .' She let her sentence trail off. She remembered that night in such specific detail that it replayed itself to her over and over, like a movie she'd watched a hundred times. That night at Lars and Agneta's house, where Agneta had hung hundreds of little fairy lights around the garden, the porch and through the house. There were scented candles that smelled of lilac and rose. She'd got caterers in to serve canapés – Anna recalled the tiny circles of toast with the perfect little toppings – creamy cheese and sweet quince, beef tartare and sharp redcurrants. The drinks had been wonderful colourful cocktails, served by pretty, young things in the skimpiest interpretation of 'black tie'. And then the drugs, of course. Delivered to the guests in tiny organza gift bags.

Peter had been away that night. He'd been away a lot around that time. Spending time with male friends that she had never really got to know well. Those football-watching types who thought that authors were too posh to spend time with.

And then, later, when they were all in full swing, came the knock on the door that would change everything. Well, a knock was putting it mildly. There was banging, shouting . . . and then the door had been knocked off its hinges before anyone had a chance to answer it, and the armed police had come in. The smells of lilac and rose were replaced with sweat and fear and something sharp and spiky that comes through your pores when adrenaline kicks in.

'I didn't stick to the story,' Anna said eventually, snapping herself back into the present. 'I'd made up another one, you see. One where Lars was behind everything. And that's the one I told the police.'

Peter made an unimpressed *hmph* sound. 'Surely he told them you were lying?'

Anna shook her head. 'According to the police, after I'd made my statement, he changed his and corroborated my version of events.' She bit her lip. 'I was shocked. I hadn't really expected them to believe me, but there was no evidence either way, and Lars knew that. I thought after my betrayal, he would do what he could to bring me down with him, but he stuck to it, and they convicted him. I think the gang were more important, and that's why he didn't get the maximum sentence. I mean, it's him who should be scared, not me. But I suppose maybe the gang were OK with it, given that they all got caught anyway.'

'Right . . . so what are you so worried about then? He's let you off the hook.' He tried to laugh, but it was forced. 'I always thought he was a fucking idiot, despite all his business-shit and his money. Still not entirely sure what Agneta saw in him. I'm still surprised that she didn't divorce him the minute he got arrested. Hardly good for her society image.'

'That's the thing,' Anna said. 'I met with Agneta before we left. She told me exactly why she didn't leave him. Yes, there's the money, the lifestyle she wants to keep. But she showed me some pictures. Pictures of her – naked, tied up. That sort of thing. Bruises too. She was scared of him. Terrified. He told her if she tried to leave him, or if she told anyone about any of it, he would have someone throw acid in her face so that no one would ever want to look at her again. He knows people. The whole drug-dealing, gang thing was just a game to him, Peter. He duped me. I didn't know any of this when I gave my statement, and if I had, I would never have tried to blame him for it all. I would've told the truth and asked the police for help.'

'Help with what? They gave you help. They set us up with a new life in this dystopian hellhole with a pretty seaside view, didn't they?'

Anna felt tears springing to her eyes, wiped them hastily away. 'Agneta gave me a message from Lars. He said that I should never stop looking over my shoulder, because wherever I went, he would find me . . .' She reached across the table, took Peter's hands in hers. 'He said he's going to kill me, Peter . . . and I believe him.'

Peter gave her an odd look. His calm demeanour shifted, ever so slightly. He glanced away for a moment, as if composing himself.

'That's ridiculous,' he said. He wouldn't meet her eye.

Anna stared at him. He'd sat and listened to everything she'd said and remained calm, impassive throughout it all. So calm that she'd felt like leaping over the table and shaking him, just to get a reaction.

But right there at the end – something had happened. The revelation that Lars wanted to kill her. It was almost as if he'd known everything else she'd been frantically telling him, but this last part – this last, crucial part – was a shock.

A thought sprang into her mind and she wondered why she hadn't considered it before. Peter had met Lars first. Peter had introduced her to Lars. Peter was always conveniently away when Lars had a party.

Had . . . had everything that had happened to them been a set-up? Was Peter behind it in some way? Was that why he seemed so unfazed?

Unfazed, that was, until she'd uttered those final words.

'He's going to kill me, Peter . . .'

Anna stared at her husband and realised that she didn't know him at all.

Maybe she never had.

Forty-Four

A Police Station: Now

DS Marcus Cole ran his sweaty palms down the front of his trousers, before sitting on the hard plastic chair and shifting slightly to try to get comfortable. It was the first time he'd been in this station, spending most of his time 'in the field' since his transfer. He spoke to his new boss regularly, but mostly by phone or text via the secure phoneline.

Detective Inspector Lydia Mills was sitting behind her desk. She had steepled her hands and was leaning forward on her elbows, her face fixed into a completely unreadable expression. Marcus wasn't sure if she was about to say a prayer or blast out a stream of obscenities.

After a moment, she took her elbows off the desk and leaned back in her chair, putting her hands behind her head. 'Sorry about that chair you're on. I did have a nice leather one but some idiot swung back on it and the leg snapped.'

Marcus let out a sigh of relief. She sounded OK. Definitely not about to bollock him. It was odd, seeing her in the flesh, getting some facial expressions and body language for a change. He hadn't known quite how to read her. He shuffled back in the chair, making himself more comfortable.

'Right then,' Lydia said. 'How much of a shitshow are we talking here? On a scale of one to ten, one being "Actually, guv, we can carry on as normal with a couple of minor lessons learned," and ten being "I would like to have myself put under the care of the protected persons service and have myself shipped to Australia in a packing crate with no air holes"?'

Marcus shifted in his seat again. He swallowed a lump of air so hard he wasn't sure he was going to breathe again after it went down. This was not good. This was really not good. This was so far from being good that it was all of those things in that Alanis Morissette 'Ironic' song. He could think of a few others too. It was a drinking game he played with his mates sometimes. Like the Top Trumps of bad things.

'It's, er, it's like being trampled by camels just as you reach the oasis.'

She narrowed her eyes. 'Sorry?'

He'd misjudged this. He'd assumed from the phone relationship they'd cultivated over the last few months that she understood his humour. But maybe his timing was off. In fact, OK, his timing was definitely off. The problem was, it was such a mess that it almost felt like it couldn't really be happening. After that meeting at one of the residents' houses, he was half-expecting a TV crew to jump out with a hidden camera while people pulled off their prosthetic faces and laughed at him. 'Gotcha!'

'It's probably a twelve, guv. If I'm being honest.' He couldn't look at her. She didn't say anything, and the temperature in the room seemed to drop about ten degrees. He actually shivered. When he finally met her eye again, she was just glaring at him, no doubt imagining all the ways she could punish him with as much pain as possible. The airless packing crate seemed almost too humane.

'I should just fire you right now and have you escorted out of this station. But considering how much I've personally and professionally invested in this programme, I would like some sort of explanation.' She picked up a bound set of papers and tapped it on the desk, levelling out the pages. 'And we need to do an immediate risk assessment on the residents. Do you agree?' She laid the papers flat and flipped over the front page.

He tried not to show his relief. Maybe there was a way to come out of this looking like slightly less of an incompetent fool than he felt. Maybe he might be allowed to stay on the force, albeit in a much less exciting role. He suspected he had traffic management and crowd control in his not-too-distant future.

'Yes, of course,' he said, sitting up straighter. 'I've already made some notes.' He took his phone out of his pocket. 'I think first, Finlay Wallace. I'd like to get her moved as soon as possible. She's grieving, and she's angry—'

'And no doubt ready to blow the whole operation out of the water . . .' Lydia checked her notes. 'She used to be a journalist?'

Marcus nodded. 'The surviving half of Eve and Casey Bell. Eve was a nurse. Before her attack. She set up her own baking business when they moved to The Street. Casey . . . I mean, Finlay . . . she'd just started doing some gardening jobs. Nothing fancy, no landscaping or anything like that. She told me she liked the serenity of it all after her previous job.'

Lydia frowned. 'I believe Raymond White was apprehended this morning. He'd been sleeping rough in a derelict pub in Tranent. Builders went in to start an assessment for a potential buyer. He'll plead diminished responsibility, I expect. He'll likely get it too. Either way, he's going to be locked up for a very long time. I'll send someone to talk to Finlay. Not that it will be of much comfort.' She leaned back, rubbed her eyes with the heels of her hands. 'Eve . . . Beth was supposed to be safe. We let her down.'

Marcus nodded. There wasn't really any more he could say about that.

'Jonas and Kayleigh Grant, aka Lindsay and Ritchie Walker . . . Their families have been informed. We think there's been a whisper about The Street making its way around the prison system. Someone's revealed the location, but we don't know the details yet. I've got informants on the case, people on the inside who owe me some favours. But yet again, this disaster is on us. Moving them after that breach should have kept them safe, not made it worse.'

'They were only meant to be in that accommodation in Musselburgh for one night. They were meant to lay low.'

'But they'd already been compromised, yes? That's why we had to take them out of The Street? Why didn't you move them further away? The top dog from their case wouldn't have had to look very far to find them.' She sighed. 'Let's save it for the inquiry, Marcus. Next?'

'John Alfred. Previously known as Simon Glass—'

'He's the one who reckons he sussed it all out, is he? Did he actually give you any information that wasn't publicly available?'

Marcus shook his head. 'No. But the things he found were the result of more sloppy mistakes. By us. I've no excuses, guv.'

'Please stop calling me that, Marcus.'

He nodded, carried on. 'He was a human rights lawyer in a past life. Blew the lid off a big trafficking case. He's kept to himself a lot. Savvy. Works for a charity in Edinburgh now and I think he'll want to stay there. We can move him somewhere in town.'

'Fine. Simple enough. What about the Knights? Brooklin and Asya.' She gave a little snort. 'They could choose any names they wanted for themselves and they chose those?' She ran a hand down the page. 'And they chose to become Instagram influencers? When they're supposedly in hiding?'

'Mainly photos of their dog,' Marcus said. 'I guess Colin and Dawn McKee wanted a more glamorous existence after they escaped their scummy lives amongst the Glasgow drugs elite.'

'Right. Move them to our place in Newcastle. The further from Glasgow, the better. Exploit the joint initiative across the forces as much as possible. Tell them to consider new names and some normal jobs.' She flicked a page. 'Next is Mary Congleton, aka Frances Bailey. Witnessed a brutal murder from her bedroom window.' She shook her head. 'Poor woman. As if she wasn't traumatised enough, she's had to deal with her neighbour suffering the same fate. These people are all owed a huge apology, Marcus.'

'I know. I expect they'll get compensation too.'

She rolled her eyes. 'I expect they will. I expect they'll all get anything they want in exchange for keeping their mouths shut about this whole ridiculous debacle. You know, I was looking for a change of scene, anyway. I hear the beaches on Shetland are nice. Low crime rate too – unless you watch that ridiculous TV show where someone gets killed every week.'

Marcus didn't tend to watch detective shows. The last one he'd attempted had made him want to kick the screen at the ridiculousness of it all. That would never happen, he'd thought, but now look. Anyone watching this one would be laughing their heads off at the nonsense of it. Talking of fictional nonsense . . . 'Then we have Peter and Anna Clarke, our newcomers.'

'Ah yes.' Lydia ran a hand down the page again. 'Patrick and Amanda Barton. She testified against her *friend* and local Swedish cartel wannabe, Lars Kristiansen.'

'Who, despite being on the hook for a much bigger operation that has little to do with drugs shifting and more to do with people moving, happens to have been relocated to HMP Castle Huntly, as of about two weeks ago.'

'Marvellous. Expensive lawyer?'

Marcus nodded.

'Have the Bartons been informed?'

'Not yet. Had a few other things to deal with. Besides, I can't see him absconding. He struck some sort of deal. He's biding his time. I'm waiting on more detail, but—'

She waved a hand in front of her face. 'Whatever. I'm not worried about them.'

He swallowed. That fat lump was back. He wondered if anyone had died from swallowing their own breath before.

'You're right,' he said. 'I think we both know our biggest concern is what to do with the Whitelaws.'

Forty-Five

Anna: Wednesday

'We can't stay here. Not for another day, or night. Not for another minute.' Peter watched silently from the doorway as Anna pulled things out of drawers and tossed them on to the bed. She had barely unpacked since they arrived, and here she was, ready to pack it all up again. Why was she even bothering? She didn't need any of this stuff. What she needed was to get herself away from this completely unsafe show-home in this ridiculous street, where broken people from various parts of the country had been flung together to save some fat cats in suits a few quid.

This was her life. She wasn't intending on having it ended prematurely.

As for Peter . . . He had been acting off since they got here. Disappearing down to his shed, or in the car. Acting like he wasn't bothered about their vanishing neighbours.

His reaction to her revelations about Lars was off too. If she'd told him about the affair a couple of years ago – not least that she'd even started it – he would've flipped his lid. But all he did was leave the house, and when he came back in the morning, he seemed to be fine and ready to move on.

This was not the Peter she thought she knew.

She thought back to when they met . . . She'd been offered a ticket last minute to go to a comedy club in central London, one of those ones in the bowels of an overpriced hotel, with aggressive bouncers and lurid drinks. Really not her scene, but her friend had just split up with her boyfriend and she didn't want to stay home. She'd called round and thrust the ticket in Anna's face, insisting that they go now and they get very, very drunk.

The comedians had been awful. She'd recognised the name of one, an Edinburgh Fringe favourite, but not someone she'd have chosen to see again. His material was overly political and too try-hard. The others were clearly much lower on the pecking order of the comedy circuit and as much as she sympathised with their plight, it wasn't really her idea of fun to be subjected to their awful jokes and terrible delivery. She'd gone outside for some air, and he'd approached her within seconds, introducing himself as he crushed his cigarette on the pavement.

'Terrible habit. I'm only out here because I'm scared I'm going to die of a cringe attack.'

'Oh God, me too! I can't even find my friend. She came here to get over a break-up and I think she's already found herself a replacement!'

He laughed. 'What's that saying? The best way to get over someone is to get under someone else?'

Anna had found this ridiculously funny. Not because it was the best joke in the world, but because it was better than anything she'd heard in the last hour, and the bright blue cocktails had made her quite giddy.

'So what do you do, when you're not lurking around seedy comedy dives?' he said, leaning back against the wall.

'I'm a writer,' she said. 'Currently crime novels, but I do some other things too—'

'Crime novels? Hmm. I've read a Mark Billingham book. Didn't care for it. Felt like he was making it up as he went along . . .'

She giggled. 'I'm pretty sure that's what we all do. The clue's in the name, you know . . .' She made air quotes with her fingers. '"Fiction."'

He shrugged. 'Whatever. Hardly a literary genius, though, is he, that Billingham bloke? So violent! I mean, what do you expect from an ex-SAS guy? I'm surprised he can read, never mind write. Anyway, I prefer real books.'

She'd felt her jaw drop, wondering if he realised how incredibly rude he was being. But then she saw the glint in his eye, and realised he was joking. He knew there were two Mark Billinghams. Didn't he? He'd wanted to entertain her. He wanted to let her know that her world was not alien to him. He'd wanted her to notice him.

It was a shame that things had gone so horribly wrong.

She shook away the memory, tried to refocus herself on the here and now, with this new version of Peter that she wasn't sure she knew any more.

'Are you even listening to me, Peter?' She turned around from the bed, where she had been shoving pairs of shoes that she didn't even need into the last remaining holdall.

He was gone.

She wasn't sure how long he'd been gone for. She sighed, and threw a pair of socks into the bag before sitting down on the end of the bed. Her shoulders slumped, and she felt overwhelmed with tiredness all of a sudden. The adrenaline that had fuelled her was gone. The house was weighted with a heavy silence. She realised that she hated it here. That she always had. She looked around the room, at the clean lines of the furniture, the minimalistic design. She missed her old place, with the walls that weren't quite straight and the peeling paint on the old sash windows. All the bric-a-brac she'd collected over the years. Stuff that meant things. What did she have now? Luckily she'd gone against Jasper's advice and put it in a storage unit instead of taking it to the dump, so one day, she hoped, she might be able to move back to a house with character again, and make it her own.

She hadn't realised how eerily silent this place could be, with its triple-glazed windows and nothing outside to make a noise. When was the last time she'd heard a wailing siren, or a bunch of drunks stumbling home from the pub, talking too loudly and singing outside her window? She concentrated on the sounds of nothing, and realised she could hear voices.

Anna stood up from the bed and walked carefully over to the bedroom doorway. She could hear Peter talking but she couldn't quite hear what he was saying. She walked to the top of the stairs, and his voice grew louder. Then he stopped talking and she heard the other voice coming through the phone. It wasn't on speaker, so it was just a tinny, distant sound – but she was pretty sure it was a woman, from the pitch. She wanted to walk down the stairs. Ask him who he was talking to and why the hell he'd been so antagonistic earlier, but something stopped her. He spoke again, once more, then he hung up.

She started humming a tune as she walked down, trying to act normally and not let him realise that she'd been trying to listen in. Why was she so suspicious, anyway? He could've been talking to anyone, for any reason. But there had been a furtive feel to it, like he was trying to keep his voice low. For someone who normally annoyed people on the train with how loudly he spoke, this was a definite red flag.

He was coming out of the kitchen. 'Oh, there you are,' he said as he slid his phone into his pocket. 'Have you stopped your mad packing? Shall I make us a tea?'

'A tea would be nice. Who was on the phone?'

'Garage. After-sales call about the car. They're sending me some questionnaire to fill in or something. I couldn't get rid of her.'

It was plausible, Anna supposed. The car was only a few weeks old, and the dealership had said they would follow up to make sure they were happy with it. 'Right, yeah. Talking of phones, I need to get myself a new one.' She sat on the couch and pulled her legs up under her. She was actually in no real rush to replace her phone. It was nice not to have that stupid app beeping at her, reminding her to watch what she was saying and who she was talking to. She leaned back into the cushions, thinking how nice it would be to just drift off to sleep and forget about everything for a while. Peter had to be tired too. Neither of them had slept the night before and it had already been such a long day. It would be better to leave in the morning, anyway.

'Earth to Anna . . . Do you still want this tea, or shall we just go to bed?'

She woke with a start. She must have drifted off after all.

'I'm sorry I was a pain in the arse earlier,' he said, handing her a steaming mug. 'It's just all this . . . everything. I'm exhausted. I just want to run away and never see any of these people again.' He paused to take a drink. 'I know that sounds harsh. I feel awful for Finlay, although I don't even really know her, or Beth. And the neighbours too – it all feels like it was some sort of fever dream.'

The scent of the tea woke her up a bit. It was too hot to drink, so she blew on it. Peter had already drunk half of his. He always did have the weird ability to drink almost boiling water, where she liked to wait for it to be lukewarm. He was being nice to her again, but she was fed up with him blowing hot and cold. 'I want to leave, Peter. I haven't changed my mind. But it would probably be better for us to go in the morning? It's light at about 4 a.m. anyway.'

'I agree. But . . . aren't we supposed to be waiting for Jasper to tell us what to do next? Also, don't the police need to know where you are? I don't think we can just run away, as much as I'd love that right now.'

'Fuck Jasper. Or whatever his name actually is. Seriously. I don't want to be Anna Clarke. I want to go back to being Amanda Barton. I want to go back to London, to our lovely house next to Clapham Common. I want to go back to the never-ending sounds of sirens and maniacs and god knows what else.' She put the mug on the coffee table. 'I don't want to live this life. I know it was meant to protect us, but I feel stifled. Stuck. I'm never going to be able to write here. I'm never going to make any real friends. I think we should go to bed and get a few hours' sleep, and then we should get up, throw what we can in the car, and leave. See where the roads take us. I know we're not meant to leave, but I honestly don't even care.'

He laughed. 'Are you serious? I don't think we can do that, Anna. I really don't, after what you told me about Lars, I—'

'I don't want to talk about him. I don't even want to think about him.'

The truth was, he was never far from her thoughts. While her heart was urging her to run away as fast as she could, as far as she could – she knew deep down that she would never escape what had happened. What she'd done. She truly believed that Lars would find a way to get to her. He was obviously just biding his time.

Peter's phone rang, and he held it out to her to answer.

'Hello, Jasper. I'm going to have to keep calling you that I suppose, as I doubt you're going to tell me your real name.'

She heard him sigh down the phone. 'I'm sorry, Anna. It was part of the risk planning to protect everyone. What if you'd all known me by the same name and one of you let it slip to another? You'd have worked it out in seconds.'

'Hardly. We're all here trying to protect ourselves, aren't we? Who'd be looking for the possibility of shady experiments where we're all kept together in this luxury pen? Anyway, as I'm sure everyone else is, I'm done with it. We're leaving in the morning.'

The tone of his voice changed instantly. 'Anna, I'd really recommend that you don't do that. We're working on it at our end, I promise you. We'll get you a new place as soon as we can. Just you and Peter. You won't be near anyone else from this street, and of course, we won't be publicising what's gone on here – I assume we can rely on your discretion? After all, we're the ones who brought you here, to keep you safe.'

'Lars Kristiansen is a resourceful man. I'm sure it's only a matter of time before he tracks me down. I'm not willing to sit here and wait. I don't think I'm safer here than anywhere else. Do you? Look what happened to Beth!'

He swore under his breath. 'Look, Anna . . . there's something you don't know—'

She'd pressed the red button to end the call, then handed the phone back to Peter. There was no doubt plenty she didn't know, and as far as she was concerned, she didn't want to. She picked up her mug and downed her lukewarm tea.

'I'm going to bed.'

Forty-Six

ANNA: THURSDAY

Early-morning sun stung her eyes. Anna rolled over and pulled the duvet up over her head. So much for getting a good night's sleep. Anna had been wired, and overtired, and spent most of the night tossing and turning, trying to fall asleep. Occasionally she'd lapsed into one of those deep sleeps that bring kaleidoscopic nightmares, where she would wake suddenly, heart beating too fast, taking a moment to work out where she was.

After the third of those, Peter's patience had left him, and he'd disappeared off to the spare room.

She'd spent most of the hours since then staring at the window, watching the sky change from indigo to violet to the lemon-or-ange sunrise that gradually filled her bedroom with light. In those post-nightmare hours, all of her plans to escape from the mess of her life slowly ebbed away.

Yes, she could run. Maybe she could even make it abroad. She didn't have a new passport yet, but there had to be a way, didn't there? Plenty of dodgy sorts managed to find their way to Spain without raising any red flags. But if she ran, then she would always be running. Always looking for that man on the beach, on the street, outside her house. She had no doubt that Lars would track her down. It had worried her all along that he had taken his punishment so easily when she had lied to the police about him. It had worried her too that they had believed her so easily. All those years of writing fiction had finally paid off.

Except they hadn't. It was all a lie. And she didn't want to live a lie.

What would she actually get, if she went and confessed? She'd be charged with several things, she supposed – perjury, for lying in court. Perverting the course of justice – was that still a thing? Plus, the original charges that had been levelled at Lars – all those things that were linked to him instigating the deal, setting it up, running it – were still on him. But the big part – the instigating . . . that was on her.

Sometimes she tried to convince herself that she had only done it because she'd been carried away with the fantasy life with Lars, the two of them like a couple of gangsters or something. It was ridiculous, really. Because what did she even know about any of that? And yet it had been her. That night when Lars told her his usual cocaine supplier was no longer available. And she – high as a kite and full of complete shit – said that she would find him a new one. She knew she'd taken too much that night. Her head had been fizzing with it as she ran across the common towards the trees. And Lars had been the opposite, he was flat. He wasn't playing. He'd sat on a bench and shouted at her to not be so stupid . . . and she had taken off her shoes and run away into the trees, and then she'd bumped into him. Right into him.

And that was the start.

Anna set up that first deal. Anna went back and asked for more. Anna told Lars that it was stupid that there was this supply issue when they could sort it, they could organise it – and he'd laughed at her and said, 'So you're a dealer now,' and she'd rolled her eyes at him and said, 'No . . . I am in charge now.'

And here she was, just sitting in this house, waiting for something to happen, with only Peter to save her – and he clearly didn't give a shit; she could see it in his eyes.

She had to take charge again.

She threw off the duvet and waited a moment for her eyes to adjust to the bright light, then she picked up yesterday's clothes from the floor by her bed, where she'd discarded them only a few hours before. She sniffed them and grimaced. They were not fresh. All the stress hormones had pumped their nasty little scents into the fibres. But she had packed everything else. So she pulled them on anyway, and doused herself in a heavy cloud of body spray.

Peter was sound asleep when she passed the open door to the spare room. He hadn't closed the blinds, but he was oblivious to the sunlight that bathed the room with a pale golden glow. He'd got used to it. She wasn't sure she ever would. She carried her shoes down the stairs, waiting until she was almost at the front door before she put them on. After she'd laced them, she peered up the stairs, holding her breath to try to make out any noises from Peter. His gentle snores drifted down, and she was glad he was sound asleep. If she told him what she was doing, he would only try to talk her out of it.

She slipped out of the house, closing the front door gently. Across the street, a car door slammed a little too loudly for the early hours. Anna watched as the car drove away. The Whitelaws were in it. Three of them, at least. Donna was standing on the front doorstep, arms crossed and face etched into a scowl. She spotted Anna and stared, her impression barely changing.

'Weird time to take a holiday, right?'

Anna hurried down the path and across the road. She didn't want to be shouting over the street, especially at this hour. The Whitelaws' behaviour had always struck her as odd, but this was the oddest yet. How old was Donna? Should she even be left alone in the house? Especially after what had happened?

'Are they really going on holiday? And leaving you here on your own?'

Donna smirked. 'Not really. They've got to drive my brother to a hospital appointment. It's in some specialist place near Glasgow. That's why they've gone so early. They wanted me to go. They're lucky I even got out of bed to see them off.'

'Ah, OK. So they'll be back later today?' She wondered what was wrong with Donna's younger brother – Max – but decided it wasn't her place to ask.

'Yeah, I suppose. Unless they keep him in.' Her face softened. 'He's not a bad kid, you know, as little brothers go. He was really sick when he was younger, but now he just has to get annual checks. He's actually been going to that hospital since he was a toddler – it was a lot further to drive there from where we used to live.' She looked down at her feet. 'Not that I ever went with them.' She looked back up at Anna, and there was a look in her eye that said, *Ask me more stuff, why don't you . . . I know you want to know . . .* Donna half-turned to push open the front door, which had been left ajar. 'Anyway, I'm going back to bed.'

Donna disappeared back inside her house. Anna watched for a moment, until she saw Donna upstairs. She looked down at Anna as she closed the blind. *Well*, Anna thought. *Just more strangeness from the strange house.* She shook her head. The sooner she was out of here, the better.

She passed Finlay's house, and then Mary's, glancing into both, but all the blinds were drawn. When she got to Bradley's, it was the opposite. It was what she expected from a dog owner, and as it turned out, a police officer. He would definitely be an early riser.

She saw him in the living room, looking out, and he'd opened the front door before she even got to it. 'Fancy a cuppa?'

She followed him inside, and through to the kitchen. 'Thanks, that'd be lovely.'

'Lacy's taken the dogs out. I think she's planning a longer walk than usual. Wants to clear her head.'

Anna nodded. 'I know the feeling.'

Bradley bustled around the kitchen getting the tea things together. Flicking the kettle on, rinsing mugs, checking the tea caddy and then frowning, rooting around in a cupboard for a fresh box. He sniffed the milk then left it out on the side. 'I was wondering if you might come over.' He poured water into two mugs. 'With you finding Beth—'

Anna sat down on one of the kitchen chairs. 'I'm not here about Beth. I'm here about me, and . . . why I'm here. And why I probably shouldn't be.' She looked down at her hands, picked at a cuticle. 'I need to tell you something . . . and then I need you to tell me what to do. I can't keep it a secret any more. It's too hard.'

He placed the mugs down carefully on the table. 'You can trust me, Anna.' He poured milk into his mug, then pushed the bottle gently across towards her. 'I haven't had a chance to tell anyone this yet, after all that's gone on in the last few days . . . and I don't know what's going to happen next, or where any of us are going to end up, but I want you to know – I want all of you to know – that I took this job because I wanted to help people. I know that's a cliché – and yes, I did join the force initially because I fancied the thrill of catching bad guys . . . but then when this role came up, and I had the chance to protect people instead of running around after the country's scumbags . . . well, I took it. I—'

'I'll have to stop you there, I'm afraid. As much as I'm a fan of your altruistic life choices, you might not be so accommodating when I tell you my dirty secret.'

He took a sip of his tea. 'Try me.'

Anna took a deep breath and blurted everything out. It took two more cups of tea before the story was done. She looked for judgement in his eyes and found none, and it felt as if the tight band of fear around her chest had loosened. Not completely. Not yet. But somehow, she was able to breathe a little easier.

Afterwards, he told her to go home. To wait. And to say nothing else to anyone until he'd made some calls.

Forty-Seven

PETER: THURSDAY

He was upstairs packing his things when the doorbell blasted out its annoying fucking tune. He looked over at the half-filled cases and bags – all his things, not hers. Her stuff was mostly scattered over the bed. *She* wanted to leave, though. He would just tell her he had changed his mind – decided she was right. Of course they could flee. He would just have to find a way to disappear sometime later.

The most important thing was that he got himself away from here sooner rather than later.

The doorbell went again. She must have forgotten her keys, but that was good because it had given him enough time to think up his story. If she'd let herself in and walked upstairs to find him packing only his own stuff . . . yeah, that might have looked bad.

He flipped over the lid of one of the cases, then pulled out another of the empty ones and tipped Anna's underwear drawer into it. There. That looked better. That looked more like both of them were meant to be running away from this mess.

Not just him.

The doorbell went again, followed by knocking.

Fucksake.

'Coming!' He took the stairs two at a time, slipped a bit at the bottom. Righted himself.

He yanked open the door. 'OK, OK . . .' The words died in his throat.

The person who had been ringing and knocking so insistently was not Anna.

'Hello, Patrick,' he said, pushing his way past and into the house, kicking the door closed behind with his heel. 'You seem surprised to see me! I did say I would pop round as soon as it was feasible.'

'Lars. You're . . . They let you out?'

Lars grinned his terrifying, mirthless grin. 'Not as such, no. The video you sent in helped. Got me moved to their little playground prison up north of here. Easy to slip out of there for a day trip, you know. I'll be back there for tea.' He paused, stepped in closer. 'Probably.'

Peter backed towards the kitchen. Lars always stood too close. He'd originally thought the man had no concept of personal space, but had soon realised that this was just one of his intimidation tactics.

If he could just get into the kitchen, he could get a knife, or . . . something. Anything. Peter felt very vulnerable. He didn't even have any shoes on.

'Can I get you a coffee? Something to eat?' He tried to sound confident, but there was an underlying tremor in his voice. He should have known that the last job he'd agreed to in prison that day was not going to be the last he'd hear of Lars. That's why he'd been ready to run. It was fine to bat it all towards Anna, but Peter . . . Patrick . . . whoever the hell he was now – he knew this was all on him.

'No, thank you,' Lars said. The grin had slid off his face. 'I won't be staying long. Your wife . . . ?'

Peter swallowed. *Please, Anna. Don't come back now.* 'She's not here. She's visiting a friend.'

Lars nodded. 'It's nice that she's found some friends here. She's a good person, your wife.' His eyes gleamed. He took another step towards Peter, closing the gap. 'Not. Like. You.' He stabbed his finger into Peter's chest, punctuating each word.

Peter's breath caught. The pokes hit him hard in the sternum. 'Lars, I—'

'Save it. I'm not interested in the likes of you, Patrick. The type of man who'll betray his own wife for money. That was all you ever wanted, wasn't it? Her nice little earner with her books had you feeling small? You thought you could schmooze me and turn yourself into some sort of big man?'

Lars laughed that horrible laugh that Patrick remembered so well from before.

And Patrick knew he was fucked.

It didn't matter that The Street was supposedly surrounded by police. That they were all supposedly under surveillance. He'd given Lars his way in, and now he was in his house, and he wasn't going to leave until he got what he wanted. Whatever that might be.

Peter realised now that it was not, as he'd thought it would be, Anna.

'You know,' Lars continued, 'my relationship with Agneta was really quite good before you came along. Filling her with ideas. Telling her to get out, that you . . . *you*!' He laughed again. 'That you could give her a better life?' He shook his head. 'What did you think was going to happen, Patrick?'

'Lars, please . . .' Peter held up his hands, backed himself further away. 'If we could just talk? I was trying to help you. Agneta was getting itchy feet and I was trying to placate her, I was—'

'Lies!' Lars shouted it into his face, sour spittle spraying on to Peter's own open mouth. 'You let me fuck your wife! You let me set her up, and you'd have been more than happy for her to go to prison . . . She still might, you know. I assume the police have not spoken to her yet, but it's only a matter of time. I suppose your protected status has messed up procedures in some way.' Lars sighed, pulled away slightly.

Peter breathed a sigh of relief. 'Look, she'll be back soon. You can talk to her, you can . . . We can sort this. Can't we? I mean, you're out now. You don't have to go back. There must be ways for you to just . . . disappear.'

Lars glared at him. Then a smirk played on his lips. 'You're right, Patrick. There are definitely ways for people to just *disappear*.'

He moved too quickly for Peter to react.

Lars grabbed him by the throat, and Peter's hands flew up, fingers trying to prise Lars's hands off his throat, but the pain was intense. Already he felt light-headed. He felt his feet lift off the floor.

He had definitely underestimated Lars's strength.

Peter tried to kick out, but he was too weak. He felt every ounce of strength slowly drain down through his body. He blinked, his vision clouding. Breathing was difficult. He opened his mouth wider, trying to gulp in air.

Lars turned towards the front door, carrying Peter with him like a giant ragdoll, hands still firmly on his throat.

Peter felt warm liquid run down the inside of his trousers. He tried one last time to dig his nails into Lars's hands. To get his hands off . . . to . . .

Then he heard a loud snap, as if someone had angrily broken a twig, and everything rushed past his blurred line of vision – stairs . . . door . . .

There was a dull thud as he landed hard on the carpet. Then a brief moment when Patrick realised that he no longer felt any pain . . . and then . . .

Black.

Forty-Eight

THE DIARY

So much for the police cordon. I know that Anna snuck out earlier, taking the route through the trees and out of the back gate. I watched her from the window, then I followed her.

It's no wonder these people find themselves in bad situations. They have no awareness of the danger that surrounds them. Too trusting. Too stupid. Don't they realise that there are nasty, evil people everywhere they go? Watching and waiting, ready to pounce when the opportunity strikes?

There's so much defence of these sorts when they inevitably get caught. So many explanations – so much about their bad upbringings and lives of poverty and degradation. All these psychologists think they have it all sewn up.

Take my therapist, for example. That woman thought she had me all worked out. Don't they realise we're manipulating them while we pretend to manipulate them? It's some sort of psychotic double-bluff and I see it a lot. I watch people. I read people.

I know when they're like me.

Take this man out on the street right now. This man who is definitely not one of the police. This man who has managed to bypass our protection and infiltrate our street . . . He's like me. He's one of the ones that look so normal. One of the ones who you'd never suspect – he didn't come from a broken home. He wasn't beaten and abused. If anything happened to him when he was a kid, he was part of it.

I'm not sure that makes a lot of sense – but I know I'm right about this. After all, I'm inside my own mind. All those fancy doctors might think they know, but I'm telling you, Dear Diary . . . they really, really don't.

I'm probably going to have to stop writing in a while, to deal with what's going on here. But for now, I'm happy to keep scribbling down my thoughts as I watch. It's a kind of live feed, except it's in my notebook and it's just for me. I doubt anyone will ever read this. I'll probably burn the lot soon. When we all leave.

I'm quite excited to move again. I'm not sure I ever really gelled with this place, and it makes total sense now after finding out that everyone is here under false pretences.

What an absolute joke! Some crackpot experiment that someone in a suit cooked up to save money while playing around with our heads.

Oh, hang on. This is interesting. Did he come out of Number Six? Maybe he's a friend of the new people. I didn't see him go in there, but then I wasn't staring out of the window the *whole* time. He's left the front door ajar. No, wait . . . he's gone back to close it. He's looking around now, seeing what's what. He looks pretty pissed off, actually. He's marching across the street. I'm starting to feel a bit . . . fizzy thinking about it. About what he might be up to.

Beth got herself killed. Finlay reckons she knows what happened, knows who did it. Knows why. But what if she got it wrong? What if we all got it wrong?

What if there's just a psycho on the loose, looking for prey?

Oops – has he seen me? I've ducked down a bit, slid in behind the curtain with my notebook balanced on my lap. The next few lines might be a bit wobbly, but it doesn't matter. It's only me who's going to read them back. I'm going to wait for a bit before I look out there again.

If he is some psycho, I'd really rather he didn't know I was here.

◆　◆　◆

I'm doodling the outline of a roadkill crow in my notebook when I hear the sound of a door opening downstairs, and my heart pitter-patters. Then a skitter of goosebumps runs up my arms. I hold my breath for a moment, as I stand up slowly from my crouched position to peer over the window ledge. I smile to myself, then I lay my notebook on the floor and shuffle over on my knees towards my luggage chest. I'm going to need to protect myself.

I look out of the window again, just to check. But I know I'm right.

The man is no longer outside on the street.

There's a creak on the stair. I think about that old film with the babysitter . . .

The call is coming from inside the house!

I'm lying on the floor as I scribble down these last few notes, then I'm going to have to ditch it and deal.

Was that another creak?

Yes, Dear Diary. In true horror-film fashion – the bad man is in my house.

This is gonna be fun.

Forty-Nine

ANNA: THURSDAY

Anna didn't want to go back home. Not yet. She wasn't ready to face Peter, to tell him what she'd just done. She wanted some time to herself before Bradley made his calls and everything kicked off.

Would they come here and arrest her? Or would they ask her to voluntarily go to a police station and make a proper statement? Was what she told Bradley legally binding? He hadn't cautioned her. He hadn't recorded it. She could change her mind and it would be her word against his.

But she wasn't going to change her mind.

She glanced around The Street, at the houses with their blinds and curtains still drawn. Still early. Maybe some of them couldn't face getting up. She couldn't blame them. She was about to cross over to her own house, where Peter probably still slept, when she remembered the other early risers. The Whitelaws . . . and Donna left on her own. She would probably be back in bed by now, sound asleep. That's what teenagers did, wasn't it?

Anna's eyes were drawn up towards Donna's window. There was a chink in the heavy curtains, darkness beyond. Downstairs, it looked like there was a light on in the kitchen. Maybe Donna would welcome a visitor. Some company. She'd been friendly enough to Anna and Peter at first, only retreating again when she was in the company of her weird family. Plus, Anna felt like there was a story that the girl wanted to share. She'd got the impression earlier that Donna had wanted to ask her questions – like why was it that she never went to the hospital when her brother was younger? Or maybe she was making it sound more mysterious than it actually was.

Anna walked past the Whitelaws', trying to get a look into the living room as she passed, but she couldn't tell if Donna was downstairs. She cut up the alley at the side, and decided to go around the back to see if she could spot any sign of life. The fences were lower on these houses. She had noticed at the barbecue. And they weren't the transparent one-way Perspex like hers, it was just a normal fence, and she would probably be able to see through the gaps between the slats.

As she rounded the bend it became obvious quite quickly that she wouldn't have to do any covert peering . . . the back gate was open, and it was hanging at an odd angle. The small hairs on the nape of her neck stood on end.

Something was wrong.

She quickened her step until she reached the gate, then she stopped. Should she go back to Bradley? Tell him that Donna was home alone and that someone had broken the back gate?

But she didn't know that yet, did she? Maybe the gate had been broken a while. Maybe the Whitelaws were aware of it. Maybe she was letting her imagination run away with itself again. Or maybe . . .

Anna stepped into the garden, past the broken gate, just in time to see a figure disappearing into the Whitelaws' house. A man. He was dressed in grey tracksuit bottoms and a pale blue t-shirt. Slim build, hair cut short. She hung back around the gateway, worried that he would turn around and see her.

This wasn't the man that she had seen on the beach the other day – the one that the police assumed had hurt Beth. That man had been younger, his hair darker and cropped even shorter – that distinctive tattoo on his neck. Even from behind, she could tell that this man was older. Something about the way he moved. Something about his energy.

She knew she should have left then and gone straight back to Bradley, but she wanted to deal with this herself. Maybe it was a misguided attempt at fixing what she had failed to do for Beth. If she could save Donna, maybe her stomach would stop churning over with guilt. Maybe the burning bile would stop trying to destroy her from inside her own gullet.

A final glance around. A final decision to go it alone.

Anna took a deep breath and curled herself back around the gatepost, eyes searching the rear of the house for signs of the man. There were none. He was definitely inside. She hurried up the path, jogging on her tiptoes, trying not to make a sound.

The back door was standing open.

Anna crept into the house. She stood just inside the kitchen doorway, held her breath. Listened. If this had been her old house, she would know in a second where anyone might be – the creaking floorboards were a dead giveaway. But in these new-build cubes with their concrete floors and soundproofing insulation under the thick carpets, it was more of a challenge.

She knew she was being reckless, but again the thoughts swirled around her brain, telling her to carry on, because what did she have to lose? Bradley was making his calls. The police would be coming for her soon. It was only a matter of time.

Might as well use the time in a last-ditch attempt at salvation. Donna's and her own. It would be much easier to go to prison knowing she'd done all she could to help someone, instead of the earlier scenario – where she'd done the opposite.

Anna kept light on her feet as she made her way further into the house. She held her breath again, listened. The house was in complete silence. Donna was nowhere to be seen. Probably still in her bedroom, maybe even asleep. Maybe with headphones on. She would have no idea that she was in danger.

She felt her heart rate start to speed up again. Rubbed her clammy hands on her t-shirt. Crept closer to the stairs. Listened again.

Still nothing.

At the bottom of the stairs, she stopped, looked up. No sign of anyone. It seemed darker up there, as if all the doors were closed. In her own house they kept the upstairs doors open during the day, letting the light flood in. There was less light too, perhaps, on this side of the road. The atmosphere felt thick and heavy. Stale, as if the air had been trapped inside to fester for a long time.

She started to climb the stairs.

Halfway, she stopped again, strained her ears to try to pick up the slightest of sounds. Nothing. She took another step. Stopped again.

There!

A rasp of breath, unmistakable.

Icy fingers trailed down the back of her neck. She shivered, although it wasn't even slightly cold.

Go back, Anna! Get help!

She ignored the voice in her head. The one making the sensible suggestions. She breathed in and a scent caught the back of her throat. A musky, sweaty smell. A manly smell.

Goosebumps skittered across her bare arms.

She reached the top of the stairs and stopped. She'd half-expected to find herself face to face with the intruder, felt like her heart was about to jump out of her chest, but there was no one on the landing. Blood whooshed in her ears.

Just as in her house, there were four doors. Bathroom, straight ahead. The other three were bedrooms. Her and Peter had no need for them all, but in this house, she knew they were all put to use. She assumed that Lorraine and Kevin were in the first room to the left, the master, same as hers. The one next to that was Donna's – the second biggest. She'd seen Donna at the window – knew it was her room. The other room was the smallest, and that must belong to Max. Youngest child, smallest room – this was the way it always was.

All of the doors were closed, but only Donna's and the master bedroom were closed tight. The doors to the bathroom and Max's room were slightly ajar. Anna swallowed. There were still no sounds coming from anywhere. Not a peep from Donna. Her heart lurched. Had he already hurt her?

Where was he?

If he wasn't in Donna's room or the master bedroom, then it was fifty-fifty. She hadn't heard any doors open or close – of course, being new, none of them made the slightest squeak. But there would've been a click, if one had been closed.

The bathroom was closest to Donna's. She imagined him in there, biding his time. She'd have to go to the toilet at some point, right? He would wait. Pounce. And then what? Anna shook her head, trying to dislodge the thought. It didn't bear thinking about.

It was too late to back out now.

She would have to take a gamble and hope she was right, and at least she would be here, ready. She could also wait.

Holding her breath again, she pushed open the door to Max's room. When no one jumped out, she released the breath again slowly, and stepped inside. A quick glance confirmed that no one was in there. There was only a single metal-framed bed, a narrow wardrobe and a desk with a few drawers at one side, and a red gaming chair pushed into the gap underneath. The bed was neatly made, the duvet tucked in around the edges. She crouched down to check underneath, but she knew there was no one there. The room smelled of Lynx body spray and fresh laundry. No hint of that other scent that she'd noticed in the hall.

That scent that she'd tried to convince herself was completely unfamiliar.

It was funny how people had their own unique scents. She remembered first noticing this as a teenager, getting into perfume. One of her friends had *Lou Lou*, and it had smelled so good on her, but when Anna had tried it on herself it had been thick and cloying and had made her feel sick. She could remember the smell of her mum – never one to wear perfume but she had liked to dab essential oils behind her ears – lime blossom and neroli. She could conjure up that smell with a single thought. Just like the smell in the hall.

She'd really hoped that she was wrong about that one. But the hint of a certain soap had mingled into the thick, sweaty air.

Anna returned to the doorway. She peered out into the dark hall, at the bathroom door. It had been slightly ajar before, but now it had been opened further. Just a little. Just enough.

Enough to see the face staring out at her. Thinner. Angrier. But unmistakably the face of Lars Kristiansen – the man who she'd put in jail.

The man who'd threatened to kill her. Or so his wife had claimed . . .

'Hello, Amanda. Aren't you looking well?' He pulled the door open wider. 'I popped round to yours first, but you weren't in. I had a lovely chat with that husband of yours, though.' He grinned, showing his row of perfect white veneers. 'You know, he really should have treated you better.' He stepped into the hall.

Anna felt sick. 'The police are coming, Lars . . . you should get out of here.'

'Oh, I will,' he said, still grinning. 'This won't take long.'

Fifty

THE DIARIST

Donna had been crouched behind her bedroom door for what felt like hours. After seeing Anna and returning upstairs, she had considered going back to sleep. She'd climbed into bed and lain there with her eyes shut, but nothing had happened.

There was too much going on.

Usually, writing in her diary was enough to keep the mountain of confusing thoughts at bay. It had been her therapist's suggestion. The first therapist. The one who'd asked her to draw her feelings and then been too disturbed to analyse them.

Seemed like anyone could be a therapist these days. No real qualifications needed. Like lots of these silly jobs. Sure, there were actual professionals out there doing lots of professional things, but there was also a plethora of chancers and charlatans, ready to prey on the vulnerable.

She'd read a disturbing news article the other day, about women booking massage therapists using online apps. Letting unknown males into their homes, who then went on to sexually assault them. It was easy to judge, to say 'what kind of idiot would invite a man she didn't know into her house' – but nothing was ever that simple, was it? Some of these male massage therapists were legitimate. This kind of shit must threaten their businesses. But whatever. It didn't take away from the facts.

The facts right now, though, were that there was a man in her house. The same man that she'd seen on the street when she'd been peeking out from behind the curtains. That man who'd clearly seen her there, and who'd come around the back and broken down the gate.

The man who had come up the stairs, and who was now hiding in her bathroom, waiting for her.

These houses were well insulated, of course, but when you live somewhere for long enough you start to pick up on the tiniest of changes – noises, smells, whatever. A shift in the atmosphere.

She'd taken what she needed from her luggage chest. It was an old army knife – a six-inch blade. Something else she'd picked up in one of those junk sales, along with the chest. No one had seen her take it. She hadn't dare pay for it, in case the seller alerted her parents, who'd been mooching around a bunch of old paintings in case there was a Renoir hidden amongst the rubbish. It had been rusty and blunt, but she'd seen the potential in it. She liked the look of it and wanted to restore it. She had others too. She'd never actually thought about using them for real.

Sometimes she had fantasies about creeping through to her parents' bedroom in the middle of the night and stabbing them to death. In the fantasy, Max appeared in the doorway, quiet as a mouse, mouth frozen in a silent scream. She'd finish what she was doing, then walk carefully past him, then she'd climb back into bed and sleep. A real sleep, like the one she had after that day when the thing had happened that she tried her hardest not to write about in the diaries.

It was coming, though. She was starting to feel ready. Not to talk about it, but to write it. To start at the beginning and let the words pour out until the end. Then maybe, just maybe – she could get some real sleep again.

But not now.

She'd heard the bathroom door open earlier, then close. And it had opened again now. It was the only door in the house that you could really distinguish, and only if you were near it. Because behind it, there were two hooks that were meant to hang towels or dressing gowns, but she always hung her own things on there, under her dressing gown. There was one of those wiry body puff washer things, and there was one of those foot things, with the cheese-grater side and the pumice side, on a string. It hung on the hook, and when you opened or closed the door, it rattled gently against the wood. It was the most familiar sound, and she'd heard it just now.

The man had gone in there, and now he was coming out. What she didn't know was why . . . but she had an inkling that it wasn't only the man who was in the house. There had been no other sounds to suggest this, no other doors had these little tapping things hung on hooks, but like she'd felt earlier when the man had come in – again, a shift in the atmosphere.

There was someone else here.

An accomplice? Given all the shit that had gone down recently, it was clear that the location of this so-called safe street was out there, circulating around the whisper networks. There would be people, still, who wanted to come for her. There would always be people who wanted to come for her.

She stood behind her bedroom door, clutching the knife. She tried to keep her breathing as quiet as possible. She was hoping for the element of surprise. Hoping that the man, and whoever else was with him now, didn't suspect that she knew they were there.

Had they waited for a time when they knew she was alone? Start with her first? Would they wait for her parents and brother and deal with them too? People get irrational when they're angry. When they want something.

But Donna wasn't ready to be found.

She had one hand on the door handle, the other gripping the knife. She took a deep breath, ready to yank the door open . . . and then she stopped.

A voice came from the hall. A man. Not a voice she recognised. 'Hello, Amanda . . .'

Who the hell was Amanda?

She let her hand fall away from the door handle, but kept a tight hold on the knife with the other. She leaned in closer, listening.

It became apparent quite quickly that this man wasn't here for Donna or her family. He was here for Amanda. He had the wrong house. But there was no Amanda on this street.

Who else was in her house?

Then she heard a familiar voice. A woman's voice.

'The police are coming, Lars . . . you should get out of here.' Anna's voice was pitched high, coming close to a whine.

Whoever this Lars was, Donna imagined he wasn't going to be susceptible to cajoling. His words, when she first heard him speak, were calm and clear, but they dripped with venom.

This was a mess. It had nothing to do with her. She could just stay in her room, barricade the door. The luggage chest would work for starters, then she could drag the bed over. She could make a rope from her sheets and escape out of the window. She could yell for help – the police cordon staff might have been half asleep earlier but they were surely up and about now? Someone would hear her. Someone would help her.

Someone would help Anna.

Anna had been the first person on this stupid street to talk to her like an adult. OK, so she wasn't quite an adult yet, but she wasn't a kid either. Her parents wanted to wrap her in cotton wool for ever. They didn't want her going off to university after she finished her home schooling. They didn't want her out of their sight. She was still surprised they had left her this morning, but she had refused to go and they knew they couldn't miss Max's appointment. Besides, she really had planned to stay in her room all day. She rarely left the house. She had no desire to leave the house. The beach might only be metres away, but she saw no point in going there. She could see the sea from her bedroom. The sea was boring.

But maybe she was the boring one. Maybe it was time to stop living inside her head, inside the pages of her diary. Maybe it was time to get back into reality.

Maybe it was time to live again.

A scuffle started in the hall. Something – someone – slammed against her door. Someone screamed. Anna.

She had to help Anna.

Donna gripped the knife tighter and yanked the door open.

Anna was on the floor at the top of the stairs. The man she had called Lars was on top of her, pinning her arms down with one hand. He had a knee up between her open legs, pressing into her. With his other hand, he was pressing down on her mouth. Anna bucked and kicked and tried to roll free. He was leaning in close to her head, loud whispering to her, telling her to stop struggling. That he was only giving her what she wanted . . .

Anna's eyes widened when she saw Donna. The man hadn't noticed her yet, still intent on pinning Anna down, spewing his twisted words into her ear.

Donna felt a rush of euphoric calm that she hadn't felt for a very long time. Anna tried to signal to her with her eyes.

Stay away! Run! Hide!

But Donna was done with hiding.

She lunged forward and thrust the knife into the man's side and slid it out fast. His head flipped up and he let out a cry of surprise. Anna used the distraction to roll out from under him.

What happened next was fast, but slow. The actions blurred, her mind drifting elsewhere into the clouds.

He got on to one knee to push himself up. A dark, bloody stain blossomed through his t-shirt. He yelled something at Donna, but she couldn't quite hear it above the rush of blood in her ears. She was in another place. A place she had never expected to visit again, except in her mind. In her fantasies.

This was so much better than her fantasies.

She lunged again, spearing him in the chest. She pulled the knife out quickly and a torrent of blood soaked the front of his t-shirt. Anna was screaming something now, but Donna couldn't make out the words. Anna had shuffled back against the wall, knees pulled up tightly towards her chest. Her eyes were wild. She was still saying something, shouting something, but it was just white noise in Donna's head.

Lars toppled back, somersaulting backwards down the stairs, until he came to a hard stop at the bottom. Donna walked down towards him. Anna's muffled voice was still there in the background, but she ignored it. Lars lay on his back, crumpled. His eyes were wide open. One of his hands twitched.

He tried to speak; she read his lips. 'Please . . .'

His eyes had begun to change. He didn't have long. But she wasn't going to risk going any closer. She'd seen those films. The hand grabbing the ankle. The final showdown. He was bleeding out quickly.

This was the final showdown.

Donna took her phone out of her pocket and hit 999. 'Come quickly.' She was smiling as she spoke. 'I've just killed an intruder.'

Fifty-One

ANNA: THURSDAY

Anna had never really understood how those foil blankets worked, but the paramedics had wrapped her in one and given her a bottle of water, and as she sat on the grass outside her house, watching the goings on at Number Seven, she felt oddly serene.

They had taken Donna into the ambulance to do some checks. Despite her protestations that none of the blood was hers and that she wasn't in shock, they had used professional judgement and insisted she go inside. Anna could see her through the open door, hooked up to the machine where they check your pulse. She was staring straight ahead, and although Anna had tried to catch her eye, given her a little wave, the teenager hadn't responded.

Her parents and brother had been called, but it would take some time for them to get back from the hospital in Glasgow. Anna hoped the police had explained that Donna was fine, and that Max was able to have his appointment before they returned.

It wasn't as if there was anything they could do. Donna, it seemed, *was* fine. Physically, at least. Although her vacant stare made Anna think that she was not quite OK mentally. And might not be for some time. But she was in the right hands.

She hadn't returned to her own house yet since the events at Number Seven. The windows were in darkness, and she assumed that Peter must've headed out somewhere again – although the car was still in the drive. She'd been about to text him when she remembered she still didn't have a phone. If he'd been inside, surely he'd have come out when the sirens screeched on to the street. He would have seen her, sitting there on the grass. If he wasn't back soon, she would ask someone to call him.

Meanwhile, the police had started their door-to-door enquiries, asking people if they'd seen anyone they didn't recognise on the street earlier. It was strange that Lars had managed to find his way here so easily, and to get in without being questioned. But she no longer trusted any of the security measures and she had little faith left in the police team who'd been supposed to be looking after them all.

The nice detective from Beth's case, DS Russel McLean, walked out of the Whitelaws' house just as a couple of white-suited CSIs walked in. He pulled down the hood of his own suit and started to unzip as he made his way across the road towards her. By the time he reached her lawn, he'd pulled the top part down to his waist.

'Anna,' he said, by way of greeting. 'Give me a second.' He rolled the suit to the ground and climbed out of it, then he pulled off the booties and rolled the whole thing up. A uniformed officer rushed over to him and held out an open plastic bag, letting him stuff the suit inside. The officer sealed the bag and took it away.

DS McLean sighed. 'Well, then. Quite the drama this week. Are you OK?'

She opened her mouth to say something, but he carried on before she got the chance.

'I mean, obviously you're not OK . . .'

Anna rubbed her eyes. 'Did you know that Lars was out of prison? I mean, what with him and that one who came after Beth, you're not doing very well at keeping track of your inmates.'

He gave her a pained look, then sat down on the grass beside her. 'Anna . . . I didn't even know your real identity until about an hour ago. As for Lars, well, that is a bit of a mess, to be honest. It turns out that he was moved to an open prison recently, after a successful appeal. In Scotland, funnily enough. We've only got one of them. It's up near Dundee.' He pulled his knees up to his chest. 'You should have been informed.'

Earlier, when she'd left Donna's house, she'd been furious about what had happened. About Lars being able to find her so easily. She'd had no idea about him being in an open prison. It was laughable now. She couldn't even find the strength to be angry.

'I suppose Jasper knew . . . I mean, DS Cole.'

Russel nodded. 'Aye. Marcus knew. I've only spoken to him briefly, but he told me he had plans to meet up with you. I guess this latest incident kind of scuppered that, eh?'

Anna bit her lip. She wondered if Bradley had made his calls. If she was living on borrowed time. She hoped that Peter would come back soon. She'd have to tell him what she had told Bradley. Hopefully before someone came to arrest her.

'I've spoken to Bradley too,' Russel said, as if reading her mind. 'He told me quite the tale.' He turned to face her. 'We'll get to that. Probably need you to come down the station and have a chat soon. But first things first, eh? My main priority right now is making sure that you and Donna are OK.'

Anna nodded. She was scared to say it. She'd seen them loaded on to the ambulance. 'Is there any update on Lars?'

'Stable, they said. But he's lost a lot of blood. The next few hours will be critical, and I can keep you informed if you'd like. I realise that your relationship with him is a complex one.'

It was certainly that. Despite her fear, there had been a moment in Donna's house when she wasn't sure that he had actually come to hurt her. There was a moment when she thought he'd actually come to get her, to run away with him. But no . . . that was stupid. He'd pinned her down. He'd tried to . . . She thought back to some of the times they'd spent together in bed. There'd been some roughness there. He was very different to Peter, but . . . no. He had come to hurt her. He'd come to kill her. Hadn't he? Donna had seen that. Donna had reacted.

She glanced around towards her house again, looking to see if Peter was at one of the windows. But he wasn't there. The door-to-door officers were leaving Number Four and heading towards her house. Anna knew there was nobody at home, but they didn't. They walked across the grass and on to the path. One of them lifted a hand to ring the doorbell.

She turned back to face the detective, her eyes drawn to the rest of the street. The other residents were milling around, either in their own gardens or on the pavement.

Mary was chatting to Finlay on Finlay's doorstep. Both of them looking out at the street. Mary was saying something, making the occasional arm gesture towards the Whitelaws' house.

Asya was holding her little dog. She stood at the end of her path, just staring down the street at all of the activity. More cordons – this one around Donna's house. A cordon within a cordon. Suited CSIs were coming in and out of the house, carrying bags and equipment. Anna hadn't seen John, or Bradley and Lacy, but they wouldn't be far away. Donna was still in the ambulance opposite.

Anna watched her as the paramedics checked her vitals again. After a moment, they unclipped the finger monitor and Donna shrugged off the foil blanket. She lifted her arms above her head, stretching them out. Then she clocked Anna and dropped her hands into her lap. An unspoken signal passed between them, and Anna gave the tiniest of nods before she looked away.

'Sarge?' The female voice came from behind her, and Anna turned around just as the sergeant replied.

'What's up?'

'You need to come and see this.'

Anna felt a prickle of something reaching across her shoulders. She noticed now that the front door to her house was slightly ajar.

'Sergeant McLean?' she said, pulling herself up to her feet. 'What's wrong?'

He'd already started walking towards her house, and Anna tried to hurry after him, but her foot had gone a bit dead from the way she'd been sitting, and she stumbled, almost tripping on the path.

'If you could just wait here for a moment, Mrs Clarke,' the officer said. She was walking towards Anna, holding a hand out in front of her. 'We just need to have a look inside your house. Is that OK?'

The prickle had turned into something sharper, gripping the back of her neck. A horrible, fluttering wave rose through her chest.

'There's no one in there . . .' she said, trying to convince herself.

Maybe there *was* someone in there. Perhaps Lars hadn't been alone. He'd sent his accomplice into her house to find her, and . . .

No!

The thought came back to her like an ice-pick to the back of her skull. Lars had said it earlier . . . *'I popped round to yours first, but you weren't in. I had a lovely chat with that husband of yours, though.'*

'No!' she said again, running across the grass, elbowing the officer out of the way. Detective McLean was still on the doorstep, but he'd pushed the door open further. One of the other officers was on his way from the CSI van, a new pack of forensics gear in his hands.

McLean grabbed her by the shoulder just before she managed to enter the house. 'Anna, please . . . you need to step back.' He put an arm around her, pulling her away, calling over his shoulder, 'I need some help here . . .'

And Anna heard all this, and she felt the weight of him, the heat of him, as he enveloped her and tried to stop her from seeing something that no wife should ever have to see. But it was too late, because she'd already seen it. She'd smelled it now. In all her research, people who worked at crime scenes always said the same thing . . . There's no mistaking the scent of death.

She closed her eyes and felt herself falling. Felt the arms tighten around her. She tried not to think about what she'd seen, but it stayed with her as the darkness slowly descended.

Peter.

Patrick.

On the floor. His head turned to face the door, neck twisted at an impossible angle. Eyes wide. Staring, but seeing nothing.

She felt herself being lifted, then laid down. A soft blanket pulled over and tucked under her.

And everything dissolved.

Fifty-Two

ANNA: ONE WEEK LATER

Anna hadn't expected Lars to survive. Donna had done a good job with that knife, and she'd believed she was doing the right thing – protecting Anna. Yes, she had taken it one step further, and although no one was telling her anything more about Donna – other than that her and her family were safe and had been relocated – Anna was pretty sure that Donna wasn't in hiding because she was in danger . . . more that she was the dangerous one. Anna had read up on the psychology of children who killed, and it was a minefield – not a place she wanted to go. If this was Donna's background, then it was probably best for everyone that it stayed in the past where it belonged.

Lars was handcuffed to the hospital bed, despite the fact that he was in no fit state to run away. He'd regained consciousness after twenty-four hours, and the first thing he'd said was 'I need to see Amanda.' She'd refused, at first. But a week on, she decided that she was ready. He was asleep now, and he looked peaceful. It was hard to believe that he was the same man who had caused her so much pain.

Peter had not been so lucky – but she knew that the minute she saw him lying there on the floor. The police had suggested at first that it might have been an accident. He was near the bottom of the stairs. It wasn't beyond the realms of possibility that he could have slipped and fallen. But then they'd seen the finger-marks on his neck . . . and then Lars had confessed.

Why, though? That's what Anna wanted to know. She'd thought it was her he wanted to get rid of . . . unless Agneta had been lying.

Anna was more confused than ever, and despite everything, she had wanted to make things better with Peter, and now she would never have the chance. If she asked Lars why he'd killed him, would it open up a can of worms that she would wish had stayed closed?

You can do so much better than him, you know . . .

Why had Lars said that to her? He'd hardly known Peter.

Had he?

She was torn. Detective McLean had already told her that there would be no charges brought over her 'confession' – he said that Lars had exonerated her – again. So she had to thank him for that, at least. But did she want to talk to him? She couldn't imagine that anything he said was going to make her feel any better about losing Peter.

She looked down at him in the bed, still sleeping peacefully. There was a guard outside his door, but there was no one in the room. It would only take a second for her to take one of the pillows out from under his head and press it hard on his face. He was so weak . . . it probably wouldn't take long. She would be caught, of course. There was no way she could do something like that, with a police officer right outside, and manage to get away with it. They would know he'd been smothered. It was almost impossible to kill someone like that and not leave any trace. Burst blood vessels were only the visible part of it. Again, something else she'd learned about during her research for her books.

She wasn't sure what she was going to write after this. Living through so much violent crime had left her feeling tired. Soiled.

The thought of writing about it for cheap thrills felt grubby. Her mind went back to that first conversation with Peter . . . when he was Patrick, and she was Amanda – and he'd joked that crime books weren't real books, and she'd been mock-offended.

Well, living through it, she could confirm that crime was most definitely real. And she was going to need a lot of palate cleaning before she even considered writing anything dark again.

She was only at the start of her grieving process for her husband. She didn't even know where she was going to live next. What she was going to do.

She had no idea where she wanted to be, but she knew that it wasn't here, with Lars.

Anna stood, picking up her bag from the floor.

He opened his eyes.

'Amanda?' He smiled. 'You came.'

She swallowed. Gave herself a moment to think. Then she turned away and walked towards the door, stopping just before she pushed it open.

'Goodbye, Lars,' she said. Then she walked out into the corridor.

The police officer looked up, raised his eyebrows. 'OK?'

She nodded, then walked quickly down the corridor, trying to get as far away from Lars as she could.

McLean was waiting for her outside. He was sitting on a low wall, phone glued to his ear. Two coffees beside him. He saw her and raised a hand, then gestured to the phone. She slowed down, waiting for him to finish up.

She had negotiated a lot with the police over the last week. That detective from before – DS Georgia Lawrence – had driven up from London with her boss, and DS Marcus Cole, aka Jasper, had been involved too. Mclean had been her contact from the Scottish police side – and he'd been great. The whole lot of them had been working together, trying to unpick everything that had gone on. The head of the witness protection programme – the specific one that involved The Street – had been there too.

Because the programme had failed. Badly. The investigation was already underway. Secretly, of course, given that the identities of the witnesses still had to be protected.

She hadn't seen any of the other residents since the day that Lars turned up. The handling team had decided that enough was enough, and they had all been taken to temporary accommodation, while they worked out what to do next.

Anna hoped that the other residents would find new lives elsewhere – happier and more peaceful than the ones they'd had on The Street. She hoped that Finlay would find a way to rebuild her life without Beth; that Donna would find some peace in herself. Anna had continued with her version of events, the version where Donna's actions were in self-defence, and in the end, the police had stopped asking.

And of course Peter was gone, and Anna knew she was still completely in denial about all that had gone before. Peter had to have known about her and Lars, surely – and he'd had his own reasons for keeping that quiet. Their relationship had started to fail when she'd seen a bit of success. She could pretend all she liked, but he was bitter about it. Bitter that he wasn't the big earner. Bitter that she had a much more exciting life than he did.

Peter was not Patrick.

Not *her* Patrick. That man had been lost long ago.

But none of that mattered now.

Did it?

One thing was certain – she no longer had to stay here and be *Anna*. She knew that Lars wouldn't come after her. Whatever it was that he was really up to with his shady dealings, Anna was small fry, a distraction – something he needed to forget about.

Just as she needed to forget about him.

So . . . she could go back home. She could call her agent, say she'd changed her mind – she'd had a break and she was ready to come back and be *Amanda* again. Write her novels. Write anything she wanted.

Or . . .

She could just walk away from all of it.

Start over.

Go wherever she wanted.

Be whoever she chose to be.

She'd spent her entire adult life writing stories.

Maybe it was time she put some work into her own.

ACKNOWLEDGEMENTS

I moved around a lot of rented flats when I was younger, and most of the time I never saw much of the neighbours. But there was one instance where we moved into a flat in South London and bumped into the people who lived below us on our very first night in the local pub. We got on really well, and it was great to think that we might have made new friends in the building – something that's mostly quite a feat, especially in London. But then the next day we saw them in the garden – they were moving out!

The rapid high/low of that ill-fated friendship stuck with me – and became the nugget of the idea that led to this . . .

The site of the development is real – I grew up close to Cockenzie Power Station – and it was a sad day when they demolished the iconic chimneys, years after the place shut down. At the time of writing, the site is still vacant. Sadly, there's no chance of building a private beach there, but the cruise-liner terminal *was* a real possibility at one point. I made up the café near Prestonpans beach. Someone should put one there though – it would do well.

The other part of the story – the 'why are they all there' bit – came from a WhatsApp chat with fellow author and excellent plotting fiend Ed James. Cheers for that!

Lindsay and Ritchie Walker . . . well, that's not two people, it's one. Huge thanks to Lindsay, who bid very generously for her name to be in the book – glad I managed to squeeze all of your names in there, and I hope I bumped you off satisfactorily. Your donation was gratefully received by Young Lives vs Cancer.

I actually know Lindsay from fifth year Chemistry, where I sliced my hand open with a scalpel one day and she had to help me drive home from college, where we were doing a placement. Good times! She also lived on the same street when we were growing up, so it's only right that she is in this book!

Thank you to my brilliant editors – Vic, Russel and Kasim – you all rock . . . to Melissa for her excellent copy-edits, Sarah for her diligent proofreading and to all at T&M who made this book happen.

Huge thanks as ever to the Superstar that is Phil Patterson and the wonderful Marjacq gang.

I exist within an incredible community of crime writers, readers, reviewers, event organisers, booksellers, librarians, cheerleaders and book lovers – and without them all, I don't think I would be writing this. Massive thanks for your support. I'm grateful to you all, for the chats and the laughs, especially when this writing life gets hard (i.e. every day . . .)

Special thanks to Steph Broadribb, who had the dubious honour of reading my first draft chapter and declaring it (not) shit.

To my family and friends – I love you, and I thank you, as always, for putting up with me being so busy all the time.

And of course, to JLOH, the best egg boiler in Brentford.

THE HIKE BY SUSI HOLLIDAY

If you enjoyed *THE STREET*, why not try *THE HIKE*, Susi's dark, twisty thriller set in the Swiss Alps?

Four hikers enter the mountains. Only two return. But is it tragedy? Or treachery?

When sisters Cat and Ginny travel with their husbands to the idyllic Swiss Alps, it's an opportunity to reconnect with each other after years of drifting apart.

But as they head into the mountains and the terrain turns treacherous, cracks in their relationships begin to appear.

When only two of the four hikers make it down from the mountain, the questions quickly follow. What really happened on that ridge? How did they survive? And what are they trying to hide?

Prologue

SUNDAY MORNING

He is in much worse shape than she is. Half of his face is obscured by dried blood and muck. One of his eyes is puffed up and squeezed shut. His shorts and t-shirt are ripped. Muddied. Bloody. She knows she doesn't look too great herself. Sweat patches under the arms of her sweatshirt. Grazes on her knees. She tries to stay focused. Keep the pain at bay.

They're sitting, far apart, on the steps outside the wooden chalet-style building that allocates most of its space to an outdoor equipment shop. Only the small blue sign stuck on the wall to the right of the glassed entrance gives away what's inside. She swivels around to read it, wincing as her back protests.

POLICE

Below that, another small sign stating that tourist-season opening hours are 11 a.m. to 12.30 p.m. and 3.00 p.m. to 4.30 p.m. Three hours to wait.

She turns back around, rests her elbows on her knees. Takes in the empty street. It's still early in the village. Most people are probably tucked up in bed, while the early risers are starting on the croissants and coffee as they scroll through their phones and glance out of the windows, soaking up the views.

He coughs. 'What now?' His voice is ragged, hoarse. His breathing laboured. He needs medical attention.

She stands up, wipes a hand across her face, smearing the mud and tears that have replaced her make-up. She walks carefully around him, leans in close to the sign next to the door. 'There's a phone number here. For emergencies.'

He coughs again.

'We don't have phones, remember?'

She sighs. Walks away from him, glancing up and down the street. 'Something must be open.' She pauses. 'I could go to the hotel.'

He shakes his head. 'Not sure that's a good idea, is it? You said we need to stick to the plan.'

She hesitates. Unsure. 'Yes, but . . .' Her eyes travel over him. His injuries. His pain. After everything that's happened, maybe this is too much. 'I could go somewhere else. Get help. We need assistance now, not in three hours . . .' She walks further away from him, takes in the street filled with closed shops, hotels still sleeping, no public phones in sight. She starts to walk along the street. Her heart starts to beat faster. She could change the plan. It's not too late. Is it? She glances back. He's clinging on to the railing, trying to stand up.

He calls out to her, his voice barely a rasp. 'Don't leave me here. Please.'

She stops walking. She is torn. She turns back fully and takes a long look at him. He's broken. Maybe enough is enough. She walks back to him, sits down on the step again. Lays a hand on his arm, guiding him back down. She shuffles across, lets him lean against her. Feels his warm body against hers. His breathing slows.

'Thank you,' he whispers.

Side by side they sit, waiting. They are in this together.

One

If someone had asked Cat Baxendale to draw a typical Alpine village, then Villars-sur-Ollon would be it. Pointy-roofed wooden chalets, swathes of lush greenery. Pine trees as far as the eye could see and, behind it all, framing the scene, the jagged-topped mountains; majestic and looming. The August heat was stifling, but the Swiss Alps remained snow-capped all year round. In winter, the whole vista would turn from green to white. But on this blue-skied summer's day, cold weather and ski boots were the last things on her mind. All Cat could think about was a glass of chilled white wine outside one of the pretty Alpine bars, soaking up that killer view.

Cat had spent a lot of time planning this trip, making sure that every little detail was perfect. It was almost a shame that things would inevitably end on a sour note, but she'd had enough. She wasn't going to put up with the situation for one day longer. Well, two days, actually. At least this evening would be fun for them all before she lit the touchpaper.

The drive from Geneva Airport had been quicker than expected, hardly more than an hour. The tall grey buildings and advertising billboards on the fringes of the city had soon made way for open roads and parched green fields. The ascent up the mountain had been exhilarating and twisty, and often precarious, but before they knew it, they'd arrived in the village and Cat was inwardly bouncing with excitement before they'd even stopped the car.

She had never been to Switzerland before, but her year-long stint in France as an exchange student meant that her language skills should just about hold up, as long as the group didn't veer into the German- or Italian-speaking regions. Her three companions – her husband, Paul, her younger sister Ginny, and Ginny's husband, Tristan – seemed less enthused. Paul, because he'd been green with travel sickness since they'd got into the hire car, and the other two because they'd been bickering since the departure lounge at Heathrow. It wasn't unusual for Tristan and Ginny to fall out, but luckily it usually passed quickly, like a cloud on a windy day. Cat's plan would definitely lead to more than a bit of bickering, however, and the thought of that cheered her even more. Her sister, of course, remained oblivious, despite Cat's obvious glee.

'Let's just dump the bags and head out,' Ginny said, yanking her small suitcase out of the back of the car and dropping it on the pavement. 'I have an urgent need for cheese and wine.'

'We can sort the bags,' Tristan said, slapping Paul on the back. 'Can't we, mate? Sorry . . . are you going to puke?'

'You took those corners far too fast.'

'Oh, come on. You need to drive like that, ascending so high in one of these stupid little cars.' He kicked the driver's-side back tyre. 'I thought you'd ordered a four-by-four?'

Paul was gulping lungfuls of fresh mountain air, his colour slowly returning to normal. 'Cat said she did. It's not my fault they messed up the booking.'

Ginny grabbed hold of Cat's arm, dragging her away. 'There's a bar over the road. Let's leave them to it.'

Cat grinned at her, and the two of them hurried towards the cute little hut with wooden chairs and tables outside. The tables were covered with red-and-white-checked cloths, held down with metal clips. In the centre of each table was a small stone vase holding a bright-yellow flower.

'This is just perfect,' Cat said, pulling out a chair. 'It's exactly as I'd pictured.' She glanced around, soaking up her surroundings. 'I feel like Heidi.' She lifted her honey-blonde hair out to the sides in two bunches. 'Can you do plaits?'

Ginny laughed. 'I think Heidi was German.'

'Yeah, but she lived in the Alps, didn't she? I'm sure it's not that much different in the German cantons.'

'Well, let's hope we don't bump into the evil Fräulein Rottenmeier. She was horrible.'

Cat was about to start dredging her memory for the exact details of the book that she'd read so long ago, when the waiter, dressed in a typical French black-and-white ensemble, appeared by their table, an expectant look on his face.

'*Bon après-midi, mesdames. Vouz avez choisi?*' He waited a beat, then spoke again, this time in heavily accented English. 'Good afternoon, ladies. Have you chosen?'

Ginny grinned at him, holding up two fingers. '*Grandes bières. Merci.*' Her accent was terrible, and the waiter forced an indulgent smile before disappearing back inside.

Cat rolled her eyes. It was just like France then – the locals finding the tourists' attempts at their language barely tolerable. Especially tourists with terrible accents. 'I thought we were having cheese and wine?' She had been looking forward to the wine. It was typical of Ginny to change her mind. Sometimes Cat wondered how she managed to get through a day, with all her dithering and indecision.

'We need a livener first.' Ginny blew out a long breath. 'I am *so* glad to be here. One more of those hairpin bends and I thought we were all goners.'

'Me too,' Cat said. 'Tristan wasn't exactly taking it easy for someone driving on the wrong side of unfamiliar roads.' She paused, smoothing down the edge of the tablecloth from where the breeze had flipped the corner up. 'Are you going to tell me what you two were arguing about?' She kept the 'this time' to herself.

Ginny took a packet of Marlboros and a lighter from her handbag. 'Everything. Nothing. You know what it's like.' She offered Cat the packet, knowing she would shake her head because she hadn't smoked in years – despite her sister's attempts to lure her back to it, to 'keep her company'. Eventually, Ginny shrugged, then popped a cigarette into her mouth, lighting it quickly and inhaling deeply. 'I think he might be having an affair.'

This time it was the word 'again' that Cat added, only to herself. She tried to keep her expression neutral. There was no way her sister could know the truth about what she had planned for this trip, was there?

'*Deux bières.*' The waiter reappeared, placing two large bottles of beer and two stemmed glasses on the table, setting down a small bowl of peanuts between them. Then he was gone, and Ginny's sentence hung in the air. That cloud, again. But this time it wasn't shifting so quickly.

Cat nibbled on a peanut, crunching it hard between her teeth. 'What makes you say that?'

Ginny waved her cigarette, blew out a plume of smoke. 'A few things. I don't know, Cat. Maybe I'm overreacting.'

Cat picked up her glass, tipping it to the side as she slowly poured in the beer. 'Like what?'

Ginny drank hers straight from the bottle. 'It's so clichéd, I don't know if I can even be bothered to tell you. Late home from work. Not paying attention to me. New clothes . . .'

'Maybe he's just busy at work.' *Some of us actually do some work*, Cat thought, taking a long, slow drink. The beer was ice-cold and tasted heavenly.

'Not too busy to buy new clothes, though?' Ginny stubbed out her cigarette, crushing it hard into the metal ashtray. 'He used to always ask me to help choose his clothes.' Ginny pouted like the spoilt child that she had always been. 'God, you're so lucky with Paul. He'd never cheat on you, would he? The two of you are so bloody perfect.'

Cat kept a poker face. Ginny knew nothing about her relationship. She was far too self-absorbed to care. A classic Daddy's Little Princess, her sister had grown up to be the ultimate city boy's trophy wife. The fact that she was supposed to have an actual job helping Cat run her events company barely registered on her radar, especially over the last few months. Ginny's life was all about looking pretty and searching for the perfect recipe to wow Tristan with every night, despite the fact that he usually got home late, half-pissed, having already eaten out with clients at a posh restaurant. It was no wonder that Tristan had got bored and gone looking for some fun.

At least Paul was always home for dinner. He usually cooked it, in fact. Things had changed a lot since he'd started his new job. Since he'd been *forced* to start his new job. He was making an effort, but it was mostly in vain because Cat couldn't bear to have him near her most of the time. Even the thought of his hands on her when she knew they'd been all over someone else was enough to turn her stomach. Just one of the many things that this weekend would fix, once and for all.

Cat had zoned out of her sister's chat. It was *The Ginny Show*, as always. Her photos *did* look good on Instagram though. Festooned with her humble-bragging captions about how she knew it wasn't as good as the original, but she'd tried her best, hashtag blessed. Cat wondered what her Keto-diet yoga-bunny Insta devotees would think if they could see her now – carb-laden beer and a second cigarette on the go. Cat took another large drink. The beer was nearly gone already. Her sister's moaning was in danger of ruining her mood.

'How about we forget all that for the weekend, eh? We're meant to be here to relax and enjoy ourselves. The four of us haven't seen each other properly since your birthday party.' Cat clocked the change in Ginny's expression and smiled inwardly. *Oh yes. We will be discussing that, dear sister, along with some other very important things. But not right now.* She signalled to the waiter for two more beers, then spotted the men heading towards them from across the street, and called him back for another two.

Ginny frowned, making her nose wrinkle – but not her forehead, because it was Botoxed to the max. 'I hope this hike you've planned isn't too strenuous. I really fancy a mooch around the shops and a long soak in the hot tub.'

Tristan stood behind Ginny and placed his hands on his wife's shoulders. He gave Cat a wink. '*Au revoir*, ladies! *Mange tout?*' he said, in an awful Del Boy from *Only Fools and Horses* accent, the words making no sense in the context, but turning Ginny's frown into a smile. She really did love Tristan, didn't she? The poor cow. Tristan reached over and took a swig of Ginny's beer. 'Hope you're not trying to weasel your way out of my carefully planned hike, Wife.'

Ginny wriggled her shoulders, shaking him off. 'What do you mean *your* hike. I thought Cat was arranging it all?'

Cat shrugged. 'He offered to help. I was busy with all the rearranged event bookings, so . . .'

Ginny pulled herself completely away from Tristan, turning awkwardly to address him. 'Nice of you to find some time for my sister, when you barely find time for me.' She turned back to face Cat, crossing her arms tightly. 'You don't even *like* each other—'

'I could've helped,' Paul cut in, his face falling as he pulled out the chair next to Cat. 'I've got far more time than any of you.'

'That's because you don't have a job, mate,' Tristan said, punching him on the arm. He pulled out the chair opposite and took a handful of peanuts from the bowl, tipping them into his mouth and crunching noisily.

Paul took a breath. Cat could see from the flush rising up the neck of his t-shirt that Tristan's barbs were getting to him.

Good.

The waiter arrived, depositing the four beers, and more peanuts, on the table. The moment passed.

Paul did have a job, of course. For the last six months he'd been a part-time delivery driver, and he loved it. But Cat knew that all Tristan could see was a city boy who'd burned out, and he refused to let him forget it. Cat had agreed to keep the real reason behind Paul's career change a secret, and she had no plans to reveal it, even over this weekend. She had other things in mind to deal with that.

'You guys . . .' Ginny lifted her bottle. 'We're on holiday? Let's have some fun. Cat and Tristan have worked *so* hard to arrange this for us. Cheers!' Her voice was light, but Cat could hear the tension bubbling just below the surface. Ginny was good at painting on a smile. Cat knew that Ginny didn't want to be here. Cat knew her sister hated hiking, but she was making the effort to keep things friendly. More fool her.

Cat glanced across at Ginny and mouthed a silent thank-you. She didn't want them all arguing. Not right now. Not tonight.

They all chinked their drinks together, to a chorus of 'cheers' and '*salut*', and Cat smiled, pleased with herself for pulling this weekend together. Because there were a few surprises that she planned to deliver.

And not everyone was going to like them.

FREE *DARK HEARTS* BOX SET

Join my readers' club and you'll get a free box set of stories: 'As Black as Snow', 'The Outhouse' and 'Pretty Woman'. You'll also receive occasional news updates and be entered into exclusive giveaways. It's all completely free, and you can opt out at any time. Join here: sjihollidayblog.wordpress.com/sign-up-here

ABOUT THE AUTHOR

Susi Holliday grew up near Edinburgh and worked in the pharmaceutical industry for many years before she started writing. A lifelong fan of crime and horror, her short stories have been published in various places, and she was shortlisted for the inaugural CWA Margery Allingham Prize. She is the acclaimed author of ten novels and a novella. A film adaptation of her Trans-Siberian-set thriller, Violet, is currently in development.

You can find her website, social media links and newsletter sign-up at www.linktr.ee/susiholliday.

ABOUT THE AUTHOR

Follow the Author on Amazon

If you enjoyed this book, follow Susi Holliday on Amazon to be
notified when the author releases a new book!

To do this, please follow these instructions:

Desktop:

1) Search for the author's name on Amazon or in the Amazon
App.
2) Click on the author's name to arrive on their Amazon page.
3) Click the 'Follow' button.

Mobile and Tablet:

1) Search for the author's name on Amazon or in the Amazon
App.
2) Click on one of the author's books.
3) Click on the author's name to arrive on their Amazon page.
4) Click the 'Follow' button.

Kindle eReader and Kindle App:

If you enjoyed this book on a Kindle eReader or in the Kindle
App, you will find the author 'Follow' button after the last
page.